THE PRIVATEER

VOLUME **2** OF THE FLIGHT ENGINEER

JAMES DOOHAN

THE
PRIVATEER

S.M. STIRLING

VOLUME 2 OF THE FLIGHT ENGINEER

THE PRIVATEER: THE FLIGHT ENGINEER, VOLUME II

This is a work of fiction. All the characters and events portrayed in this book are fictional, and any resemblance to real people or incidents is purely coincidental.

A Baen Books Original

Baen Publishing Enterprises
P.O. Box 1403
Riverdale, NY 10471

ISBN: 0-671-57832-4

Cover art by David Mattingly

First printing, October 1999

Library of Congress Cataloging-in-Publication Data
  Doohan, James.
    Privateer / by James Doohan & S.M. Stirling
      p.   cm. — (Flight engineer : v.2)
    ISBN 0-671-57832-4
    I. Stirling, S. M. II. Title. III. Series: Doohan, James.
  Flight engineer : v.2.
  PS3554.O566P75   1999   99-38132
  813'.54—dc21   CIP

Distributed by Simon & Schuster
1230 Avenue of the Americas
New York, NY 10020

Typeset by Windhaven Press, Auburn, NH
Printed in the United States of America

THE
PRIVATEER

VOLUME **2** OF THE FLIGHT ENGINEER

CHAPTER ONE

It's a formality, Commander Peter Raeder thought. *The fix is in. It's not a* real *Board of Inquiry any more, much less a court martial. I'm the hero, not the goat.* He suppressed an urge to rub his midriff. *Then why does my stomach still hurt?*

Of course, there was the previous visit to this self-same courtroom not so very long ago. Then his second in command, Second Lieutenant Cynthia Robbins, had been suspected of sabotage and murder, and he, too, was looked on with a gimlet eye. The look of the polished dark teak of the high table at the other end of the room, the scent of wax, and the ever-so-slight rustle of the crossed Commonwealth and Navy banners behind the senior officers spelled *danger* to his subconscious now. In fact, the sensation wasn't altogether different from the way he'd felt in a Speed when the compensator started going collywobble and the lock-on alert said a Mollie interceptor was targeting him. . . .

Back before I lost the hand, he thought. Though there had been a lot more in the way of combat stress than he'd anticipated, when they made him a flight engineer. Raeder shifted in his seat.

1

Just a few weeks later the room still boasted the same lustrous mahogany paneling, the same painting of a space battle on the back wall, flanked by the starred flag of the Commonwealth and the blue and black flag of Space Command. The row of stern senior officers seated behind the sturdy teak table in their comfortable leather chairs still faced the smaller table with its single unpadded seat. All too reminiscent of that previous occasion.

Well, some of the faces have changed.

And this time he had a personal reason for anxiety. After all, he *had* left his post in the middle of a battle with the Mollies and their alien Fibian allies.

And you can never be too sure that the powers that be won't decide to make an example of someone, despite things turning out right in the end, Raeder mused. *Someone like me, for instance.* It wasn't that he didn't *want* to obey orders. It was just that he kept being the one on the spot who knew what his commanders didn't. . . .

The fact that he looked a little like a recruiting poster—square chin, blue eyes that the newsvids insisted on calling "volcanic," black hair, pale complexion—didn't help either. He *looked* like a self-centered hotshot, you had to admit that.

He'd left his post for the best of reasons, naturally; risking his life to save a precious five-month supply of enemy antihydrogen that would certainly have been lost without his interference. It was an open secret that the Commonwealth's supply of A-H was running perilously low. And without antihydrogen fuel, the Commonwealth couldn't continue to exist and the war with the Mollies would be over. *And* he'd saved what remained of the *Dauntless,* the ship transporting it, *and* the life of a very fine engineer.

Which made him a hero.

Bigtime.

The captain had recommended him for a Stellar Cross.

A corner of his mouth twitched up.

Y'know Raeder, sometimes you worry too much.

On the other hand, there was a nasty undercurrent here that kept him shifting in his seat no matter how he reassured himself. Someone in this room was going to be damn lucky to walk out of it with nothing worse than a reprimand. Of that he was perfectly sure.

Because just now Admiral Einar Grettirson, the presiding officer, was grilling Captain Jill Montoya of the *Dauntless* with an attitude that raised the hairs along the back of Peter's neck.

"*Cap*-tain Montoya," Grettirson drawled, thick gray eyebrows drawn down over ice blue eyes, "you lost a total of one thou-sand seven hundred and *ten* of your people, as well as twenty-five Speeds in this action. Did you not?"

"Yes, Admiral," she answered stiffly.

And no one could have tried harder to save them, Peter thought resentfully. Captain Montoya had actually carried one wounded crew-woman to the lifeboats on her back.

But Grettirson was a well-known martinet, and a slave to the book; it was rumored that he slept with a copy of the Commonwealth Standard Manual of Operations under his pillow.

Montoya had managed to get her crippled ship to the edge of Ontario Base's defensive perimeter, and *with* the antihydrogen.

To me, Peter thought, *that kind of a save says, "Wow! What a leader!"*

"And just how do you explain such cat-a-*strophic* losses?" Grettirson asked, his thin, ascetic face as cold as space.

Clearly the admiral doesn't agree with my assessment. Peter shifted in his chair again, drawing Grettirson's glittering eye. He froze instantly, like a buck under the eye of a hungry mountain lion. *Oops.*

Not that the admiral was a total monster; he was simply convinced that today's subordinates emerged from a very inferior mold to the one that had shaped him.

Peter examined the other members of the board, trying to read reactions in their impenetrable expressions. Vice-Admiral Paula Anderson he knew from Cynthia's hearing, and he felt her to be intrinsically fair. Commodore Wayne Gretsky and Commodore Margaret Trudeau of the Intelligence Corps were complete unknowns. But Marine General Kemal Scaragoglu was a power, if not truly a known factor. Conspiracy, rumor and paranoia followed him around like besotted puppies.

Scaragoglu was so Machiavellian that he even looked like an African copy of the sixteenth-century statesman. He had the same tight-lipped, sharp-eyed intensity, coupled with a high-bridged nose and sharp chin; some said it was biosculp. Raeder didn't think so; he figured the Marine general was more likely a reincarnation of some extremely successful *condottiere*.

"And how is it," Admiral Grettirson was saying, "that neither you nor your chief engineer thought of Commander Raeder's rather simple fix for the damaged antihydrogen bottle?"

"I'm not an engineer by training, Admiral," Montoya answered quietly. "As for Chief Casey, I cannot say. Perhaps it was the heat of the moment. But, of course, the flight deck had taken a direct and catastrophic hit. It was a shunt from a Speed's engine that Commander Raeder used to empty the damaged bottle. Such an item would have been unavailable to Chief Casey, even if he had thought of using one."

"Have that checked," Grettirson said, and an aide in the audience spoke a reminder into a wrist filo.

The interrogation of Captain Montoya went on and on, and Raeder cringed mentally. *If this is how he's handling people who behaved like a perfect textbook scenario of responsible and heroic behavior, what's he going to say to me?*

As if he didn't know.

His own captain, Knott, had torn a nice long strip off Raeder for, as he had put it, "Going off to perform one of the most harebrained pieces of showboating I've ever seen in my entire career!"

At last the board was finished with Captain Montoya, which is to say that Admiral Grettirson had vented as much spleen as he possibly could on her innocent head.

Paddy Casey, the *Dauntless*'s red-haired and, at the moment, furiously red-faced, engineering chief was called.

He lumbered up to the table, a solid six foot slab of heavy-world muscle, and sat, fixing the admiral with a glare that should have dissolved the strong, weak and electroweak forces maintaining the integrity of his atomic structure. He folded his big hands before him, the knuckles white from the pressure of his grip.

Grettirson glowered back, but without nearly the conviction, making the staring contest a hollow gesture. The Chief didn't remain on the stand long, perhaps because every one of his quiet, polite answers sounded threatening somehow. And it was well known that Paddy was an impulsive man with a long and sorry history of physically attacking senior officers.

Something to keep in mind, given that the admiral was far less fair to Montoya than he might have been, Peter thought.

Fortunately for Grettirson, Paddy was deeply in love with Lieutenant Cynthia Robbins and was determined to get into officers' school so as to pursue their relationship. Otherwise the rule-bound Robbins would be forever beyond his grasp.

"You—did—what?" Grettirson enunciated carefully.

"I jury-rigged a magnetic bleed from a Speed's acceleration system and brought it over to the *Dauntless* in one of her abandoned lifeboats," Peter said matter-of-factly.

"You *abandoned* your post in the middle of a battle?" the admiral asked slowly, in genuine horror.

"I made certain that I had people in position to take over for me," Raeder assured him.

"*You* are the senior officer in charge of the Main Deck, Commander! No one can *cover* for you!" A blood vessel in Grettirson's temple writhed. He glared over Peter's head at the audience behind him. "I shall have to ask Captain Knott why you were not put on report." He lowered his gaze to meet Peter's. "You may step down, Commander. But you haven't heard the last of this, I assure you."

Raeder nodded and rose, giving a quick glance over the other members of the board. Gretsky and Trudeau looked at him in disgusted disbelief, Anderson looked disappointed. But Scaragoglu . . . Scaragoglu looked interested.

Peter walked stiffly back to his seat, feeling the Marine general's eyes boring into his back. *This is not a guy I want to take an interest in my career,* he thought. *Avert! Avert!*

Captain Knott came in for his own share of sharp questioning and blame, as did Squadron Leader Sutton and the captains of the *Diefenbaker* and the *MacKenzie.* But at last it was over and the board chairman made his summing-up speech. He ended it with remarks made directly to Commander Peter Raeder.

"Recommended for the Stellar Cross, indeed," he sneered, giving Captain Knott a dismissive glance. "If you had gotten yourself killed, we'd very likely have presented your family with some posthumous decoration. As it is, I shall recommend that you be given a reprimand for the record and be reassigned planetside to a desk. And consider yourself lucky that it's not worse. Because you, Commander, are a standing menace to discipline and order!"

With that he rose, banged the gavel on its plaque and led the rest of the board out of the room.

Aides rose from the audience and followed them, while Peter and the rest of the defendants, for that's what it had felt like, stood to attention.

"I need a drink," Paddy said, speaking for all of them, both high and low.

"Patton's?" Mai Ling Ju, the XO, suggested, receiving nods all around.

Peter glanced at Captain Knott out of the corner of his eye, wishing they could include the Old Man in the group. But protocol forbade. It jolted Peter for a moment. *I never thought before about how alone you must be in the captain's chair.* And then he thought, with a rush of surprising fierceness, *But there are compensations to command.* Deep in his heart he wondered if he would ever know them now.

"An interesting man, Commander Raeder," Scaragoglu remarked, his dark face placid. A violin concerto played softly in the background.

Captain Sjarhir, the general's aide, merely sipped Scaragoglu's excellent whiskey and said nothing. There was an idea in the works here, had been since Raeder had taken the stand, and he knew better than to interrupt the general's thought processes.

They were in the Marine general's private quarters, relaxing after a long and strenuous day. Even his rooms revealed little about Scaragoglu. All that one could really say of them was that they were appropriate. Appropriate to a man of his rank, and a man of his age. *Totally*, unnaturally appropriate—even to the still-holo pictures of various planets, most of them badly damaged. The planets, that was, not the holos.

Scaragoglu laughed dryly.

"That boy is in trouble, Captain. Grettirson meant what he said about a desk assignment for him."

"At least he'll be alive," Sjarhir said, meeting the African's eyes.

"Oh," Scaragoglu said, raising his brows in polite inquiry. "Is that what you'd call it?" He leaned forward, his dark eyes hardening. "For a man like Raeder you'd call that *living*?" The word was freighted with contempt. "That man is a warrior, Sjarhir, not a data twiddler. It would be a waste of his talents and a waste of the man. A year in a job pushing statistics around and he'll be as useless to himself as he'll be to us."

"Then it's pure altruism, sir?" the captain asked casually. "You'd rescue him by giving him an assignment that's likely to get him killed?"

Scaragoglu leaned back slowly, his eyes never leaving Sjarhir's face.

"Is that what you think I do, Captain? Choose people solely to get them killed?" His gaze sharpened, and though this was a game they'd played for years Sjarhir's mouth went dry. After a moment the Marine general spoke again, but he allowed Sjarhir to see that he was angry, though his voice was calm. "Dangerous, high-risk assignments are constantly coming our way," he said. "That is a fact of war, Captain. I choose the men and women least likely to get killed on those assignments.

That is my particular gift and my curse. Fact," he said and leaned forward again. "Raeder can either be alive and at risk, or he can be a zombie in a dead-end cubicle job. I know which I'd choose." He tilted his head. "And I can guess which you'd choose for yourself. Are you going to help me or not?"

Sjarhir allowed himself to look surprised.

"Why do you need my help, sir? You pretty much have carte blanche when it comes to recruiting."

Scaragoglu laughed, this time with genuine amusement.

"Because I could see by the way he looked at me that Commander Raeder has heard all the nasty rumors about my puppet-master proclivities. All the really independent ones have trouble with that at first. If someone he can trust gives him the nod and tells him I'm okay—" Scaragoglu shrugged "—it'll smooth the way."

"But General, *I* don't trust you."

Scaragoglu raised his brows.

"You've been on assignments for me before this, Captain."

Sjarhir smiled. "That's why I don't trust you, sir."

The Marine general grinned.

"More to the point, sir, there's no reason for Raeder to trust me. He's never even met me."

"Well," Scaragoglu shrugged, "he soon will, and he'll like you too. You have a winning way about you, Sjarhir."

"Thank you, sir."

The general smiled benignly, then gazed into space for a moment, one hand gently beating time to the music.

Reminded by the gesture, Sjarhir said, "Raeder has a prosthetic hand, sir. He's not cleared to fly a Speed."

The general waved dismissively.

"That's hardly a real reason not to tap Raeder for a mission," he observed.

"No, sir."

"You're my devil's advocate, Sjarhir," the general remarked with a sardonic smile. "I'd think that the devil would win more arguments."

"I think he does, sir."

Scaragoglu barked a laugh. "You've been with me too long, son. I'm going to have to have you reassigned."

"Whenever you like, sir." But Sjarhir knew it wouldn't be soon.

Peter sat at the bar in Patton's; not drunk and not wanting to be, but nurturing a nice little buzz. It kept his mood just elevated enough that he wasn't crying in his beer. Or, in this case, actually, single-malt whiskey. *The trick,* he thought, *is to stay just on the edge of euphoria, but not try to actually achieve it—because then I'd probably get maudlin and start to cry.*

The others had left him here alone at his request. "I've got some thinking to do," he'd said, cheerfully enough. And his thoughts had been running rings around each other ever since.

They're going to ground me. Just when I can fly again. They're going to ground me. It wasn't doing him any good, but he couldn't stop himself.

He glanced up at his glum face in the mirror behind the bar. The mirror was augmented to make the viewers look younger, handsomer, happier than they actually were.

It's having a hell of a time with me, Raeder thought. He looked extremely serious. But in a positive way, rather than reflecting the overdose-on-sleeping-pills-slit-your-wrists-and-jump-off-a-cliff mood he was actually enduring. *Which means that in reality I must actually look like I feel.* He forced himself to smile. You could almost hear the mirror sigh with relief.

Raeder looked around. *I really like Patton's,* he thought. *It's a nice place.* He wished Sarah James was with him. He doubted he'd feel the need to suck down liquid solace if he were in the lieutenant commander's excellent company. But he'd sent her away with the others and, to his dismay, she'd gone without argument. *Ah, well.* He sighed, and added that brick to his pile of misery.

He took another sip of his whiskey and forced himself to contemplate the type of desk job a man of his experience and training might be given. And sighed more deeply still.

"Whoa. That sounds like the weight of the world being shifted."

Reader glanced to his right. A Marine captain was taking the seat beside him. The man had a pleasant grin and the gold complexion and jet-black hair of an Indonesian.

"Not quite that bad," Raeder said with an easygoing smile.

"Jason Sjarhir," the Indonesian said, offering his hand. Peter took it. "Peter Raeder."

Sjarhir shook a finger at Raeder.

"Aren't you the guy . . . yeah, you are. You're the guy who brought in the *Dauntless*, aren't you?"

"No. Montoya brought in the *Dauntless*. I'm a glorified mechanic, is what I am. Nothing happens to me. I just did a little repair work. . . ."

"The hell you did!" Sjarhir exclaimed. He grabbed Peter's hand and started shaking it vigorously. "I'd like to shake your hand."

You are, Peter thought in bemusement.

"Can I buy you a drink?" The captain raised his hand to attract the bartender. "I insist," he insisted.

"I'm not saying no," Raeder said. *Free booze sounds good to me.* When the drink came he raised his glass and said, "To Captain Montoya. A truly gallant officer."

Sjarhir raised his brows. "And gallant of you to salute her, Commander." He lifted his glass. "Captain Montoya." And took a sip. Over the rim of his glass he assessed Peter's condition and resolved that this would be the commander's last drink. He didn't want to be accused of taking advantage of a man in his cups.

The Captain looked around and leaned closer to Raeder.

"Word is that Grettirson wants to censure Montoya."

Peter's jaw dropped. "Censure?" he said in disbelief. "He can't do that! She did everything humanly possible to save that ship."

Sjarhir shrugged and grimaced. "Grettirson's always

been a fanatical disciplinarian. But he's gotten measurably worse since his son was killed."

Raeder frowned. He liked a commanding officer who hated to see his people killed. It was by far preferable to the alternative, an officer who treated his troopers like inanimate game pieces, fungible goods to be expended like ammunition.

"Still . . ." Peter murmured, shaking his head.

"I don't think he'll get away with it though," Sjarhir said. "I heard that Anderson practically pulled him out of his chair by the lapels when he suggested it." He laughed. "She is one officer I wouldn't like to get on the dark side of."

"What can she do? She's only a vice admiral," Raeder pointed out.

"Yeah. She's his junior, but she's got a lot more respect than he has." Sjarhir nodded wisely. "He'll pay attention to what she says, even if it makes him break out in boils."

"How do you know all this?" Raeder asked. How was a lowly captain of Marines aware of the intimate details of relationships in the upper echelons of Star Command?

"I've got a bud on the vice admiral's staff," the captain said easily. He leaned towards Raeder confidentially. "It's what the old man wants to do to you that worries me."

Peter hunched down over his drink with a scowl and didn't answer. There was nothing to say.

"Y'know what you oughta do," Sjarhir said.

Raeder looked at him. "No," he answered. "What?"

"You ought to volunteer for some spectacular mission. When you come back they'd never dare to send you to a desk job."

Peter snorted and grinned. He held up a hand as featureless as a rubber glove. "First, this is the sort of thing that gets you rejected when you try for that kind of mission. Second, where am I going to find this mission, volunteer, and be accepted in time to overrule Grettirson's ardent desire to make a scapegoat out of me tomorrow morning?"

The captain smiled slowly and in a way that filled

Raeder's stomach with ice. He could almost hear the Indonesian thinking, "Gotcha!"

I should not have serious conversations with strangers after the third Glenlivet, he thought.

"If it's convenient," Sjarhir suggested, "I could take you to someone who can help you right now."

"Who?" Raeder asked, suspecting with dawning horror who it had to be.

"Marine General Scaragoglu." Sjarhir's dark eyes were inscrutable and his face was as bland as dry toast.

Even expecting to hear that name, a cold ball of panic flashed into being in Raeder's stomach. *Get a grip,* he ordered himself. *You've only got two choices. One: let Grettirson ship you back to Earth in disgrace. Two: go have a look at whatever rattlesnake Scaragoglu is passing around. I mean, how bad can it be? I can always turn it down.*

"C'mon," Sjarhir urged, "what have you got to lose just by listening? Besides, the general's whiskey is better than this slop."

"Then by all means," Peter said, rising, "lead the way, Captain."

CHAPTER TWO

Lieutenant Commander Sarah James tapped her fingers on the arm of her chair and recrossed her long legs yet again. She knew her fidgeting was distracting to the captain's secretary but simply couldn't stop it; waiting in offices wasn't her forte.

Odd, considering that as a WACCI pilot (the acronym stood for Warning, Assessment, Control, Command, Information) a lot of her working life demanded waiting in perfect stillness. And James was extremely good at her job.

But waiting in an office for an appointment was just dead time. It made her think guiltily of reports that she should be working on, or frustratedly of things she wanted to check on her craft, or her equipment. She put both feet flat on the floor, tapped her toes for awhile, then crossed her legs. There was a muted chime and the captain's voice said: "Send Lt. Commander James in now, Lieutenant."

James and the secretary looked at each other with *Thank God!* written on both their faces. Sarah rose and tugged at her midnight blue uniform, brushed one hand through her short auburn curls, then with a nod to the lieutenant she walked to the door and entered the eagle's nest.

Captain Roger Knott's craggy features did put one in mind of an eagle. Especially the piercing glare of his pale eyes and his aquiline beak of a nose. Right now she was getting the full value of that famous glare of his. He returned her crisp salute more casually and indicated a chair before his desk.

"Have a seat," he said.

"Thank you, sir."

Knott studied her for a moment. He saw a competent young woman in her mid twenties, with a lean intelligent face and warm, sherry brown eyes. He liked James, he trusted her work, and he wasn't especially happy about the reason that brought her here.

Ordinarily he wouldn't be taking appointments this late in the day. But he needed distraction from Grettirson's board of inquiry and he saw no reason to keep either the lieutenant commander or himself in suspense regarding her request.

"This is sudden," he said, tapping the document displayed on the screen built into his desk.

"I've been considering it for several weeks, Captain, and this seemed like an excellent time to request a change of this nature."

Knott raised his brows and leaned back in his chair. "It does?"

"Yes, sir." Sarah leaned forward. "There are a number of vacancies in the Speed squadron and I'm a qualified Speed pilot."

"You haven't flown a Speed in four years, Commander," Knott demurred.

Sarah nodded. "But I've hardly been in dry dock, sir. I'm prepared to take a simulation exam." She met Knott's eyes calmly and when he nodded she went on. "In addition, there's a pilot officer on Ontario Base that's amply qualified to replace me. I'd like to commend to your attention Lieutenant Barry Chueng. He was scheduled to head the *Dauntless*'s WACCI crew." She stopped.

The *Dauntless* no longer had a WACCI division, nor any Speeds of her own. Those that hadn't been blasted apart by the Mollies or their Fibian allies had, perforce, been left behind in Mollie space while the *Dauntless* made the desperate leap to Ontario Station. Subsequent missions to that area had found nothing but some charred debris.

"But the *Dauntless* might very well be decommissioned," she continued, "and in any case she's in no condition to do anything right now. A good many of her people have already been reassigned. Chueng is in an odd place, though. He hasn't been able to present his orders to Captain Montoya and so he can't be reassigned as yet."

Knott permitted himself a small smile.

"And you recommend that I put in a request for his services?"

"Immediately, sir. He's good." Sarah began to allow herself to hope that the Old Man would allow her to do this. Meeting Barry Chueng had given her the impetus to get rolling on it, and now that her mind was made up she was impatient to make the change.

Knott looked down at her transfer request and pursed his lips.

"I thought that you enjoyed what you were doing, Lt. Commander," he said quietly.

"I have, sir. I've learned a lot and I've enjoyed every minute of it." She hesitated. "But I think it's time to get my career back on the fast track. I don't think I'd like to be a WACCI pilot for the next twenty years. There are other things I want to learn and to do, sir."

Knott leaned back and tapped his desk thoughtfully. He was disappointed. After a lot of effort he'd obtained, in almost every instance, exactly the people he wanted. He'd been pleased at the way they worked together, respected and liked one another. Naturally he'd hoped to keep them together for a longer period of time; they'd help prove that fast light carriers were a worthwhile use for scarce antihydrogen and shipyard space. He'd fought hard to prove the concept, and having the right people was a big part of it.

As well, James was a known factor and he didn't relish giving that up. By the same token, if he trusted her judgement, then he should accept her word when she said Lieutenant Chueng was a suitable replacement. He should also trust her judgement if she said it was time for her to move on. Stepping on a request like this was no way to nurture a junior officer. And she had to do it this way. She was taking a step sideways, surrendering command of her highly specialized group, in order to be in line for a step up in a more general command position. WAACI pilots didn't become ship commanders; Speed pilots did. One hoped in the near future.

He met her eyes. Hers were calm, confident.

"It does seem that Speed pilots get promoted faster, doesn't it?" he said with a smile.

She smiled in return. "Yes, sir."

"All right." He nodded decisively. "If you'll agree to, and pass, a flight-simulation test, I'll approve your request for a transfer to the Speed squadron." He rose and extended his hand to her. "Good luck, Lt. Commander."

Sarah rose and took the captain's hand. "Thank you, sir," she said, barely able to contain her joy. She saluted, and he returned it, crisply this time. She pivoted neatly and left his office. Inside she was turning handsprings.

Sjarhir suggested that they walk. It didn't take a genius to figure out why.

"It's halfway across the station," Peter protested, half amused. "I'm not drunk, y'know."

The Indonesian smiled, a mere quirk of the lips.

"I do know. But when dealing with the Marine general it's always best to have as many of your wits about you as you can manage to scrape together."

Raeder gave him an old-fashioned look. "Oh, yeah? Well, I've never heard a story about someone who'd scraped together enough to outsmart him."

"That's because," Sjarhir said, starting off, "it takes

more than intelligence." He stopped and looked over his shoulder. "You coming?"

Peter frowned and looked around. Not that he wanted to get into Scaragoglu's hands any sooner than necessary, but a five-klick walk would just prolong the agony. He grimaced. There weren't any cabs available anyway. And Sjarhir was already sauntering off. Raeder watched him go, certain the captain would turn around again. But he didn't.

With a soft hiss of impatience Raeder started after him. *Why should he wait for me? He knows I've got nowhere else to go.*

They walked in silence for awhile. Peter trying to square what seemed to be a desperate move with himself, and Sjarhir thinking whatever dark thoughts spooks think.

"All right," Raeder said, "what does it take besides intelligence?"

Sjarhir's lips quirked.

"Not that it will do you any good to know," he said. "But it takes sheer ruthlessness and a great deal of power. The general can do almost anything he wants with, or to, almost anyone he wants." He cast a sideways glance at Raeder. "I say almost because it seems logical that there would be *some* limitations on his power." He smiled. "But I could be wrong."

Raeder grunted and picked up the pace.

"And for all I know," the captain said, easily keeping up with him, "it could well take more than that. Because to the best of my knowledge, which is extensive, no one ever has gotten the best of him."

Raeder glanced at him, and grunted skeptically.

"Why does the high command put up with that sort of thing from a lowly line general?"

"Because he takes the dirty little jobs nobody else wants, and gets them done—successfully, so far."

"God help him if there's a major screwup, then."

"Oh, yes. But I wouldn't bet the integrity of my hull seals on that happening, if I were you, Commander."

Raeder considered that. Then he marched resolutely down the cool, night-dimmed corridors of Ontario Base, his arms swinging freely at his sides. He looked like a man with a purpose instead of a man running from one doom into another.

Raeder's lurid imagination had clothed Scaragoglu in a burgundy satin smoking jacket, seated him in a deep armchair in a dimly lit, luxuriously furnished room and given him a brandy to swirl around a balloon goblet. Maybe there had been a pipe or a cigar in there too.

The reality was a rather spartan, well-lit office with the general wearing a slightly rumpled undress Marine uniform.

And it was whiskey.

Raeder saluted and the general returned it without looking up from the document he was scanning. He indicated a chair before the desk and Raeder, with a glance at Sjarhir, sat down.

After a moment Scaragoglu sighed and turned off the screen. He kept troubled eyes on his desk as he raised his whiskey for a sip. Then he leaned back and looked at Peter.

"The results were good," the Marine general said without preamble. "I commend you for that." And he raised his glass to the commander. "But you were very much out of line." He gave Raeder a level stare.

Raeder returned the general's stare without comment.

"Personally," Scaragoglu went on, "I believe you need a little more seasoning before you take on that flight engineer's job. I'd be interested in your take on that," he said after a moment's pause.

Raeder looked down at his hands, loosely folded in his lap, and gathered his thoughts. He assumed that he'd be made an offer of some kind. But it was dangerous to make assumptions with a man like Scaragoglu. *I hate it when someone wants something from you, but they just have to give you a test first. I want something, he wants something. Let's get to the horse-trading part, already.*

"You may well be right, sir," he said at last. "But the point is moot since I'll be relieved of that command and shipped Earthside come morning."

Scaragoglu took another sip of his drink.

"Is that why you accompanied the captain here? So that you could tell me you're going back to Earth?"

Raeder had to suppress a smile. An inconvenient, fey part of him had always found that there was something inherently ridiculous in almost any crisis situation. Even when it was his career in the balance. But Peter doubted that the general, like every other authority figure in his life, would appreciate, or understand if he showed his amusement.

"I followed the captain here, sir, in hopes that you'd have a more attractive proposition."

Scaragoglu's Turko-African face might have been carved out of scarred basalt, but Raeder thought he detected a smile in the slight narrowing of the dark eyes. The captain shifted his stance as though uneasy, and Scaragoglu's glance found him. Peter wondered if they'd had a bet riding on his reactions.

"I don't think 'attractive' is quite the word I'd have chosen, Commander. Your report says that you are, basically, sane. But I do have an alternative. Are you interested?"

"Very."

The general smiled. "What I have to show you is highly classified. Nothing that I tell you, regardless of whether you decide to accept this mission or not, is to leave this room. Do you understand?"

Unless you're planning to use me as a human hand grenade, I'm in, Peter thought. *So discretion won't be a problem.*

"Yes, sir."

Scaragoglu gave him an appraising look, then activated a holo display. The room lights dimmed automatically and a view of an asteroid field snapped into clear focus.

Tumbling rocks scanned by, sixteen centimeters above the surface of the general's desk. A little scale marker at the bottom of the image told Raeder that they ranged from palm-sized to the magnitude of small moons. And those were just the ones that could be seen at this magnification.

Raeder winced. *Messy,* he thought.

"This asteroid field is in Mollie space," the general explained. "No habitable planet in the system, but plenty of nice rich rocks with shallow gravity wells. Used to belong to the Consortium, but it's been abandoned since the Commonwealth won the war." He shrugged. "You can see why; it's in the middle of nowhere. There are always a few misanthropic miners that are looking for a berth like this, but the proximity of Mollies drove even them away."

Peter smiled at the mild joke.

"There's still a lot of palladium to be harvested there, but it will have to wait until we've won the war."

The general did something and the recording speeded up, then stopped. Scaragoglu touched one particular asteroid with a laser pointer, and the computer brought the undistinguished lump of rock into magnified view. The scale made it three klicks long, approximately, and a half a kilometer wide. It looked vaguely like a sausage.

"This was the miners' hutch." The general touched the nose of the big rock with his pointer and the view switched to give Peter a head-on view of the asteroid. As usual with holos taken in space there was no sense of depth to the huge black circle on one end. "This shadow indicates the opening to a rough, but endurable base."

Peter nodded thoughtfully. It would be rough, the Consortium wasn't inclined to coddle the miners they'd all but enslaved. But there would be perfectly reasonable conditions for a covert military operation.

"You want to put a spy post there?" he guessed.

Scaragoglu shook his head.

"We have every sophisticated spy device known to man deployed in that block of Mollie space. They're extremely efficient and damn near undetectable. There's nothing that could be learned from this base that they wouldn't find out just as well as a human operator. Less, actually, since this field is in proximity to a spinning neutron star. It's far enough away from the hutch that hard radiation shouldn't be a significant problem, but close enough that it will play merry hell with sensors. Ours as well as the enemy's." His lips quirked in a smile. "Think bigger."

Bigger, Raeder thought. *Rescue mission?* His mind went to the missing WACCI crews and maybe even some of the Speed officers from the *Dauntless. Naw, we're looking at a permanent base.* In Mollie space. The hutch was too small for a ship like the *Invincible.* So it must be for . . .

"You mean to harry the enemy. You need a base for a small squadron to launch on hit-and-run missions." Raeder looked away from the holo to meet Scaragoglu's approving eyes.

"Not unlike the privateers in the ancient Caribbean," the general confirmed. "You'd harry their shipping. Interrupt their supply lines and in general wreak havoc on their morale. These are damned suspicious people, Commander. Not knowing how ships that lack interstellar capability are showing up to destroy their supply lines is going to make them even more paranoid. You'll make it look like their pirate allies. I'd just love to drive a wedge between the evil and the insane."

Raeder grinned. It was an appealing thought. Then his face sobered.

"And my place in this mission, sir?"

"You'd be in command." The Marine general's eyes sparked, but his dark face was unreadable.

"Why me, sir?" Raeder asked. The obvious and unattractive answer was that he was exceedingly expendable. He didn't particularly relish the idea of being a human sacrifice. They hadn't yet talked about how he and his people would be evacuated. *Maybe after the* Dauntless *thing he thinks I'm too gung ho to even ask sensible questions and won't notice we're as likely to be recalled as a plasma beam once it's fired.*

"Because you're the only hero I happen to have on tap at the moment," Scaragoglu said dryly. "You've proven you can think fast in a tough situation. That you're willing to take risks without being overly concerned with intangibles like, 'Will the admiral approve?' " He smiled thinly. "But I don't think you're going to throw your life away. Or anyone else's for that matter. And I need a cool, clearheaded leader who can think on his feet, not a berserker. I think that makes you my man."

"I'm not cleared to fly a Speed," Raeder said. *Might as well be up front about it.*

"I'm aware of that, Commander." Scaragoglu glanced over at Captain Sjarhir.

The captain had gone so still that Peter had almost forgotten him.

"I mentioned it to the general earlier, Commander," he now said.

Peter nodded. *Glad I mentioned it then,* he thought.

"However, thanks to an innovation by my second, Lieutenant Cynthia Robbins, I now can fly. Without the slightest difficulty."

The general frowned and looked at Sjarhir, who shrugged.

"Unfortunately, we've never heard of this invention and therefore it hasn't been approved for use by Space Command, and therefore might as well not exist," Scaragoglu said, giving Peter a cautionary look. "Which means you are not cleared to fly for the foreseeable future. I would describe that as a *slight* difficulty."

"The patent has been submitted, sir. And since it works I'm sure it will be approved. We're likely to lose too many highly trained pilots otherwise." *Read expensive,* Peter thought. *Expensively trained pilots. Space Command is going to be screaming for something like this and soon.* "Therefore you might say it would merely be a formality to give me permission to fly a Speed, sir."

For the first time in years Scaragoglu felt his chin loosen preparatory to dropping. *The brass of the man!* Clearly it wouldn't be an easy ride having a *muntu* like this under his command, but it certainly wouldn't be boring.

He leaned forward and gave Raeder a steely eye.

"A formality?" he asked coldly.

"Yes, sir. On a mission like this it's only logical that I be cleared to fly."

"Oh, really?" The general's eyebrows were almost up to his receding hairline. He leaned back with a sigh and stared at the ceiling for a moment. "I see you haven't learned anything from your recent adventure with the *Dauntless,*" he said casually.

Raeder flinched within.

Scaragoglu flicked off the holo and, drawing his chair in to the desk, leaned forward again, fixing Peter with a glare the way a bug collector pierces a butterfly with a pin.

"A commander . . . Commander, doesn't leave his or her post to go haring off to hell on a whim. That is what being in command is all about. This is why we delegate tasks, even when we'd rather do them ourselves." He set his teeth. "It's *hard.* It's not going to make you popular. It will be misunderstood at every turn. But it's what makes a leader. I thought that you might have picked up on this little lesson by now." His voice deepened to sarcasm. "Or was Grettirson right in his assessment for a change?"

Raeder swallowed. Captain Knott's angry words came back to him. "If you don't know that yet you've risen as high as you're going to, or ought to." *But that isn't the only reason I'd want to fly.*

"Sir, I wasn't necessarily saying I'd like to regularly fly a mission. But I feel that on an assignment like this everyone should be cross-trained and cleared to perform any task. Otherwise an individual could become dead weight at any moment. I've no desire to find myself in such a situation." *Sounds plausible to me,* Raeder congratulated himself. Now to see if the Spider bought it.

Scaragoglu stared at Raeder expressionlessly. Then he glanced at the captain, then back to the commander.

"Cleared to fly a Speed in an emergency," he conceded.

"Emergency to be defined by me," Raeder countered.

The general allowed the moment to stretch. It didn't do to let a subordinate think they had you. *And it would be very unprofessional to let Raeder see I like him. How much better to be forced to restrain the noble stallion than to prod the reluctant mule!* It was going to be enjoyable having Raeder on board; a challenge, but enjoyable. Finally he gave a curt nod of consent.

"Will I be allowed to pick my own people?" Raeder asked.

"I'd like to recommend a couple of Marine flyers, if

you don't mind," Scaragoglu murmured. "This could turn out to be a plum assignment if it's handled right."

"Very true, sir. I'd welcome any suggestions you may have. Especially since it's essential to match personalities in a case like this to minimize friction in close quarters." *There goes Paddy,* Raeder thought with regret. The big New Hibernian couldn't abide a Marine.

Scaragoglu rubbed his hands together and conceded to himself that Raeder's comment was well phrased. He'd let the general know that he expected to have final cut regardless of anyone's preferences, however highly placed they might be.

He nodded briskly and stood.

"All right," he said. "We'll work out the details later. But if you work for me you have to understand two things, Commander. One, I will not tolerate any willfully self-aggrandizing stunts." *Like the one that got you into my hands in the first place,* went unsaid. "And two, this is *my* mission you're on. However far away from this base you may be, you are under *my* direct command, representing *me* in the field. I expect you to behave accordingly." He stared into Raeder's eyes for a long moment. "Is that clear, Commander?" he barked.

"Yes, sir!"

"Is that acceptable?" he asked more softly.

Raeder paused a moment before answering.

"Yes, sir."

Scaragoglu's lips quirked. *Brass balls, sure enough,* he thought—he knew full well how intimidating his presence could be, especially backed up by his reputation. *I wonder if the commander's aware that he's already picking up some of the Spider's tricks?*

"Dismissed," he said. Raeder snapped to salute and Scaragoglu returned it with an economical precision.

Peter turned on his heel and strode from the office, buoyed by hope for the first time in days. *Rescued in the nick of time,* he thought happily.

It didn't occur to him—then—that there was a certain irony in thinking of this mission as a *rescue* from a safe, comfortable staff post on Earth.

✧   ✧   ✧

The door closed behind Raeder, and Sjarhir and Scaragoglu looked at one another for a long, silent moment.

"I like him," Scaragoglu said at last.

"Is that because you think you can predict what he'll do?" Sjarhir asked.

"Hell, no. It's because I've no idea what he'll do. Although I was right about his wanting to fly," he said smugly.

Sjarhir nodded, sighed, and slipped his currency card into the desk reader, wincing as it clicked away a fair portion of his last month's pay.

"Why do I keep offering to bet you on things like this?"

"It's a futile attempt to keep your self-esteem intact," Scaragoglu said, as he accepted it with a chuckle and a thumb on the screen's surface.

"That boy is going to work out just fine," he went on happily. "I'm looking forward to seeing the expression on Admiral Grettirson's face when I tell him the good news," he said.

"Now *that*," Sjarhir said, "makes losing the bet really worthwhile!"

CHAPTER THREE

Admiral Einar Grettirson walked into the Board of Inquiry the next morning looking as though he'd spent the night tippling pure vinegar.

Or just eating his heart out, Peter thought wryly. *Which would amount to the same thing.*

The admiral sat silently, his hands folded in front of him, looking as though he were praying as fiercely as he had ever fought.

The moment lengthened until some of the members of the board began to stir restlessly. Grettirson's head rose slowly; pale furrows traced a path from his thin nose to the downturned corners of his mouth; his ice blue eyes flashed coldly. The Admiral's thin lips twisted for a moment, then his expression became as stiff as wood.

"In the matter of the conduct of the captain and crew of the *Dauntless*," he said at last in a dry, bitter voice, "the board finds that their behavior was in full accord with the highest traditions of the service. The board directs that it should be so noted in the permanent records of each one of them."

27

His eyes narrowed to slits and flashed in Raeder's direction, resting on him like an accusation.

"In the matter of the conduct of Commander Peter Ernst Raeder . . ." The words slowed to a stop, as though Grettirson could barely force them out. He took a deep breath and continued. "Due to the demands of the service . . . this board is to be indefinitely adjourned . . . and will reconvene at some future date to consider the matter."

He slammed the gavel down and rose, rushing from the courtroom before anyone could react properly.

Confusion and pleasure were equally mixed among the spectators, who had risen raggedly on the admiral's departure and remained on their feet uncertainly.

He did it, by God! Raeder thought in wonder and relief. *He did it!*

Vice Admiral Paula Anderson leaned forward and said, "I would like to offer my personal congratulations to the captain and crew of the *Dauntless*. Well done, ladies, gentlemen."

"Hear, hear," the other board members said, smiling, tapping their academy rings on the table in approbation.

"This Board of Inquiry is adjourned," the vice admiral said and struck with the gavel again. And with a smile she turned and led the others from the room.

At the door Scaragoglu turned and, with a wicked smile, crooked a finger at Peter. "My office, twenty minutes," he mouthed, and followed the others.

Knott's head snapped round to glare at Peter.

He did it, Raeder thought gleefully, trying to look innocent. Then his heart sank with the thought: *And now I'm in his debt.* Peter wondered how it would be to owe his career to one of the most ruthless men in existence. *Like selling your soul to the devil?* They didn't call General Scaragolu the Spider for nothing . . .

Knott had made his way to Raeder's side.

"I'll see you in my office at eighteen hundred, Commander. That should give you plenty of time to finish your business with the Spid . . . with the general."

"Yes, sir," Raeder said and saluted. The captain stared at him, and then shook his head—it was a fatherly gesture, somehow. *It certainly makes me feel like a small boy on the carpet.* Knott snapped off a salute and left the courtroom, leaving Raeder to dread both of his appointments.

Flying a Speed was different. The pilot half reclined, fingers planted in cups lined with sensors that responded to every tiny movement. That response moved the sleek fighters through their deadly acrobatic, and, with the aid of an eye-tracking mechanism built into the face shield, fired their considerable weaponry with deadly accuracy.

The face shield also showed the pilot a one hundred and eighty degree sweep of the field of stars around her as well as a heads-up display which overlaid the view. With a precise series of blinks an object could be brought up to intense magnification. Useful at the speeds and distances the fighter craft could travel.

Sarah James blinked the asteroid she'd spotted back down to size. It glinted as it tumbled, which was what had first attracted her eye. She was assigned to a routine convoy escort and was just skirting the edges of boredom.

Not that escorting convoys had been all that routine of late. Especially as they approached the jump point. Still, things had gotten somewhat better now that the powers that be had begun to allocate real weapons and the trained crews to use them to the merchant ships. At the very least they'd succeeded in thinning the ranks of the pirates.

On the other hand, like natural selection, sometimes the results were not what had been intended. Humanity was now left with only the most deadly pirates, and cockroaches that could breathe vacuum and eat insecticides.

She looked down at the convoy of freighters. Her Speed looked like a sparrow beside a crocodile in comparison to the smallest of her charges. But she was the dangerous one despite her relative size. The ships below were reasonably armed now, but they lacked her Speed's agility.

There was quite a disparity of character among the freighters. Some were glitteringly new from the factory

space-yard, some old but well tended, some barely
spaceworthy, if that.

Sarah dipped her head and sucked on her water tube.
Instruments pinged and automatically checked on the
spaceborne bodies they located. So far, all asteroids. The
lieutenant commander frowned. Rather a lot of asteroids.

"Computer, is there usually this much clutter in this
corridor?" she asked.

"Checking. It varies, Lt. Commander," the AI
responded. "However, I have no previous reports of an
asteroid field containing such large specimens in this area
before now."

Interesting, Sarah thought.

Asteroid fields didn't just happen. Bodies large and
small did drift through space, true, but it was vanishingly
unlikely that a conglomeration of pieces this large would
appear without anyone noticing them. The computer
showed they averaged no less than fifty meters long and,
depending on the angle, thirty wide.

*They're a navigation hazard for one thing, so they should
have been one of the top items in my briefing.* Sarah frowned.
There was also a distinct lack of smaller pieces accompanying them. *I think my life just got more exciting,* she
thought with dawning suspicion.

Had to be more than was meeting the eye here, had
to be.

"Escort to convoy," she said, then spoke the coded
phrase that would bring the merchants to red alert. "You
are drifting. Adjust your course on the leader by ten
degrees."

"Escort," said a surprisingly young voice, "this is
Murphy's Queen. What are you talkin' about? My instruments say we're all perfectly aligned."

Sarah's eyes widened. *What the hell . . . ?*

"If you will check your briefing papers, *Murphy's Queen,*
you will find that *I* am in charge out here. And if I tell
you to adjust your alignment by *ten degrees,* you *will* adjust
your alignment by *ten degrees,*" she said loudly and with
heavy emphasis, hoping that someone within hearing
distance of this kid *had* in fact read the briefing papers.

"La-dy! If I adjust our course by ten degrees we're gonna be a big silver splat on one of these rocks out here."

Give me strength, Sarah prayed to whoever might be listening.

After a long pause she snapped, "Let me speak to your captain."

The youngster left the com open and she heard him call out, "Da-ad."

Good grief! she thought. Sarah was aware that merchanters trained their children by letting them help out on the ship. But surely, even the most raggedy-assed ship knew better than to leave what sounded like a twelve-year-old in charge of the bridge during the most dangerous period of their crossing!

Captain Dad came on with a gruff, "What's happening?"

"Sir," Sarah said, biting off each word. "If, as indicated in your *briefing papers,* you would please adjust your course alignment by *ten degrees,* I would appreciate it."

"Whaddayoutalkin'about? We're in perfect alignment." *AAARRRGGHH!!!*

"Did you read your briefing paper?" Sarah demanded.

"No-o."

"Go read it now," she insisted. "I'll wait." *And if there are pirates out there and they're listening to all this briefing papers,* ten degrees, *wink, wink, nudge, nudge stuff, they should be powering up any second now. If I get my hands on this guy, assuming I live through the next twenty minutes, I'm going to clean his clock!*

"Ooooh," said *Murphy's Queen's* captain with elephantine obviousness. "Adjust my course by *ten degrees.* Yes, ma-am!" And he was gone without signing off.

"Neutrino output detected," the computer said calmly. Flashing lights indicated four of the larger asteroids. "Signal is commensurate with ship power plants activating."

Nooo kidding, Sarah thought sarcastically. She brought her weapons online automatically.

"Designate which came first, second and so on," she ordered the computer. The blinking lights flashed red, yellow, blue and green in sequence. Next came the part she hated most. "Unknown ships, please identify yourselves immediately or be fired upon."

Nothing like warning the enemy. But it couldn't be helped. People did stupid things, like hiding in the bushes, then shaking them and growling when their well-armed hunting buddies came back to camp. Similarly, this might be a cluster of tramp merchants hoping to join the convoy rather than a group of pirates. It was never wise to be too trigger-happy. She forced herself to count to ten. *Okay, long enough,* she thought.

Sarah fired on the asteroid marked in red just as a ship burst free of its cover. Fusion-driven particle beam met carbonaceous chondrite rock and turned it into small but high-velocity shrapnel, slashing into the raider before it could build up enough delta-v to escape. The front part of the fuselage spun off out of control and crashed into the massive side of one of the freighters, in a mist of frozen air and volatiles from both craft.

Sarah winced, hoping there wouldn't be many casualties. But she was only aware of the disaster peripherally. She'd already fired on the yellow asteroid, and apparently destroyed the ship lurking behind it. But now blue and green were out of cover and swooping down on her.

All right, roughly corvette-sized. Pirate ships weren't built to order, but they usually had fairly massive power plants for their mass. Pirates were in business to intimidate and loot, not fight—and they liked to be able to run away, too.

Blue came on aggressively, while green hung back. Sarah's fingers twitched in the sensor gloves, and a small light strobed in the corner of her vision—the missile's sensors locking on to green.

"Away," the AI said passionlessly, and the Speed shuddered briefly as the weapon streaked away. She put her Speed into a roll and snapped off a barrage of energy-beam fire at Mr. Blue. . . .

Care-ful, she thought calmly, *don't lose control.* She came out of it to find her opponents doing just fine. *Well, hell.* There was a fading nimbus of plasma where a close-in defense weapon had intercepted her missile.

And they were both approaching her with a bit more respect. But they were still willing to fight.

"Following trajectory," she told her AI, and traced a curve that would put the pirates between her and the merchanters . . . and their newly formidable armaments. Even then, some part of her consciousness was aware of the backdrop, stars innumerable and burning with the clear bright colors of vacuum.

Let's distract Mr. Blue, she thought, and took the Speed looping over in a dive almost as abrupt as a winged craft in atmosphere. She faked a drive towards blue, then fired on green. The Speed bucked slightly as the particle beam slashed out, invisible to human eyes, marked on her vision by the fighter craft's systems . . .

Woah. *That* was visible to the naked eye, a corona of light expanding around the green marker that the sensor system had painted on her vision. Nobody who'd seen combat in space could mistake what it meant; a containment vessel had failed, and matter and antimatter had come into contact . . . and the rest of the pirate craft was now an expanding ball of ionized gas.

Blue flashed past at an angled vector and took off for the tall timber, or at least for the hyper limit. Sarah killed her velocity and boosted in the ship's wake; it was a stern chase, but she had a lot more normal-space boost than a craft burdened with interstellar capacity, even a compact and powerful one like the pirate corvette.

You took them down or you took them in, but you never left this scum to run free.

Firing solution, she thought. Too much in the way of fields and energetic particles for a beam attack, crawling up their butts like this, but a missile . . .

"Bogie on your tail," the computer announced with obscene calm.

With a gasp and a sharp stab of adrenaline Sarah's hands moved in the gloves, wrenching acceleration slamming the Speed into a random course. But she felt a hard impact and the craft was shaken like an old sock in a Doberman's mouth. The lights flared, went from green to red to overload as systems failed, lethal secondary radiation sleeted through all shielding . . .

And her board blanked and the power went offline with a descending whine, leaving only a "YOU'RE DEAD" signal blinking at her.

Sarah sat in the darkness and pouted.

Where the hell did that bogie come from? she wondered. *Why didn't the computer tell me that there were fresh neutrino signals in that neighborhood?*

"Simulation over," the computer announced in a prim little voice. "Pilot and Speed both total casualties. Probable outcome of exercise, loss of one merchant ship."

Sarah winced, already assessing where her errors had lain. *For one, I didn't make sure that every merchant bridge crew was familiar with the plan.*

Wearily, Sarah pushed up her helmet and unclasped her harness. The door to the simulator opened and a tech peeked in with a waft of cool, sterile station-side air. Sarah rose from her pilot's couch and stepped out, bracing herself for the inevitable techie good humor.

"You did really well in there, sir," he said, smiling, but respectful. "Only person who's ever had a higher score on this run is Commander Raeder."

Sarah's brows went up. "Raeder's run this sim?"

"Yes, sir. He's here most every day. That new prosthesis that Lieutenant Robbins made up for him works like a charm. He could fly rings around just about anybody on board. If they'd let him fly," the tech finished with a shrug.

Sarah just said, "Huh!" and walked away to write her report on this simulation. It gave her a little lift though, to know that Peter wasn't giving up. Speed pilots as a group were hard to get down. But taking their wings away was one of the few things that could do it. Raeder's determination to get his back pleased her.

Though why it should, she thought with a shake of her head, *is beyond me.* Then she stopped, cocked her head and turned back to the tech.

"So I've got the second-highest Speed test rating on board?" she asked.

"Yes, sir." The tech grinned. "Unofficially, of course, since the captain is the one that's s'posed to tell you."

Sarah returned his grin and gave him a thumbs up. *I'm in!* she thought happily, as she walked away. *Now all I have to do is keep from overdosing on testosterone.*

Peter walked jauntily, returning the occasional salute; the corridors of the station felt a lot less drab and confining, now that he knew he wasn't staying here long. Even the recycled and carefully "scented" air felt better. . . .

On the other hand, he thought, *I'm on my way to see His Arachnidness Marine General Scaragoglu.* Even that wasn't quite enough to dampen his mood . . . but then he turned a corner to find Admiral Grettirson coming towards him. When Grettirson noticed him the admiral's lips jerked back from his teeth like a man stabbed in the backside by poisoned mandibles.

Peter's step slowed, but he continued walking. As they came closer to one another, he snapped off a salute and stepped to the side.

The admiral slowed, then stopped, standing very close to Raeder. He did not return the salute. Raeder kept his eyes stubbornly downcast, rightly afraid of the nervous laughter he knew would betray him. This was exactly the sort of situation that brought it out in him.

How do you explain to a man this serious about himself that you're not laughing at him? I'm not laughing at you, sir, I'm laughing at the situation. I am the situation, Raeder. But I'm not laughing at you, sir. Then why, Raeder? I'm laughing because, because . . . Because, sir, just because. Oh he'd had that conversation many, many times. *But not with this man,* he warned himself. *You don't ever want this man to think you're laughing at him.*

Grettirson leaned closer, until Peter could feel the admiral's breath on his face.

"You lit-tle *pissant!*" the admiral said softly.

Raeder's eyes snapped up in surprise and met the full force of Grettirson's ice blue glare.

"You think you've put one over on me, don't you?" the

admiral asked him. He leaned closer. "You're probably laughing at me right now, aren't you?"

No, sir! No laughing here, sir! But Peter could feel it tickling his ribs. He shook his head, trying to look sincere. *Oh, God, oh, God. Don't smile, don't smile.* Sweat popped out on his forehead as he struggled manfully.

"Well let me tell you, *boy*," the admiral's teeth were clenched and muscles in his cheeks danced with the stress, "you may think you're getting away with something here, but you are in for a *big* surprise. I know my duty. *No one* interferes with the performance of my duty. And my duty is to put glory-hungry loose cannons like you where you can't get good men killed."

Grettirson paused, breathing heavily through his nose, his thin lips pressed tight, the color draining from his cheeks. Peter sensed the tension in the older man's muscles, as though the admiral would attack physically if Raeder made a move. After what seemed an eternity Grettirson seemed to get himself under control once more.

"If you survive whatever party he has planned for you . . ." The Admiral smiled and nodded. "I'm going to issue you an invitation you can't refuse."

Huh? Raeder thought, frantically trying to figure out exactly what the admiral meant. *Does he mean he's going to court martial me, or he's got an assignment that's more of a killer than even Scaragoglu can come up with? There's a cheerful thought.* Either choice would keep him up nights.

Grettirson poked the commander in the chest, hard.

"You just made yourself an enemy you can't afford, boy."

I haven't got any *enemies in my budget, sir,* Raeder thought. *Especially not admirals.*

The admiral leaned in again. "Watch your back, Commander." He hesitated and then snapped off a salute.

Raeder lowered his arm and watched Grettirson walk away. He shuddered.

There's a guy who's right on the edge. Even so, another part of him noted, the admiral couldn't bring himself not to salute. *But it cost him.* Raeder knew it wouldn't be welcome, but he felt sorry for the guy. *Losing your kid must be the worst thing that can happen to anybody.* Which did not mean he had any intention of taking it in the neck as someone's revenge against an uncaring universe.

So should I mention this . . . encounter to the Scaragoglu? No. It was doubtful that the Marine general would appreciate something that smacked of whining. *By the same token, he'd expect to be informed. Guess I'd better have another drink with Sjarhir then.*

Raeder continued thoughtfully on his way, feeling a great deal less jaunty than he had.

To Peter's surprise, when Scaragoglu's secretary let him into the inner office, Captain Knott was seated before the Marine general's desk, sipping whiskey, looking as though he'd been there for some time. There was a slight smell of fine tobacco and single-malt liquor tinging the inevitable Navy smell of recycled air and metal and synthetics.

Reader saluted and his seniors answered it. He could feel their eyes on him now, disconcertingly sharp, like the targeting lasers of a seeker missile. He had the feeling that they were expecting him to do something clever.

Like . . . ?

"Sit down, Commander." Scaragoglu leaned back in his chair and watched Peter seat himself, then he leaned forward and pulled the chair up to his desk, leaning his elbows upon it. "I've been outlining the bare bones of the plan to Captain Knott here," he said, indicating the Captain with a gesture. "Now that you're here, we can get down to some of the specifics.

"We're planning this as a thirty-day mission. The *Invincible* will enter Mollie space on what is apparently a raid-scouting mission. We've got some good information that should bring you in on the skirts of a pirate we've been tracking." He passed a chip over to the captain. "That's her dossier. She's got three genuine Speeds, four Mollie-built copies and one jury-rigged critter that still manages to do a lot of damage. The main ship is an old Earth-built bulk freighter with souped-up engines. Our information says that the Mollies are so eager for the goods she's carrying that they're sending an escort." He smiled grimly and nodded at Knott. "That should give your people a little something to sharpen their teeth on. Whatever else happens though, let at least one Mollie ship go crying home to the Interpreters. When you've chased them far enough that you're sure they won't double back on you, call back your Speeds and proceed to this location."

He called up the holo of the asteroid field he'd shown Peter the night before.

"I'll give you both a chip on this before you go, gentlemen." Scaragoglu gave Knott a nod. "It's an obvious job for a light carrier," he said. "The *Invincible* is fast, she's small, but she packs a wallop when she needs to, and best of all she can carry a whole lot of Speeds. More than we'd originally planned, in fact. Your last mission proved that."

"How many more?" Knott asked.

"Six. We couldn't hide more than that in our projected base." He touched the miner's hutch with a laser pointer and enlarged the view. Scaragoglu turned to Peter. "There's no gravity there, can't be helped. Any change in that area will draw attention and we can't risk that. So you'll just have to live with it. But it might be a factor in choosing your crew."

Raeder nodded. Space adjustment sickness was a factor, if a minor one. Most Speed pilots were only affected by SAS in a minor way, but someone inclined to vomit when it struck was a definite disadvantage. Especially in a place that probably had lousy air filtration.

"Your Speeds will be specially equipped with unusually heavy weaponry." Scaragoglu grinned. "That should make you equal to about anything you run into. If you encounter pirates, engage them," he said. "If you can take them, imprison them in their own ship. Disable their engines, weapons and communications. Then lock them away from anything more vital than the kitchen and the head." He took a thoughtful sip of whiskey. "It would probably be best to drain their fuel and then destroy any pirate ships you take after the first one. One ship should suffice to contain all your prisoners; I don't especially care if they get along together. With the weaponry you'll be assigned you should only leave a few atoms floating around. Any ship too big to destroy completely, get it deep into the asteroid field and break it up there." The general's sharp brown eyes met Raeder's. "While I don't want these people abused the fact is that you won't have enough people to nursemaid them. They'll have air, water, and food, the rest will be their responsibility.

"If, however, you encounter Commonwealth freighters shipping to the Mollies, you will take them with the least loss of life possible. Lock them in their *own* ships and hide them in the asteroid field until they can be escorted home by the *Invincible*. Intelligence, needless to say, will be very interested in any records of transactions you might obtain."

"What about Mollie patrols, or freighters, sir?" Raeder asked.

The Marine general pursed his lips.

"The Mollies are the enemy, Commander. Treat them as such. When attacking the Mollies you will do your best to appear to be pirates. Mollie patrols are fair game," he continued, "defeat them if you can. The freighters present a more delicate problem. By our lights they'd be civilians. But by Mollie standards they're as much soldiers as anybody in a fighting craft."

He shrugged. *Uh-oh*, Peter thought. That was the shrug of a superior officer saying: *Use your own judgement.* That generally translated: *If you're right, I get the credit; if you screw up, you're the goat.* The Commonwealth had a long tradition of gentlemanly treatment of noncombatants; on the other hand, the Commonwealth *didn't* have a long tradition of fighting for its life against opponents of comparable strength.

"If we'd consider them civilians, sir, then I'll treat them as such," Raeder said.

Scaragoglu smiled.

"I knew you'd say that, Commander." He shook a finger at Peter. "Just remember, *they* will fight like soldiers and consider themselves to *be* soldiers. So treat them with appropriate caution. Allow the odd one to escape, towards the end of your stay, naturally, to tell the Interpreters all about this pirate activity they've encountered. If you do it right, they should never suspect it's us. The aim of this operation isn't simply to destroy enemy shipping; it's disinformation."

He raised his brows and looked at Peter until the commander nodded.

"Excellent." The Marine general passed out a set of chips to both Peter and Knott. "These are the particulars on the location and the base, the mission brief and your orders. These," he looked at Peter, "are the dossiers of those Marines I mentioned to you. And a couple of technical people I'd like you to consider." He handed them over. "If you have any further questions on this material contact my liaison." He nodded at Sjarhir, quietly seated in his corner.

"The pirate ship the *Invincible* is going after, the *Bastard's Bait*, appropriately enough, will be coming through the jump point in three weeks." Scaragoglu grimaced. "Unless they all get drunk and forget about it completely."

Raeder and Knott smiled politely.

"It's tight, I know. But I've given orders that your resupply needs are a top priority, so I don't imagine you'll be given the usual runaround by the quartermaster." This time he smiled, and it wasn't polite.

Uh-oh, Peter thought again. There weren't very many people who'd care to talk procedure with Scaragoglu when he had a mission priority statement from the High Command. The problem was that the Marine knew that and savored it.

This guy knows what he's doing. Trouble is, he enjoys *having that sort of clout.* Which made you just a bit nervous about working for him. *I'd trust Knott to back me up whatever happened. Hell, he* has *backed me up when it put his ass in a crack too. Scaragoglu ... all I know about Scaragoglu is rumors and the fact that he's called the Spider.*

Scaragoglu leaned back, the chair creaking slightly under his massive shoulders.

"Questions?" he asked.

"None immediately spring to mind, sir," Knott answered. "I may have a few once I've reviewed this material."

The Marine general nodded affably and turned to Peter.

"I have my pick of personnel, sir?" he asked.

Scaragoglu nodded.

"With only seven days I'll have to get my candidates from Ontario Base and the *Invincible*," Raeder said. "Will I be allowed access to service records?"

"Virtually unlimited access," the general said expansively. "Your way is cleared and the rails are greased." He gave Raeder a smile. "Don't get used to it."

"No, sir," Peter answered, with a small smile of his own.

"If there's nothing else, gentlemen ..." The Marine general rose and they rose with him. He extended his hand to Knott, then to Raeder. "Good luck, good hunting, and may God and His Prophet go with you."

"Thank you, sir," they both murmured and left the office together.

They'd walked a long way through the myriad corridors of Ontario Base, each lost in his own thoughts as they made their way back to the *Invincible*.

At last, Peter cleared his throat and asked, "Did you still want to see me, sir?"

Knott gave him a sidelong glance and shook his head.

"No point," he said with a rueful smile. "I've been snookered by the old bastard myself. Who am I to give you dire warnings?"

Then the older man grinned. "Besides, this *is* exactly the sort of thing the *Invincible* was designed for, and I *did* request the command."

"In other words, sir, you're exactly the sort of glory hound you were about to chew me out for being?"

For a moment Raeder thought he'd gone too far, and

then the captain's shoulders rose and fell in a shrug. "That's one way to put it, son. The other is that I'm *extremely* focused . . . which is what you call the same behaviors once the hormonal storm of youth has passed. Let's go; we've both got a Hell-load of work to do."

CHAPTER FOUR

Raeder entered his office with a sprightly step and sat at his desk, radiating energy. He rubbed his hands together briskly, flexed his fingers and called up personnel records on his computer. There was a bright side to this whole mess. Two, in fact. If it worked and he survived, he'd have done the war effort a real service; good in itself, and it *looked* good, which he frankly conceded to himself he needed badly at this point in a more-than-eventful career. Second . . .

Anybody I want . . . and anything. His smile was so wide it almost hurt. You didn't get a better offer than this, ever. *And I intend to take full advantage of the good general's generosity,* he thought with an evil grin. *Carte blanche will come this way but once, hee hee. It's Christmas day and the sun's coming up. Toy time!*

Names scrolled up the screen; he ticked off the ones he wanted and the computer brought them up in a queue. He sipped at a cup of cocoa his orderly deposited in an outstretched hand.

Better just work up a short list first. Let's see, we'll have six Speeds, and I'll want a minimum of four alternate pilots, that's ten. Skeleton tech crew is three per, then we'll need six more just to be safe, surveillance, medical . . .

There were two people he had to eliminate out of hand for practical reasons. Paddy because of his loathing for Marines. *And if Scaragoglu wants Marines, there will be Marines,* Raeder told himself ruefully. Nor could he tap Second Lieutenant Cynthia Robbins. She was much improved, incredibly enough, by her association with the impulsive Paddy, but she still lacked those ever-important people skills.

In a high-stress, low-amenity situation like a miners' hutch in enemy territory, you don't need to come home to someone who'll tear a strip off you for getting a nick on your Speed.

And she would too. Cindy loved the Speeds in her care like they were her prize stallions, or pet lambs, or kids— God help any children she eventually had. But she tended to treat the pilots like they were plug-in parts of suspect origin that didn't function as efficiently as they should. She probably really, really regretted that nobody had ever been able to build a genuine artificial intelligence. There were times he thought she wished she were one herself.

And so, for her own good, both to preserve her newly won and very fragile self-confidence and his own sanity, Raeder flicked past her name without stopping.

Paddy now . . . there was a name he hated to pass by. *He'd be perfect in so many ways,* Peter mourned. *He's a fantastic engineer, resourceful, quick and knowledgeable. And I like him, dammit.* Raeder shook his head. Not possible. And it would be unfair. Paddy really wanted to make it into officers' training, and putting him in close quarters with a Marine was just waving a red flag in front of a bull.

Raeder settled down to choose his team. In less than an hour he had double the number he'd need and had scheduled them for interviews. *The Chief's been bugging me to do performance reviews for a week now. That'll make an excellent cover.* And no one need know that they'd been considered for the mission and rejected.

Peter felt a fleeting regret that he couldn't take arap Moi, his chief petty officer, along too. He sighed. *Gotta leave somebody around to watch the store.* And Cindy. They didn't want any backsliding into her old ways.

There was a tap on his office door and Raeder called out, "Come in."

The door slid aside and Paddy poked his head into the room like a turtle uncertainly testing the air outside its shell.

"What can I do for you, Chief?" Peter asked. His curiosity was immediately aroused. Diffidence was not Paddy's style. "Sit down," he said, indicating a chair.

The big, red-headed New Hibernian shuffled over to the seat and, sitting, swamped it. He looked at Raeder from under bushy ginger eyebrows with a sorrowful expression on a face like a boiled ham, if you could imagine a ham with blue eyes and freckles.

All at once Peter had a vision of Paddy as a seven-year-old in a striped jersey, bitterly sorry for some prank he'd pulled. Part of being an officer was controlling your expressions; he kept his neutral-friendly.

"C'mon, Chief, spill. What's the problem?"

Casey took a breath deep enough to inflate his toes and then let it out in a sigh so expressive it was almost a song. He tossed a datachip onto Peter's desk.

With a wry look at the Chief, Raeder picked it up and inserted it, calling up the information it contained. After a moment, what he read made his own shoulders slump.

"I'm really sorry, Paddy," he said with great sincerity.

"Ahhh, tis me own fault," the big man answered. "If I wasn't so in love wit' provin' myself with me fists instead o' me brains I wouldn't have a record that would make a nun curse."

Raeder glanced at the letter on his screen.

. . . unfortunately, repeated assaults upon fellow enlisted personnel and even officers force us to conclude that you lack the temperament necessary to an officer candidate.

Peter shook his head. He honestly couldn't blame them. Glancing at Paddy he thought, *Even the big guy agrees with 'em.* Pity the Chief had allowed his temper such free rein, he had a lot to offer in most respects.

"I need your help, sir," Paddy said humbly.

Peter's eyebrow went up. Paddy? Humble?

"I can write to them on your behalf," he offered.

"Nah," Paddy flung out a dismissive hand, then raised his head and looked Raeder straight in the eye. "Y'know they'll just file it."

Raeder's other eyebrow went up. "So . . . what do you want me to do?" Was he just looking for a drinking buddy?

"Ah, now here's the beauty of my scheme," Paddy began, hitching himself forward on his chair.

What scheme? Raeder thought suspiciously.

"By helpin' me ye'll be helpin' yerself, sir."

That's two sirs in one conversation, Peter thought. *Whatever he wants, it's big.*

Paddy drew himself up, blue eyes sparkling, gave Peter a confident smile and said, "I'm volunteerin', sir."

Raeder blinked. "For . . . ?"

The Chief chuckled and leaned forward conspiratorially. "You *know.*" Paddy jerked his head to the left. "That other."

"Hanh?"

That other? What the hell was "that other"?

Paddy rolled his eyes, then gave the commander an old-fashioned look.

"That other thing that the Marine general has been on to ye about," he said impatiently, in a hoarse whisper.

Raeder's jaw dropped. *What's next?* he thought. *An announcement in the* Globe And Mail, *"Captain Raeder to Head Top Secret Mission, Details Available for Download"?*

Paddy was leaning forward again and explaining himself eagerly.

"I'm your man, sir. Y'know the quality of my work, y'know ye can rely on me to get the job done, whatever it takes."

Raeder waved a hand to stop the flow. "You're an excellent engineer, Paddy, and no one could doubt your loyalty or courage. Or resourcefulness." Raeder's voice had slowed and his eyes took on a speculative gleam, then he shook his head decisively.

"'Tis me thrice-cursed temper, isn't it?" the big New

Hibernian asked in despair. "The bane of me existence, it is. But you know how much it means to me to get into officers' training, sir." Paddy's hand stroked the edge of the desk, but his eyes never left Peter's. "This is me only hope, sir. I need to do somethin' amazing or they'll never spit on me, they won't. I've never had a *reason* to hold me temper before now. But there are some things that a man will change his very nature for and this is one of 'em," he insisted.

"Lieutenant Robbins?" Raeder said.

"Aye. She is the pulse of my heart, Commander. But unless I am an officer I cannot . . . we cannot . . . *it* cannot be!"

Peter stifled a sigh. In peacetime it would be another matter. Cynthia could surrender her commission, or Paddy could leave the service. Heaven knew the merchant marine would happily employ a couple with their skills. *Happily? They'd clear out the captain's cabin for them.* But there was a war on, and resigning was out of the question for both of them. *No discharge in the War, as the poet said.* Not that the government needed regulations to keep those two in; that was just part of who they *were*.

Peter rubbed his face with both hands and said, "Paddy, there are going to be Marines."

"Ahhh, tcha!" Paddy exclaimed and waved it away. "And what of it? What sort of a fool would I be to hold that against any man or woman? Sure they can't help it but be what they are. T-sssh," he scoffed. "I'm not a bull that can't help but run at a red flag. I can be friends with anyone if I set me mind to it."

Peter felt like he'd been whapped with that salmon a second time.

"You *hate* Marines!" he exclaimed, trying to get back to a familiar reality.

"Oh, no, sir!" As Raeder started to object he hurried on, "It's not so much I hate Marines, d'ye see, as I love to fight. And who in this world or any other will give ye a better one?" he asked happily.

I've got a headache, Reader thought, wishing he could

clap his hands to his throbbing temples. *Wait a minute, I haven't denied anything yet. I've got to get this conversation back under my control.*

"Paddy," he said patiently. "This is all beside the point because there is no mission."

"Of course not, sir," Paddy said with a wink and a nod, a conspiratorial smirk on his face. "Ye never heard it here."

Raeder laughed; he couldn't help it.

"Paddy," he tried again, "what makes you think I've got some kind of a mission going on?"

The Chief looked at Raeder for a moment as though nonplussed and then exclaimed, "And didn't that divil Scaragoglu crook his finger at ye and say to come to his office? And why would he be doing that if he didn't have something major on his mind? For, sure, if it was you alone he wanted he'd never have made a public display like that." Paddy's blue eyes studied Raeder to see how this had been taken. Shaking his head, he went on. "Tis something big, I'm thinkin' and he wanted to alert those with eyes to see that an opportunity was comin' up. That's my thought on it."

Peter felt a blush warm his cheek as he realized that was exactly what Scaragoglu had done. *Maybe I ought to bring him along just to interpret the Marine general for me,* he thought ruefully. There seemed to be a definite link between the spiderlike deviousness of Scaragoglu and the sort of low cunning Paddy had picked up in a decade sliding up and down the greasy pole of rank from rating to noncom and back.

"If I hear anything . . ." he began.

"Sir," Paddy murmured with a telling inclination of his big head.

Raeder took a breath and started again. "I'll keep you in mind."

"Thank you, sir. That's all I ask is a chance." Paddy stood, grinning. Then his face grew serious again and he leaned forward confidentially. "But please remember, sir, how very much this means to me."

Twist that knife, Paddy, Raeder thought with a sick smile.

Oh, yes, I saved your life, but I'd never dream *of calling in a favor, no, sir, perish the thought . . .*

They exchanged salutes. Paddy marched to the door, where he turned and whispered, "Thank ye, sir," as the door swished closed before his beaming face.

It was with mixed feelings that Raeder confirmed Paddy as his first team member. *I'm happy,* he told himself. *I mean Paddy was my first choice.* An instinctive choice. The right choice. *I hope.* There was still that legendary temper to beware of.

But Peter was very unhappy about his missing something so obvious as the Marine general's publicly calling on him to come to his office. *Scaragoglu does nothing without a reason.* So the rumors said, and so, he thought, he knew. *I guess I was too focused on my own problems to see what was right in front of my face,* he thought. And that kind of obtuseness in dealing with someone like Scaragoglu was dangerous.

Hmmm. It would be just like Scaragoglu to deliberately leak that Raeder was being tapped for some clandestine mission, then a little more subtly leak a false mission profile, and then clumsily leak the *real* mission, using that to disinform—

He ran his hands across his face again. That sort of thinking made his head hurt. *Well, forewarned is forearmed. I'll be more aware in the future,* he promised himself as he went back to work. *I hope.*

Raeder had gone over the personnel files of all his choices to familiarize himself with any changes that had been made recently and had been pleased by what he had seen. Efficiency in his own Flight Engineering department was way up and most of the people he'd chosen had been commended for their behavior during the *Invincible*'s recent crises. Those who hadn't were new to the ship.

They'll get their commendations yet, though. I think Invincible*'s going to be one of those career-making ships.* Which would probably please her unknown mentor, a presence Peter was convinced existed. Otherwise how could an experimental ship ever have gotten the attention and the crew she deserved? And *Invincible* was beautifully constructed, no expense spared, and splendidly staffed. *Of course, ships that make careers and ships that end them— permanently, so the relatives get a folded flag and a visit from the parson—are very, very similar.*

There had been a few exceptions to the "splendidly staffed," Peter remembered with a wry grimace. Such as William Booth, the chief of security, a last-minute replacement foisted on the ship by an unkind bureaucracy.

He won't be a problem this time, Peter comforted himself. *A security officer would be a luxury on this trip.* Then added, *I hope,* as he remembered John Larkin, the saboteur he'd genuinely liked on first meeting.

Peter determinedly thrust the whole matter from his mind and began to concentrate on what supplies he especially wanted to obtain. He wondered if this wouldn't be a great opportunity to scrounge a few things for Main Deck that the quartermaster's office had been denying them for months now.

Well, sure, he thought, *as long as I don't abuse the Marine general's license.* Unconsciously, his face slipped into an expression of blatant innocence. *I'd be derelict in my duty not to.* Raeder called up the quartermaster's catalogue and dove happily in to a Tom Tiddler's Ground of spare drive coils, brand-new electronics modules still sealed in preservant film, and delicacies intended for the Port Admiral's mess steward.

Peter had been working steadily and responsibly for an hour and a half. He was quite proud of himself for resisting the urge to hog all the hard to obtain, and therefore most often needed, parts for the *Invincible.* Not that he'd want anyone to be dangerously undersupplied. Still, it was an ancient tradition of the service; if somebody had to do without, you didn't want it to be *your* ship. . . .

By the time the task was done he was whistling tunelessly with sheer enjoyment—a far cry from the stomach-churning frustration that usually attended an afternoon doing "Requisition and Resupply." After every request he'd typed, the word "Approved" had appeared. Only once had he been balked and then it was a matter of, *"Parts on order. Six (6) will be reserved and shipped to* Invincible *upon receipt at Ontario Base Quartermaster's,"* so he really couldn't complain.

Hey, for all I know, my ordering 'em will speed up the base's request at Central Supply.

Peter was making small happy sounds as he worked when his eyes lit on something unexpected. *Wow! I didn't even know they* made *these anymore.* Acquisitive lust sparked in his belly. *There's no rational reason why I should get these,* Raeder warned himself. *Hell with that,* he answered instantly, *I want 'em and I can have 'em. That's excuse enough for me.*

With glee in his heart he typed in an order for six, and exulted when the word "Approved" lit up beside his request. *YES! Come to papa my little beauties.* Peter chuckled as he imagined envy on more than a few faces when his fellows discovered this coup. *For all I know these are the last ever made and they're* mine, *all mine.*

Raeder leaned back with a wide smile. *Ah, this is the life!* He felt like a Parliamentary Committee's idea of a Naval officer, someone whose main amusement was figuring out new ways to spend the taxpayers' credits.

There came a sharp tap on his office door and he called out an affable, "C'min."

Lieutenant Oswald Givens, resplendent in Speed pilot's coveralls presented himself before Raeder's desk with a snappy salute, eyes focused above Peter's head, body straight, feet together. A totally different Givens from their previous encounters.

Raeder returned the lieutenant's salute with one markedly less crisp. *Suddenly I feel like Captain Knott,* he thought, amused. He kept his face painfully straight, however. He knew Givens, and a sense of humor—particuarly about himself—wasn't among his many virtues.

"At ease lieutenant," Raeder said. "How can I help you?"

"Sir! I would like to volunteer, sir!" Givens still looked

straight ahead, about a foot over Peter's head, and he'd shifted his stance to a very stiff parade rest.

Raeder studied him. Oswald Givens was quite a handsome young man of about twenty-four years. He was a hair under Peter's own six feet, with an equally athletic build. Oswald had honey-blond hair, regular features and a firm, one might almost say heroic, chin.

If asked, Peter would rate him an excellent pilot, almost as good as himself. Givens got on well with his fellow pilots, who also rated him as a competent fighter and a hell of a flyer.

On the other hand, I've yet to meet anyone in Technical Support and Flight Engineering who doesn't hope he breaks his neck the next time he takes a shower. It wasn't *quite* bad enough for them to want to him totalled in combat, and besides, that would hurt his Speed.

To be fair, Oswald's was an attitude common to Speed pilots. In his honest, midnight moments, Raeder could admit to himself that once in a while he'd been no better in his flying days.

After all, who could avoid knowing that the purpose of a carrier was to carry? And what they carried was Speeds, and what was a Speed without her pilot? Therefore, the whole purpose of a carrier and her several thousand crewmen and women was to support the Speed pilot. Making all Speed pilots, regardless of rank, the princes of the city.

The question now was, *is Oswald Givens more arrogant than other pilots?*

Yeah, Raeder decided, remembering Givens' treatment not only of Cynthia Robbins, but of himself on a certain occasion. *He's above the line on arrogance. He's probably exactly the kind of conceited, macho jerk that permanently turned Sarah against Speed pilots.* Peter felt a spurt of resentment towards the lieutenant which, for once in their acquaintance, Givens hadn't earned. There was a saying about Speeds, that to fly them you had to have grapefruit-and-peas syndrome.

On the other hand, he flies better than almost anyone I've ever seen. Raeder frowned and shifted in his chair.

Givens glanced down for the first time since entering the office. It occurred to Peter that the lieutenant had taken it for granted that his offer would be accepted at once, with extreme gratitude, and he smiled inside.

"Sit down, Lieutenant," he said, indicating a chair.

Givens did so, a no-expression cast to his features that spoke his puzzlement as loudly as words. He looked at Raeder with bright, green-hazel eyes that Peter was sure had broken hearts from here to Luna-base with ease and without conscience.

"Explain yourself, Lieutenant," Raeder said, leaning forward, his hands clasped together on his desk.

Givens blinked, opened his mouth, closed it, then visibly gathered himself and began to speak.

"Word is that you're heading a mission, sir. Word is it's an important mission. I'd like to go with you, sir."

How many "sirs" is that since he walked in here? Raeder wondered, remembering Paddy.

"And what, exactly, have you heard about this . . . mission? And who did you hear it from?" Something snapped behind Raeder's eyes. "Did you read it in the *Globe and Mail*, perhaps?"

"Well, sir," Givens hesitated. "I didn't *hear* it exactly, I surmised it."

Peter frowned as the lieutenant paused. *Don't make me say, "explain" again, Givens, or you can forget it.*

"I saw Marine General Scaragoglu beckon to you and invite you to his office," Givens hurried on, apparently picking up on Peter's impatience. "I figured something was up, and I want to be in on it."

"Why?" Peter held the other man's gaze, watching Givens' eyes shift minutely as he considered his answer.

"I . . . sir, the Marine general's missions are the fastest route I know to medal territory."

Raeder was genuinely surprised. His brows went up. "They're generally the fastest route *I* know to a 'The Admiralty regrets to inform you' message. Medals mean that much to you, Lieutenant?"

"They do to my family, sir," Givens said firmly.

I've got to look up the lieutenant's family, Peter thought.

His own family had a very different attitude. His mother had told him after his injury that she'd rather know he was safe than see him win a barrel of medals and a bale of commendations. She'd meant it too. But what if his parents *had* wanted to see him decorated?

"Have you mentioned this alleged mission to anyone else, Lieutenant?"

"No, sir," Givens said with a slight smile. "I wanted to get my name in before anyone else."

"Well, don't go talking it up," Raeder cautioned. "If such a mission should come up, your name will be taken into consideration," he informed him.

"Thank you, sir!" Givens said, rising. He saluted.

Raeder returned it, seated and gave him a nod.

"Dismissed," he said.

"Thank you, sir," the lieutenant answered, smiling now.

He turned and marched to the door so quickly that he had to wait an embarrassing moment for it to open, obviously convinced that he'd made it, and equally anxious to get out before second thoughts took hold.

Well, he was on the list, Raeder thought. Not at the top, but he was on it. *After all, his personality could be a factor.* Still, his ability was undeniable. *So that makes two who could be problems. At least Paddy* knows *he's not perfect. I doubt it's ever crossed the good lieutenant's mind.* And yet, the man could *fly.*

Peter sighed, called up his list and put a star beside Givens' name. *After all, he was smart enough to figure it out. Maybe this is Scaragoglu's way of having a hand in choosing my staff.* He grimaced at the thought. Maybe it was just paranoid, and maybe he was right. But if this kept up he was going to dig in his heels. For now he'd prefer to think of this as a test that his choices were passing. *I did choose these people,* he thought stubbornly. But thinking it couldn't help him shake the notion that he was being pushed.

The executive staff of the *Invincible* sat quietly in their places as Captain Roger Knott studied the information on the screen built into the conference table before him.

The device was tilted slightly forward for easier reading and it underlit the captain's stern features eerily. A similar screen lay before each officer, the blue glow stronger than the dimmed overheads in the staff room that lay just behind the bridge.

Knott touched a control that scrolled information upward, then paused. He glanced across at Truon Le, his tactical officer.

"Have we had any other problems in the larboard laser cannon?" he asked.

"No, sir," Truon Le answered. "The problem with laser placement eighteen was due to a reversed part. The part itself is functioning normally."

"Good," Knott said quietly. "Are we well supplied with replacement crystals?"

Truon Le blinked.

"We have what would be an adequate supply for a moderately active three-week cruise, sir," he said after a moments reflection. "Moderately active to be defined as one encounter per week with at least two destroyer-class vessels."

Knott shook his head, his eyes on the screen again.

"Not sufficient. If we encounter something larger than destroyers two weeks in a row . . . what then? I'd rather we were overprepared than left wanting. Is this the way all tactical supplies are stocked? On the assumption of one encounter per week of cruise?"

"Yes, sir," the young tactical officer responded. "So far, of course, we haven't been out on a three-week cruise. So we might be said to be overprepared right now." His lips quirked in a tentative smile.

The captain looked up at him and nailed him with a considering eye.

"Supply constraints?" Knott said. It was really more of a statement than a question.

"I'm afraid so, sir." Truon Le spread his hands in a helpless gesture. "That and the fact that supplies are scarce. Only priority one is getting through at the moment in this sector. Once the pirates are brought under control, things should improve."

Knott leaned back in his chair, eyes focused on some inner consideration.

Mai Ling Ju, his executive officer, watched her captain carefully. This entire unscheduled meeting had been like this: a series of rapid-fire questions regarding preparedness, repairs, supplies and personnel. Mai Ling had rarely seen Knott so utterly focused. It meant that they were going somewhere and doing something serious. The men and women around the table glanced at one another. Whatever was going on didn't have the feeling of a drill, and this talk of needing more munitions was intriguing. The captain knew the general supply situation as well as or better than they did.

"Ladies and gentlemen," Knott said at last, "I want this ship prepared for a two-months cruise under battle conditions. I want supplies laid in and I want personnel brought up to strength. We will begin immediately. I want daily reports on your progress starting this afternoon. I do not want this to be a matter of discussion with other ships or with station personnel. Preparations will be conducted on a strict need-to-know basis." He looked around at them. "Any questions?"

No one responded, but the air was thick with them. Knott was pleased. Their silence indicated that they trusted him to tell them what they needed to know when the time was right.

I like this crew, he thought with pride. It was a pleasure to serve with them.

"Very well then, let's get to work." He rose from his place and his staff rose with him. "Dismissed," he said. Knott and his staff exchanged salutes.

He turned to enter his private office, while they filed out into the hallway.

Squadron Leader Ronnie Sutton hesitated, then stepped after the captain.

"Sir?" he said quietly.

The captain turned, not especially surprised that this was the officer who had come to him first.

"Might I have a moment of your time, sir?" the squadron leader asked.

Knott checked his watch.

"I can spare you a moment, Squadron Leader," he allowed. He led the way into his office and went behind his desk, seated himself and gestured to Sutton to take a chair. "What's on your mind, Ron?"

"Sir," the squadron leader said, leaning forward and holding the captain's eyes with an earnest gaze, "does this scramble to muscle up on supplies and people have anything to do with General Scaragoglu?"

Knott said nothing, stroking his upper lip, keeping his own counsel.

"Because if it does," Sutton hurried on, "I'd like to recommend some of my people for the mission."

There was a beat before Knott spoke, as though he were waiting to be sure that the squadron leader wasn't going to add anything to what he'd said.

"One," the captain said, holding up a finger, "you have no reason to believe that there is a *mission.* Two, if there were a mission there's no reason to believe that Speeds would be involved. Three, there is no reason whatsoever to connect General Scaragoglu with the *Invincible.*"

Sutton leaned back in his chair and crossed his legs, folding his hands in his lap and studying the captain.

"Sir," Sutton said quietly, "with all due respect, I beg to differ. The general visibly tapped Raeder, asking him to attend the general in his office. Moreover, strings had obviously been pulled or the poor commander would even now be packing his bags for home."

Knott smiled. He'd foreseen this sort of interview when Scaragoglu had made his interest in the commander so public. Still, he'd no intention of discussing the mission until *Invincible* was on her way.

Sutton's people were logical candidates, because Knott knew that Raeder had taken advantage of every opportunity to watch the squadron in action. The commander knew their abilities and would no doubt prefer to choose people whose qualities and quirks were familiar.

Nevertheless, that didn't entitle the squadron leader to a special briefing. *For one thing, I don't want to step on Raeder's toes.* It might well look that way, too.

Sutton would undoubtedly approach the commander on his own, but he wasn't going to be armed with information he wasn't yet entitled to when he did so.

And Raeder's entitled to pick his own team; the only way I'd interfere is if he's doing something spectacularly wrongheaded. Though he conceded to himself that Peter Raeder was fully capable of being dead wrong and utterly sly at one and the same time. *Still, I've no intention of second-guessing him or breathing down his neck. Nor will I have Ron, here, doing it with my apparent approval.*

In any case, the Spider was undoubtedly going to try to influence the commander's decisions. Knott rather looked forward to watching Raeder deal with Star Command's own Machiavelli. *Though I've no idea where to put my money,* he thought with an inner smile.

"I have nothing to add to what I said at the meeting, Squadron Leader." Knott's voice was quiet but full of authority. "Just bring your squadron up to full strength. Anyone still in sick bay must be replaced immediately. Make me a wish list and I'll see that it gets pushed through."

He stood and perforce the squadron leader did too.

"Yes, sir," Sutton said.

Though his disappointment at being excluded from the loop was almost palpable, British sangfroid forbade any visible sign of it. He saluted, the captain returned it and the squadron leader departed.

Knott sat down with a sigh and looked over at the holo of his old scout ship.

Ah, those were the days, he thought. *The simplicity of it all. Nothing in the universe to worry about but being hopelessly lost in endless space, or breaking down with no prospect of rescue, or being devoured by some alien gourmet.* The captain sighed again. *Duty calls,* he reminded himself.

He pulled his chair up to his desk and began making more detailed notes on the reports his senior officers had turned in. Life on the *Invincible* was about to get hectic.

CHAPTER FIVE

"Come," Knott said in answer to the chime at his door.

"Good evening, sir," the XO said as she entered.

He smiled wearily at Mai and held out his hand. She dropped a set of datachips into his waiting palm, then, at his gesture, sat in the easy chair near his desk. Knott put the chips down on his desk and returned briefly to his reading. The desk here in his personal quarters was smaller, but every bit as businesslike as the one in his office, and was used almost as much.

"I think that you'll find that everyone has struggled to be as detailed as possible under the circumstances," Mai Ling said when he turned to her at last.

He grinned. "Mai, you're so inscrutable this evening," he said.

She winced slightly, but smiled in return. Then settled in to wait. If she was to be briefed, the captain would speak with her tonight.

"We're being sent on a mission to Mollie space," the captain said at last.

Ju cocked her head. "Of course," she said. Where else would they go? For what other purpose did the *Invincible*

59

exist? "But there is something about this mission that troubles you, sir."

He nodded slowly.

"Our cover is that we're supposed to attempt to intercept a pirate ship loaded with goods for the Mollies. What we're really going there for is to drop off six Speeds to do guerilla runs against their shipping."

"I see," she said. Indeed she did. *Well, that's the Spider's trademark. Bold. Daring. Unconventional. Suicidal.* Mai Ling licked her lips. "We are to return for them?"

"Yes. But there's a great deal that could go wrong. We'll be cruising in another area looking for pirates or illegal shipping, or Mollies. Meanwhile, they're going to be on their own. Which means that if for any reason we can't get back to them . . ."

"There's no backup?" Ju asked. Though it was more a statement than a question.

"Given this is one of Scaragoglu's projects I can't answer that," Knott said grimly.

"But, given that this is one of Scaragoglu's projects it's fair to assume that the answer is no." Mai Ling caught a flicker of expression. A good XO was supposed to be able to read her captain's mind. . . . "So we will have to make sure that nothing goes wrong," she said.

Knott smiled. "Now, why didn't I think of that."

Their eyes met. *Except that, by definition, in a wartime operation things* do *go wrong.*

"Well, General Scaragoglu was right . . . Commander Raeder would be wasted in a desk job on Earth."

Knott nodded. *And, of course, Scaragoglu may have decided that if he's doomed anyway, he might as well go out in a blaze of useful glory. And if he's not just lucky, if he's really* good, *he'll find some way to survive . . . and be even more useful somewhere else, later.*

"Testing to destruction," Knott murmured.

"Poor bastard."

"Commander?" Chief Jomo arap Moi's voice came from the speaker sounding unusually clipped.

Raeder, who was working hard at clearing his mind

via the judicious use of a puzzle cube, answered, "Chief?"

"Sir, could you come down to Main Deck, please? We . . . have a most unusual delivery. I'm sure it's a mistake but they won't take my word for it."

"On my way." Raeder put down the cube and headed out the hatchway.

I should brief arap Moi on what we're expecting to be delivered, he thought. There had been plenty of things on his list that would come as a surprise to the Chief. Peter hadn't expected deliveries to begin arriving so soon, though. *Working with Scaragoglu does have its benefits,* he conceded, smiling. *Maybe this is what it's like to be in the High Command; you snap your fingers, and things actually happen. You* get *things, instead of "queries" and "requests for clarification" and "profoundly regrets."*

Peter stepped out onto cavernous spaces of Main Deck and took a deep breath. The scent of machinery, lubricant, fuel and scorched plastics, pleased him as much as the scent of flowers after a spring rain, and it was far more familiar, the smell of his trade. He walked from bay to bay to where he knew the Chief waited, glancing left and right at the Speeds towering over him, gleaming in the bright light.

He began to frown as he walked. The last two Speeds seemed to have fewer techs around them than there should be.

Where is everybody?

There they were. Chief arap Moi and twenty or so techs stood about the elevator platform that delivered the more massive supplies to Main Deck. On the platform stood six enormous boxes, easily three meters by two; one of which had been opened and into which the techs were looking with excited smiles and appreciative murmurs.

The Chief, however was not smiling. As soon as he saw Raeder he broke off his conversation with a nervous-looking petty officer and came towards him in haste. He snapped off an almost absentminded salute.

"Sir," he said angrily, as soon as he was close enough, "I don't know what the quartermaster is trying to pull here but I do *not* like it." Arap Moi turned and pointed indignantly at the platform and the unlucky petty officer who'd escorted the shipment. "For some reason they're trying to dump these obsolete weapons on us. I told them we wouldn't accept delivery. He tells me that you personally ordered them. I told him, no way you'd ask for this garbage. For starters, they're useless, and besides that, where the hell are we supposed to put 'em?" He gestured around at the huge space they were walking through as though it was a footlocker. "This isn't a fleet carrier, where they can put a squadron of Speeds in a corner and forget them for a year. We're stocking up for a long cruise and we're *crowded*."

They arrived at the platform and Peter looked into the open box. His face lit up like those of the curious techs around him. He reached out and stroked the sleek side of one of the missiles—technically, the mines. Star Command hadn't ordered any of these since he was in junior prep, but it was an old maxim that you never threw anything away as long as it could be polished.

"I, uh, should have warned you that we'll be getting in a lot of supplies, Chief," Raeder said. He managed, just, to keep from sounding apologetic.

Arap Moi stared at him as though this pronouncement had been made in some foreign language. Fibian, for example.

"This?" he squeaked. The Chief cleared his throat and tried again. "So . . . you *did* order this?" He couldn't quite keep the disbelief out of his voice, or hide his own belief that "this" was a piece of junk.

Peter bit his lip. He felt a guilty urge to explain himself and yielded to it. For some reason Raeder wanted arap Moi to share his enthusiasm for these mines.

"Do you remember that movie?" he blurted out.

The Chief's head came forward. "Movie?" he asked as though he'd never heard of one.

"Yeah. That one where the Consortium ship has kicked the hell out of the Star Command ship and she's been forced to shut down her engines." Peter looked eagerly at the Chief to see if he remembered.

Arap Moi shrugged and said, "Uh . . ." uncertainly.

"Sure you do, Chief," said one of the techs, her face aglow. "It's the one where they're moving this missile from a damaged compartment to the only workable launch tube they have left . . ."

"And they have to do it by hand . . ." another continued excitedly.

"And the captain gets on the com and says everybody has to stay perfectly still in hopes of fooling the enemy sensors."

"So they have to stop in the corridor, holdin' this *missile*."

"And the sweat's pouring down their faces, and their arms are shakin' like this!" The first tech squatted slightly and demonstrated, all the others nodded in happy agreement.

"And the Consortium ship pushes their sensors finer and finer until they can detect . . ."

"Way off . . ."

"Yeah, way off, the sounds of the crew's breathing and heartbeats."

"So the Consortium captain thinks they've got the Star Command vessel right where they want it."

"And they zip in . . ."

"Right between this mine field that the Star Command captain had laid out . . ."

"And the Consortium ship triggers 'em!"

"And bam!" The tech clapped two hands together, grinning.

"Star Command wins the day," Raeder finished happily.

There was a pause while everyone looked at the Chief with big, encouraging smiles. Then arap Moi nodded slowly.

"Yeah. I think I remember something like that. Of course, in the movies they can rig a detector to hear vibrations in vacuum."

Raeder slapped the Chief's arm impulsively in a gesture of approval.

Arap Moi's dark face took on a worried expression.

"Sir," he said, moving in close, his back to the techs,

speaking quietly and confidentially. "I can see that you have a sort of . . . attachment to the idea of mines," he continued, wisely avoiding the word, *sentimental*. Arap Moi pursed his lips and thought a moment. He raised a hand, thumb and forefinger joined, and said carefully, "But these are *completely* obsolete weapons. They are entirely useless. All they're going to do is take up space that would be better allotted to supplies that we can actually use." He shook his head. "These things should have been destroyed years ago."

There was a cry of protest from the gathered techs.

"They're junk!" he exclaimed, turning to the small crowd.

Instantly there was an explosion of beseeching gestures, and a chorus of exclamations and excuses for why the *Invincible* absolutely *had* to have these mines on board.

The Chief looked from one young, earnest face to the next, noting that they'd closed ranks between him and the boxes of mines. Suddenly he felt like the mean old stepfather who wants to throw the smelly, slobbery, but deeply loved family pet out into the cold. He brushed one hand over his short-cropped, silvery hair. Glancing at Raeder he saw that it was unanimous opposition.

"This is one of those generational things, isn't it?" he asked resignedly. "The psychs fine-tune those movies to recruit adolescents and it warps their subconsious forever? Subliminal promptings, neural short circuits?"

Raeder shrugged. *Maybe so,* he conceded to himself with a lopsided smile. *I did watch the damned thing fifteen times.*

"I should have briefed you, Chief," he said aloud. "Why don't I do that now? We've got a lot of stuff coming in the next few days and you should know what to expect." Peter glanced at the precious cairn of mines, then back at arap Moi.

"There's nothing else like this," he promised, a little alarmed at the Chief's expression. It would be unbearable to make a CPO cry.

"Well," said Raeder to his second in command. "I

thought I'd save time by having you sit in on this little briefing with Chief arap Moi."

Cynthia sat up straight in her chair, looking woeful and very pretty.

I can see why Paddy's absolutely gone on her, Peter thought. *Anybody who can look that appealing when they're obviously miserable would be irresistible to a New Hibernian.*

Raeder suspected there was some genetic tic that drew Celtic men towards sorrowful women. At the moment, he felt a bit protective towards Cindy himself, even with the strong dash of Sassenach in his background.

By now she knows that Paddy was rejected by OTS, and given her home planet's rule-bound culture and Star Command's ironclad rules about fraternization she's probably thinking that their story is never to be. Well, maybe Paddy was right and this mission could give them a chance.

The acting quartermaster was still on his way, so Peter took advantage of his absence to say, "Lieutenant, you've been doing a great job in improving your people skills."

Arap Moi looked up from the manifest he'd been scanning to nod his agreement.

"Thank you, sir," Robbins said, brightening shyly.

"So." Raeder slapped his hands together. "I'm going to reward you by giving you significantly more to do over the next few weeks." He grinned at her.

The second lieutenant smiled back, but Peter could see her swallow. Star Command had a tradition that the reward for doing work well was more work. With a sidelong glance at the young woman, arap Moi changed the subject.

"We're getting *everything* on this list, sir?" The Chief's eyes were skeptical. "I mean, *all* of it?"

"Yep," Raeder assured him. *This is a great feeling,* he thought. As though he were a billionaire, or maybe Santa. *I could get used to this.*

Deep inside he knew that there was a degree of danger in that. *What would it be like if it was always like this?* If he always got what he wanted, while others stood there frustrated and empty handed. *That kind of power could go to a man's head. Pretty soon they'd give him a nickname . . . something like "The Spider."* He resolved that he wouldn't be one of those guys. "Bull Moose," maybe, or "Speed Devil" or "Ladykiller Raeder," but definitely nothing insectile. Although he had been "Peter Maggot" for a while in Basic . . .

"We'll be getting in more stuff than we've ever had to process before, so you and the lieutenant will be called on to use your ingenuity in finding stowage."

There was a sudden series of sharp raps at the door, as though a passing woodpecker wanted to come in and check for woodlice.

"Enter," Raeder called out.

A slight, nervous young man with an extraordinarily full head of hair came in and saluted, turning slightly to direct his salute at all of them. Raeder stifled a smile. This was the sort of petty officer that good scroungers always hoped to encounter. Someone so lost in detail that you could steal the pants right off them and they'd helpfully lift each leg in turn without ever noticing you were there.

"Petty Officer Bryany, acting quartermaster, reporting as ordered, sir."

Raeder returned his salute and said, "Welcome aboard, Bryany, have a seat. Draw yourself a cup of coffee—this is a new ship and the filters actually work."

The young petty officer looked at Cynthia and the Chief, then uncertainly lowered his arm. He smiled awkwardly and shifted into the empty chair before Peter's desk. Then looked up attentively, stylus poised over his notepad.

Peter allowed himself to smile then. *Was I ever that young?* he wondered.

"I've called this meeting to inform you that we'll be receiving large shipments of parts and machinery for Main Deck," he said.

"Yessir," said Bryany. "We've already been getting them. I've forwarded the heaviest equipment direct to Main Deck."

"Yes, I'd noticed," the Chief said dryly.

Raeder gave him a look. The Chief gave him one

right back and it was the commander who turned away first.

"Any-wayyy," Peter continued. "Whether we've hit the lottery, or there's a glitch in the system or whatever, now is the time to order anything you've been needing."

Bryany fairly bounced in his seat, raising his stylus like an overeager student.

"Bryany," Raeder said, giving him leave to speak. Even Cynthia was visibly fighting a smile at the young petty officer's enthusiasm.

"Yessir. Every department has been receiving back-logged supply orders in unprecedented numbers." His big teeth shone in a happy grin. "I'm seriously concerned that we might overrun our storage capacity."

"In that case, sir, perhaps we should dispose of any bulky and *obsolete* equipment we might have cluttering up the Main Deck storage facilities," arap Moi suggested.

Raeder gave him a stare from under his eyebrows.

"No," he said simply. "They stay. I'm sure you can deal with it."

The Chief raised an eloquent eyebrow.

"Put that eyebrow back where it belongs, Chief. They stay." Raeder almost lost it when he looked over at a thoroughly puzzled Cindy. "I got some mines," he explained.

"Ooohhh!" Cynthia's whole face lit up.

"Et tu, Lieutenant?" arap Moi muttered.

"So that's what those boxes were," Bryany said, almost reverently. He clutched his notepad in his two hands. "Do you suppose I could get a look at one?" he asked eagerly.

"Sure," Raeder said magnanimously. "The Chief will show you where he put them. Won't you, Chief?" He glanced over at him and watched the older man concede defeat with his eyes.

"Yes, sir. I'd be happy to."

Peter could see by the two shiny happy faces before him that a long meeting would be futile.

"I won't keep you long," he said. "The station quartermaster's office has a few details that they wanted to hammer out with us." He passed around some datachips. "So let's get to it."

They were done in record time thanks to Bryany's capacity to understand quartermaster-speak. It seemed that only a few terms and a couple of obscure accounting practices were all that had actually changed. So Raeder dismissed them happily and happily they went.

Most of them.

"Oh frabjous day," the Chief muttered sarcastically as he turned to the door.

"Cal-loh cal-lay!" Bryany, sang out. "Uh, sir."

The Chief smiled at that and led the youngsters away. *Hell, I'm starting to feel paternal–command must be going to my head.* There were times he wished he was back in a Speed, where the only thing you were responsible for was staying alive and seeing that your opposite number didn't. He was sorry that the Chief didn't understand and share his affection for the mines. He'd made up his mind to join Star Command the first time he saw that movie. The next eight times he'd viewed it had only confirmed him in his belief that there could be no better life than that of an officer in the service of the Commonwealth. But the trick with the mines had been the heart of the whole thing.

He sighed.

Everybody else gets it, he thought, perhaps a bit resentfully. Then shook his head. *Maybe it* is *a generational thing.*

The problem with selecting personnel for this sort of mission was that you felt obliged to consider things outside the usual parameters. For instance, every time he ran across someone with young children, he found his finger moving to scrub them from his list. Raeder leaned back in his desk chair, dangerously overloading its compensator, and nibbled at an oatmeal cookie, refusing to consider precisely what that meant his subconcious was telling him. *If you don't believe you're going to win, you won't,* he reflected. *Hence, I'm going to win.* He still didn't want any young parents on this one.

Still, he was proud of his choices. It was like he was

fitting together a wonderfully complex puzzle with Paddy's able assistance.

But there was one aspect of the mission that he'd been putting off and he knew that further delay was becoming impossible.

He'd been reading and rereading the dossiers of Sutton's squadron, and they were impressive. Most of them were people he genuinely liked and enjoyed serving with. Of course, in the last week all of the *Invincible*'s resident squadron had gone out of their way to say hello to Raeder. He had to grin, they'd been so transparent.

But I don't want to restrict myself to just the Invincible's *resources.* For one thing it wouldn't do to gut the *Invincible*'s squadron. *I doubt that either Ronnie or the captain would appreciate that.* The general's briefing had indicated that Sutton's squadron would see some pretty active deployment on this mission.

And besides . . . And besides, he wanted to see if he could draft the few remaining pilots from his old squadron who had remained on active duty, the ones he'd served with before he lost his hand. His squadron had been shredded in that fight, and the survivors had been reassigned to other ships, or, as in his case, other jobs entirely. He didn't know where most of them were anymore.

But I know their qualities like I can never know a pilot I haven't flown with. And if I'm handing out plums, I'm going to make damned sure they get some.

Raeder pulled up to his com and typed in: Auerbach, Espinosa, Wisniewski, and Barak, and their ID numbers. Then he sent a request for them to be placed on temporary assignment to the *Invincible*.

The last time he'd seen them, they'd been gathered at the foot of his hospital bed, looking guilty and embarrassed. They'd had a pile of bad news for him, including the news that there weren't enough of them left to rebuild their squadron. He sighed. They'd grown apart over the months of his recuperation. Sheer distance played a part in it, that and the fact that he'd buried himself in his rehabilitation and flight engineering studies.

Even if they decide they don't want to be assigned to the hutch, they'll make excellent replacements for anybody I lift from Ron's squadron. He felt a slight twinge of guilt there; he really should consult with the squadron leader before even considering such a move. But . . . *But it's in the pipe now and I don't want to call it back.* Besides, they might all be interested, which would mean that he wouldn't have to tap *Invincible*'s squadron at all, except for alternates. Need to know, as well.

He still had two places open for the general's picks. *Wonder when they'll show up?* Raeder would feel a lot better when he'd introduced them to Paddy. *Like he's a half-trained Doberman and they're the new baby-sitters.* Peter sat with his chin in his hand for a moment, imagining all sorts of mayhem when he brought the volatile substance that was Paddy in contact with the catalyst that Marines had always been for him.

Ah, well. Sufficient unto the day are the evils thereof.

Then he hit the com and called in his next interview subject.

CHAPTER SIX

The *Invincible*'s gym was empty but for Raeder and his image in the mirror; he'd set the interior g-field for 1.25. It was always more convenient to do that when nobody else was around. People would generally go along if it was already set when they came in, but getting everyone to agree at the start was like getting a crowd to order the same toppings on pizza. He moved through the kata slowly at first, critically searching for errors in his technique. Then he slid through the motions faster and faster until his breath jerked out in little gasps from the power of his moves. He went through the final spin and froze, examining his posture; then softened his pose and stood upright.

"Looking for a match?"

Peter's head whipped round in surprise, and he smiled.

Beside the mat stood Sarah James, barefoot and in her *gi*. He saw that she also wore a black belt. *I should have guessed from the way she moves,* he thought.

They'd found the traitor Larkin together, on the last cruise—and a traitor who also happened to be the trusted, competent XO of a ship under a captain like Knott was in a position to do more damage than bore thinking about. They'd saved Cynthia from being framed for treason together. They'd won an important battle and rescued a crucial shipment of A-H together. . . .

But for all that, I really don't know her well. Except in the way that sharing combat taught you the essence of someone's soul, overnight. More truthfully than any accumulation of biographical details.

"Yeah," he said. "I was hoping for one. Thought I'd have to settle for just a workout."

Hands on her hips, she moved gracefully towards him, stopped, and looked him straight in the eye.

"I've been wanting to talk to you, so I'm glad that I've found you alone," she said.

Then, touching fist to palm in a gesture of respect, she bowed. He returned the gesture, then they dropped into a stance, feet braced, hands up.

Suddenly Sarah ripped off a stunningly rapid series of blows. Peter's brows went up in surprise, but his body fell automatically into an answering set of blocks. Sarah fell back and they both dropped calmly back into a waiting stance.

That *was unexpected,* he thought. He rebuked himself for making assumptions. She was a woman and she was with the WACCIs; he'd expected her to wait for him to make the first move. *My sensei would have had something to say to me about that attitude,* he thought ruefully. Now, his eyes waited for a telltale shift of balance that would betray her next move.

"You wanted to talk to me about something," he said after a moment, "let's talk. What's up?"

Sarah's eyes never left his, but suddenly her hand flashed out and he moved to block the blow, she countered and a whirl of attack and response ensued. Then they broke off and, somewhat damp from sweat, but only slightly out of breath, resumed their waiting posture.

"You're putting together a team for some covert mission and I want to be a part of it," she said evenly.

"Oh, Jesus wept," Raeder said. *I'm heading up the best-publicized secret mission in the history of warfare. I've invented more excuses than Pinocchio. Maybe I should just hang a giant "SECRET MISSION SPECS AVAILABLE HERE" sign out of my quarters, with a datachip box beneath where* everyone *can download the details.* There were some things he could say . . . he could claim he'd started a false rumor of a secret mission to increase his popularity . . . he could claim that he was really dating Scaragoglu's niece . . .

"I'm sorry, Lieutenant Commander," he said formally. His hand flashed out and grabbed her forearm. Sarah turned smoothly, pulling him forward, pivoted her hip and flung him to the floor. *Damn!*

"*Disa!*" she shouted, the heel of one foot stopping an inch from his throat.

"But due to hangar constraints we aren't bringing along any WACCIs," he said a bit breathlessly. "So, much as I'd love to have you, it's impossible."

She raised one ginger eyebrow, then grinned and shook her head.

"Pretty vain of me to assume that everybody knows my business," Sarah said. She offered him a hand up, then backed away and set her feet, knees slightly bent. "But you've been busy. So you wouldn't be aware that I've transferred out of the WACCIs. I'm volunteering as a Speed pilot."

He feinted with a left backfist, then moved in with a right foot-sweep to the face and a spinning back-kick. The conscious part of his mind was reeling with surprise. Sarah had seemed so happy and so proud of her position as the head of the WACCI team. *And she* hates *Speed pilots. So why would she want to become one?* Was this due to some kind of demotion? Was that why she wanted to do something risky, hoping to win her old position back? If so it smacked of being a desperation tactic, and therefore, was probably a bad idea.

She jerked her torso back out of the way of the sweep and blocked the back-kick, snapping a roundhouse towards his torso. *Smack,* as he caught that between crossed hands, grabbed toes and heel, and twisted.

Oh, and Paddy had a better one? his conscience demanded. Sarah threw herself backward, landing on her shoulders and then pivoting smoothly on her head to torque the foot out of his grasp in the direction of his twist, and then shoulder-rolling erect.

Well, hell, this might be Paddy's last hope, he answered it defiantly. But this was *Sarah* who was volunteering for a dangerous mission. *And I just can't believe that her prospects are that dire.* His immediate impulse was to say no.

"I wish you'd come to me sooner," he said. "I've already selected my team."

"Really?" she asked, still crouched in expectation of his next move.

Well, he had. Mostly. Suddenly her frank gaze was unendurable.

Raeder frowned and bowed, then turned his back, walked away a few paces, turned to face the mirror and began a new kata.

Sarah blinked and then stood at ease. She narrowed her eyes, watching him through her lashes. Neither of them spoke for a few, weighted minutes.

"According to the test techs, as a pilot I'm second only to you," she said at last. "At least on this ship."

Peter didn't look at her.

"Sarah, nobody ever died because the enemy was a good pilot," he said. Raeder halted his move and straightened, glancing at her sidelong. "Can you kill, Lieutenant Commander?"

Sarah walked towards him, and in a moment she had him on his back on the mat.

"If you'll recall, Commander," she said coldly, miming a strike at his throat, "I did kill someone not too long ago. In your presence, too." She released her grip on his arm and stood back. Peter rolled to his feet and glared at her.

Damn! That's the second time she did that! And *she's right. It's not fair!*

She folded her arms, her face expressionless, but couldn't keep the irritation out of her voice.

"I didn't like it," she said, "but I most certainly can do it. You have more *direct* proof of my abilities in regard to killing than you do for anyone else on your team."

They stared at one another, unspeaking. Finally a slight frown marred her smooth brow.

"All right," Sarah told him, "I'll write up a formal request." She turned to go, stopped, then turned back. "At least consider it," she said, then walked away.

Shee-eesh! Raeder slammed through a spin kick, then did it again. *Damn! DAMN!* Once upon a time women wanted men to protect them, to watch over them. Now they wanted to kick your butt and hear you say, "Hey! Nice move!"

He didn't *want* Sarah James on this mission! He never, ever wanted to see her in danger of more than a paper cut.

But she'd be such a good *candidate.*

There was the rub. He'd said himself that he'd like his team to be as cross-trained as possible. And a WACCI pilot, with their well-known penchant for knowing their ships and equipment inside and out was already proficient in two or three different areas. *Which is way more than, say, Givens could boast.*

He sighed. *I don't wanna,* he wailed in his mind. Then he hung his head in defeat. *But she's too perfect to refuse.*

Besides, she'd never forgive him.

Raeder headed back to his office with his hair still damp from his shower and his attitude still sour. He knew he was being unfair to her. She hadn't outmaneuvered him, the leader in him had. No way could he turn down such a candidate for romantic reasons. Neither one of them would ever respect his judgement again. Whatever else he was, he was a professional.

Besides, he thought, trying to encourage himself, *she might wash out.* Something he knew was as likely as Star Command bringing back the propeller as drive unit . . .

Raeder was getting into the mood to give someone a hard time and he'd made up his mind that it might as well be Captain Jason Sjarhir, Scaragoglu's liaison.

Time and then some that they sent me those Marine candidates, he grumbled to himself. He'd much rather have full say over who joined his team, anyway. *So maybe I should put some sort of a deadline on this.*

That was only fair. Scaragoglu undoubtedly knew that
Speed pilots were knocking on his door day and night
to present their credentials. And some of the offers were
damn tempting.

Like Sarah, his traitor conscience murmured.

Raeder stopped here and there as he crossed Main
Deck to talk to this tech or that. He signed off a fuel
request presented to him by arap Moi. Then hurried on
his way, his mind far away from such mundane duties.
It was still far away when he keyed in the code that
unlocked his door.

"HUP!"

"Aiiiee!" Peter screamed, instinct throwing him back
into a defensive stance. That left him in a crouch across
from his own desk, with his bladed palms raised to
protect himself from . . .

. . . two tall figures in red-piped Marine khakis, braced
to rigid attention. It was an unconventional posture for
a senior officer to receive his subordinates in, and he
felt his ears burning as he straightened up and cleared
his throat.

"Just back from the gym," he said, feeling his words
falling limp as a politician's official explanation. Both the
figures standing to attention had ensign's bars on their
collars, he noticed. One was male, a six foot slab of
muscle with a fine fuzz of silver blond hair, azure eyes
and a massive jaw. The other was a woman, wiry, about
five foot four with short-cropped black hair and flat black
eyes.

Their heads really are *square,* Raeder thought in wonder.

"Ensigns Sam Kushner and Peggy Manning reporting
for duty," Kushner barked.

Raeder watched Manning's head move ever so slightly
and thought to himself that Kushner had better watch
his step. *This is not a woman who likes other people speaking for her.*

"How the hell did you people get into my office?" Peter
snapped.

Kushner's lips moved as though he were fighting a
smile, but he held his salute.

"We thought we'd demonstrate our abilities to the Commander, sir!"

Raeder moved around them and sat at his desk. The two ensigns turned awkwardly, their arms still raised in salute. Peter finally snapped off a salute, and as their arms came down he snapped, "At ease!"

They each assumed a proper parade rest, eyes front, faces expressionless.

After giving them the benefit of a long, hard stare, Peter spoke.

"If either of you jarheads ever invades my privacy like this again, or chooses some other inappropriate manner of impressing me with your abilities, you will be summarily dismissed from this mission. Am I understood?"

"Sir! Yes, sir!" they barked in unison.

Maybe I should tell them to impress me by jogging naked around the outer hull, he thought. On the other hand, with these two hard vacuum probably wouldn't cause more than mild discomfort—maybe a nosebleed and bloodshot eyes.

"You will be working with Speed pilots and techs of various ranks and descriptions and for the duration of this mission you will treat these people with the same respect that you would a sibling Marine. Is *that* understood?"

"Sir! Yes, sir!"

"Do either of you have a problem with that?" he asked them.

"No, sir!"

Idiots, Raeder thought resentfully. The damage was done here. He'd worked really hard at not forming any preconceptions about these people. He'd insisted to himself that Scaragoglu wouldn't jeopardize this mission by mixing in a couple of egotistical jerks. *But here they are; the pattern that egotistical jerks are made from, big as life and twice as arrogant.* He was definitely going to call Sjarhir.

"You've been assigned quarters on B Deck, section seventeen, berth F, junior officer's country—bunks ninety seventy and ninety seventy one. You're so good at finding your way into things, I'll just let you find it yourselves. You are to treat *everyone* on this ship with courtesy and respect." The commander gave them a steely look. "After this little trick you people are here on sufferance. Do not press your luck with me."

He didn't bother asking them if they understood, he knew they did and he didn't care if they screwed up. *All the better if they do. I can tell to look at them that they're trouble and I am not happy to have them under my command.*

The two Marines stared over his head, motionless, barely blinking.

"Dismissed," he snarled.

The Marines flashed to attention, snapped off crisp salutes, and upon his returning the gesture, spun on their heels, marched to the door and exited.

Idiots, Raeder thought once more. *We're into serious ramrod-up-the-butt country here.*

Outside, Peggy turned to her fellow Marine and muttered, "Nice going, Kushner." Her voice was rich as cream, the voice of a much larger, lusher woman.

"Don't push it, Manning," Sam answered her mildly. He started walking off confidently. "You've gotta let 'em know what they're dealing with straight off. It's only fair."

"Do you have any idea where we're going?" she asked. Despite being so much smaller she easily kept pace with his longer legs.

"Heck, no," he said with a lazy smile.

Manning snorted, but kept walking.

After a moment she asked, "So, what do you think?"

Kusher raised his white-blond brows and pulled down the corners of his mouth in a quick, facial shrug.

"I like him," he said.

"Ah, Commander," Scaragoglu said with a slight smile. "Good of you to call me."

Raeder blinked, certain he'd keyed in the call number that Jason Sjarhir had given him. *Maybe Scaragoglu is acting as the captain's secretary today,* he thought, dazed. *A cunning ploy by the the Spider to disorient and disinform all foes.*

"I've procured a training vessel for you and your

people," the Marine general went on. "I've also obtained the services of Daniel Molochko." He smiled benignly and leaned back in his chair, looking like a proud father who's just produced the promised pony for his five-year-old's birthday party.

"Uh, I'm . . . not sure I'm familiar with that name, sir," Raeder sounded as puzzled as he felt. *A new team member?* he wondered.

Scaragoglu chuckled, his dark eyes positively twinkled.

"If you knew his name, Commander, then he wouldn't be doing his job."

Ah, one of the general's little night creatures. Mom would definitely not want me hanging around with this *crowd.*

"Ah," Peter said aloud.

The general leaned forward, all business again.

"He'll be briefing you and your team on pirates, who they are, how they fight, rivalries you might be able to use. He'll also train you on how to enter various hatches to enable you to take a prize."

"A prize, sir?" *There's a term you don't hear every day,* Raeder thought, a little worried over the general's choice of words.

"For want of a better term," Scaragoglu said comfortably, a devilish gleam in his eye. "Two of your picks from your old team have had to bow out, with regrets," he went on. "Auerbach has been given a squadron of his own and Espinosa's on desk duties for a couple of months—scheduled pregnant."

"That's great!" Peter exclaimed. Esme and her husband had been trying for a very long time. Maybe all those rituals and folk remedies had finally paid off; the clinics had been baffled. And Auerbach deserved to be a squadron leader. "I couldn't be happier if they'd accepted," he said honestly.

Of course this *really* cleared the way for Sarah.

"Your other requests will be here in three days," the general continued.

Three days? They must have been stationed nearby . . . No, that didn't work; Ontario Base was as far out as you could get in this direction.

"I anticipated your requests," Scaragoglu said. As though he'd also anticipated Raeder's thoughts. There was no trace of smugness in his voice or expression. And yet . . . *he positively reeks of it. People used to tell me I was smug . . . I couldn't possibly have been like this, could I?* He decided not: his had been a friendly, youthful, *forgiveable* arrogance.

"What if I hadn't asked for them?" Raeder challenged. "Or accepted this mission at all?"

The general quirked his lips down at the corners.

"I'd have had them sent back, probably. Though first I'd have arranged for them to run into you." He grinned. "Jog your memory a little." Scaragoglu tapped his fingers on the desk a moment, watching Raeder. Then he said: "So that gives you three days to wrap things up over there, get ready to transfer your command. Legitimately, this time," he added dryly. "While you're training with Molochko, Captain Knott will be bringing the *Invincible* up to full strength. And when you come back, *Invincible* will leave on her mission."

"Thank you, sir," Raeder said, recognizing the tone of dismissal in that.

"Before you go, Commander. What was it that you wanted to speak to Captain Sjarhir about?"

Oh, yes.

"About your Marines, sir." Raeder kept his voice and expression neutral. *They're jerks.*

The general chuckled evilly. "They're a bit of a handful, those two," he said, almost fondly. "But I have confidence in your ability to handle them." Scaragoglu winked. "After all, Commander . . . you're an arrogant, self-conceited, prima-donna jerk yourself; if you weren't, you wouldn't have done what you did, and/or you'd have gone back to Earth to shuffle bytes. And *I* can handle *you.* You'll find them invaluable before you're through, that I guarantee you. Was there anything else?"

"No, sir." *I think I'll just sit here and contemplate my good fortune for awhile, if it's all the same to you, Spider, sir.*

"Then I'll let you get back to work." Scaragoglu broke the connection.

I did call him, didn't I? Raeder wondered. Because by the end of the conversation it sure hadn't felt like it. *I wonder what he's done with Sjarhir?* Doubtless it was better to be ignorant. *For all I know the general has him wrapped up in a silk cocoon and hanging from a net in one corner of the room.*

The com chimed at him. Raeder jerked upright and keyed it to receive. Scaragoglu's dark, seamed face showed again, an unpleasant grin making it . . .

Satanic? Raeder thought. *Dracula-inic? Just plain scary as hell?*

"Oh, I did wonder if you knew about the bomb, Commander."

"*Bomb?*" Raeder controlled his voice before it rose to a squeak.

"Larkin's bomb, Commander."

"*Larkin?*"

Scaragoglu chuckled. "Yes, our dear departed Executive Officer Larkin. It frightens me, to think what that man might have accomplished if he'd been in a civilized intelligence organization rather than with that band of fanatics. Avoid fanaticism, Commander. It's inefficient. It promotes unrealistic perceptions, which lead to defeat . . . but I must admit, he had natural talent."

The screen split, and Raeder saw an accessway deep in the bowels of *Invincible*. His mind helpfully recognized color coding on a conduit, and told him it was the main power bleed for the central containment fields in the A-H interstellar drive section.

"Eeek," he said.

Paddy, arap Moi, Cynthia, and Sarah—*Sarah!*—were grouped around the armored cable, cutting a section of that armor away with a mechanical cutter. A few of them were kept for special purposes, but it was a spectacularly slow way to do a routine maintenance job . . . which would scarcely involve so many high-powered personnel.

"What the *hell* are they doing?"

"Dealing with the bomb, Commander—I believe Ms. Robbins found it, and called in some help. Really quite ingenious. A beam cutter would be far too likely to detonate it. Quite safe stationside, when hooked into the power mains, but in the field . . ."

"There's a bomb inside the casing?"

"No, the bomb *is* the casing. Or a rather clever counterfeit thereof. A section of explosives, set to detonate *only* when the power plant goes into emergency overload."

Scaragoglu shook his head in professional admiration. "I am extremely glad you and Ms. James put paid to the nefarious Larkin," he said. "You seem to make an extremely effective team. Out."

"Captain Knott."

Knott's head came up, startled by the unexpected voice in the quiet of his ready room. He turned to his com screen, not pleased to see the image of General Scaragoglu grinning at him.

How the blazes did he manage that? the captain wondered. To get direct to Knott's desk the general had to override a number of security measures. *Very impressive,* he allowed. *Also very arrogant and extremely annoying.*

Knott assumed a pleasantly noncommittal expression. "How may I be of help to you, General?" he asked.

"Raeder and his team will be heading out on a training mission on Monday. They should be gone about five days, depending on how well they do, of course."

"Of course," Knott agreed.

It was for *this* that Scaragoglu had committed such a breach of protocol? He waited, certain there must be more. *The general is playing a little game with me,* he thought wearily. That was the trouble with spooks, they forgot that most people just wanted to do their jobs and considered this sort of thing a waste of time.

They both waited for a bit. Finally, Scaragoglu realized that Knott wasn't going to bite and he spoke.

"I can't help but notice that Squadron Leader Sutton hasn't replaced all of his wounded as yet," the general said off-handedly.

Knott waited a beat and then said, "That is correct, sir." *Damned if I'm going to answer to you like I'm a kid who hasn't done his homework!* He'd already spoken to

Sutton about the matter, but saw no reason to say so now.

"Those people, unfortunately, are not going to be cleared for duty before this mission gets underway, Captain. It is imperative that the *Invincible* be up to strength. If he doesn't want to be the one to choose new people, I will be happy to recommend several pilots to him." The general smiled benignly. "That way, if he feels any awkwardness in replacing his people, he can place the blame on me."

Knott allowed his lips to quirk slightly into a rather stern smile.

"Thank you, sir, that's most generous of you. I'll convey your message to the squadron leader. I think you'll find, though, that he's already begun to make his personnel requests through regular channels. We were discussing his selections just this morning." The captain's smile broadened slightly. "I think you'll approve of his choices."

Scaragoglu was going over the line here and they both knew it. Sticking your nose into another officer's command to this extent bordered on the irregular, since it involved an attempt to review documents that were, or should be, private. Fortunately the need for haste was something both men understood, so this incident, with its lengthy subtext, didn't need to be mentioned by either of them. Especially since Knott had anticipated the general's impatience.

Get involved with Scaragoglu and you'll never again be able to call your soul your own, Knott quoted to himself. He was angry, though he didn't allow himself to show it. *The old bastard knows, though. And he doesn't care.* As long as Scaragoglu got his way, and his way produced the right results, he'd no need to bow to protocol or even mind his manners. *God help him if he ever screws up bigtime. Everyone from me to the Judge-Advocate General will be after his hide.*

"Good, good," Scaragoglu was saying. "I'll look forward to reviewing them. I'll see to it that BuPers pushes through his requests immediately."

"Thank you, sir," Knott said.

"I won't keep you then," the general said with a smile. "I know you have a million things to do."

"Thank you, sir," the captain repeated.

"Later," Scaragoglu assured him and cut the connection.

Later? Knott mused. *I'll really thank him later, he'll see me later, don't thank him until later? Maybe I should just resign my commission now and save myself the headache of wondering what Machiavelli means by "later."*

Knott glanced at his com screen irritably. *Tell you one thing, General,* he addressed it mentally, *if it's the last thing I do, if I have to pay for it out of my own pocket, next time you want to speak to me you're going through my secretary like everybody else.* If his years in the service had taught him one thing it was that if it could be done, it could be undone.

Didn't Raeder say something about there being a spy shop on Ontario Base?

"James," the brisk voice said, before her face appeared in the view screen. "Ah, Commander." She nodded politely. "How nice to see you."

If it was nice to see me, he thought, *you'd have called me Peter.* They always seemed to be getting set back to the "Commander" stage of their relationship.

"I've got some news," he said cheerfully. "Some of my team have had to bow out." He grinned at her and waited expectantly for his thanks.

Sarah was still uncertain about Peter. She'd expected him to accept her offer when she'd made it to him in the gym and his refusal had felt like he was putting her in her place. So she decided to make no assumptions about this announcement and merely asked, "So what will you do now?"

Well, du-uh! I'm going to ask you! Why did women always have to play these games? If he'd been calling Givens and had announced that a team member had dropped out, the last thing the guy would do is ask, "So now what?" *He'd have his kit packed before I got to the words "bow out."*

"Well, Lieutenant Commander," he said evenly, "if you're still interested I was considering you for a replacement."

Sarah had started smiling at the tone of his "Lieutenant Commander" and had grinned at the spark of irritation it had brought into his eyes. She couldn't help herself, she liked Raeder. That easy, self-confident charm made all her alarm bells go off, but he was *still* so damn likeable.

"I'd be delighted, Commander," she said humbly. "Would you like me to submit a formal request, as I mentioned earlier?"

"That won't be necessary, Lieutenant Commander. We're to be ready for departure on a training mission in three days. I'll be giving everyone a briefing when I have more information myself." He smiled and nodded, prepared to sign off. Then, hesitantly, he asked, "Have you ever heard of Daniel Molochko?"

Her eyes narrowed in thought, then widened in recognition. "Why, yes." She frowned. "Though to be honest, I can't place in what connection I've heard of him." She drummed her fingers on her desktop for a moment, then shook her head. "Sorry, the name's familiar, but all I seem to know is the name."

"Thanks, just wondered," he said, and signed off. *WACCIs are a sort of branch of the spooks, maybe that's why she's heard the whisper of his name. Then again, maybe he has some way of erasing himself from your memory.* Peter rolled his eyes. *I've been connected with Scaragoglu for less than a week and I'm already forming my own conspiracy theories.*

With a sigh he turned to his usual routine. Smiling at the stray thought, *I wonder when she'll call me Peter again.*

CHAPTER SEVEN

Aardvark, Raeder thought. *Appropriate.*

The name meant "Earth Pig," and the converted freighter the Speeds would be training on certainly matched the implications. It was big and chunky and battered, looking as if some large component of an orbital fabrication plant had drifted out this way by accident, acquiring wear and patches and micrometeor impacts along the way. He watched impassively in the supply shuttle's com screen as the massive ship loomed larger and larger. For all the world it looked like a pregnant guppy; garish orange paint was smeared in gigantic irregular patches across the bulbous, silvery body of the ship, her tapering fins tipped in black. The massive circular docking door near the nose of the ship looked like a dull, silver eye.

Or maybe a giant leprous guppy. Raeder frowned. Just when he thought he'd gotten used to being exiled from the cockpit of a Speed he'd find himself being delivered somewhere like a package. Once he'd been independent, the captain of his fate.

Now I might as well be a box of adhesive indexed for delivery.

It wasn't so much that he was feeling sorry for himself—well, maybe a little. *It's jealousy, sheer unadulterated envy.* Especially now that he was pilot capable and he just couldn't get Star Command to acknowledge it. He folded his arms across his chest and permitted himself an exasperated sigh.

They were closer now and the external camera showed them approaching the circular docking bay. Raeder automatically evaluated the pilot's approach and made him/her an eight on a scale of one to ten.

He's got a slight cast to the left, Raeder thought critically. Most people saw things off center by a few degrees. That's why being a good shot was so extraordinary. *It's like perfect pitch,* he mused, *a gift and a rare one. And dammit I want to use it!*

The docking tube grew darker as the ship advanced and lights in the side were covered by the ship. Its shadow went before it with the hard, sharp-edged contours of vacuum, filling the bay like a tide of ink. There was a slight bump as the supply ship joined with the *Aardvark*, a toning vibration through the body. The pilot opened the com to announce the obvious and Raeder picked up his duffle and headed for the exit.

He liked to be the first one off. It was probably an illusion, but he'd often sensed a chill as the lock opened. Some romantic part of him insisted that he was feeling some of the chill of space. Another little illusion he never told the psychs about. It was undoubtedly just the change of air from the smaller ship to the massive hangar, but . . . he preferred his own more fanciful explanation. There was a short length of corridor, and then he was into the massive open hold of the bulk carrier. The air was cooler still, pure enough but with an overtang of esters and chemicals, probably residue from a thousand different cargos wafting up from tiny cracks and irregularities in the hold.

Raeder looked around; there were ten Speeds neatly parked nose to tail on a surface of milspec perforated planking obviously welded in place recently. The techs who'd traveled over with him headed towards their charges, spilling around him like nervous chicks gathering under the wings of mother hens. You could tell by their expressions that they expected to find damage. Any time *their* craft were not parked under their supervision there was *sure* to be damage.

Peter smiled at them and decided to leave them to it. *But I'm going to find the rest of the team.* For certain he'd be able to find his techs anytime he wanted them for the next few hours.

A lovely young black woman broke from the group of pilots that entered the hangar just then. The pilots moved towards their Speeds and the intent techs.

"Commander Raeder, I presume," she said in the warm accents of East Africa. "My name is Christa MacCauliff. I'm a technical advisor on Mr. Molochko's team. He sent me to escort you to the meeting."

"Funny, you don't look Scottish," Peter said with a grin.

"I'm not," she said with an answering smile. "But my parents were." And she turned away with a twinkle in her dark eyes.

Okay, he thought.

"What can you tell me about Daniel Molochko?" he asked.

"Nothing he can't tell you for himself," Christa said over her shoulder. She smiled to take the edge off her blunt answer.

And the girl has a charming smile. Plus a very spookish ability to say nothing politely.

Raeder decided to shut up. Beautiful smile or not, this lady was not someone who would melt for his winsome blue eyes and tell him everything he wanted to know. He could almost hear her composing her report as they walked along. *How I reacted, how I didn't react, what questions I asked and which ones I didn't.* With the unasked questions holding just as much or more interest than those he had.

Spooks! Peter thought. *They could complicate a peanut-butter sandwich.* They analyzed everything, and then questioned their results, and the person who arrived at those results and why, and on and on. *It's no wonder they're all crazy.*

But they'd all be locked up with superspook Molochko and his team for the next few weeks. He'd better get used to being down the rabbit hole.

So am I playing their little head games already? he asked himself. *I mean, by shutting up, am I participating, or not?* He marched on. *Yep,* he decided, as they ducked through a thick merchanter-style airlock into a corridor leading up the spine of the ship to the habitation modules. *If I'm asking myself questions of that caliber I'm in the game all right.*

Peter felt a yearning for the simplicity of combat. *Not that there aren't mind games in combat, mind you. But it's* during *combat, not morning, noon and night.*

Oh, the spooks would tell you that they only wanted to prepare you for what the enemy might do to you. *But where's the need in these circumstances?* Raeder wondered. *We're going up against pirates and Mollies, not the zen masters of the universe. A pirate or a Mollie's idea of subtle is wounding you first,* then *killing you.*

Though the Mollies might harangue you about your sinful ways and lack of faith before putting you out of your misery. *For them I think that's the best part. They don't get to do much serious sinning themselves, but they sure work overtime imagining us having a wild and crazy time. I've heard the Interpreters yammering about sins I'd never even heard of before they accused everybody in the Commonwealth of commit- ting 'em. No wonder they want to whack us. Jealously can be a terrible burden.*

There wasn't much sinful about his surroundings now; just standard formed-foam metal, dull gray under the light of glowrods slightly different from naval standard.

Christa turned gracefully and stepped to a door, press- ing her index finger to the pad. The door slid open.

Light security, Raeder thought in mild surprise. Then gave the door frame a surreptitious glance as he went through. There were a series of tiny dimples in the metal, probably concealing sensors.

Oooh, Peter thought, feeling a bit smug, *I must be going into spook mode.*

"It isn't noticing something one time in unusual circumstances that counts, Commander," said the man gazing into a wall-sized holo of the star field outside the ship, his back to the door. "It's being in the habit of noticing everything, at all times, that makes a good operative." He turned and looked Raeder over, obviously allowing Raeder to do the same. "And interpreting it correctly, but never getting so bound up in one analysis that you preclude the possibility of being wrong."

Peter saw a smaller, older, grayer man than himself. Bland looking, forgettably dressed, nothing remarkable about him until you looked into his dark eyes. They gleamed with arrogance and intelligence. Inwardly, Raeder smiled, knowing that they might well be dull, indifferent or bored the next time he looked into them. *I guess I'm being given a special treat,* he thought. *A hint at the master's powers.*

"Give us ten minutes, Ms. MacCauliff," Molochko said. "Then call in the others."

"Yes, sir."

Christa left without so much as a glance at Peter. Something he frankly wasn't used to.

They were in a conference room, somewhat larger than the compressed setup one usually ran into on a ship. The table was a generous oval made, unbelievably, of wood, something dark and dramatically striated. Not of Earth origin. The chairs were high-backed and well stuffed, upholstered in some silky fabric in a neutral color. The ceiling lights, perhaps in deference to the holo, were somewhat dim around the perimeter of the room, but comfortably bright over the table itself.

Raeder and Molochko continued to examine each other in silence.

"You're probably wondering why you need me if this is a straight combat mission," the operative said at last, moving away from the hologram and pulling out a chair at the head of the conference table.

Peter cocked his head, a sort of a sideways nod that could mean anything.

"But there's really nothing terribly straightforward about this mission, is there?" Molochko asked. "This is also a fact-finding mission. Those logs you'll be collecting and the pirates themselves will be stuffed with valuable information. Not just to those of us who evaluate what you'll bring back to us, but of value to you and your comrades on the site, at the time you take your prisoners." He sat back and rubbed his lower lip in thought. "I'm going to give you and your people a quick and dirty course in noticing things." His lips quirked in a little smile. "I think you'll have fun."

Fun, Raeder thought. *The spook is promising me fun. Now I'm really scared.*

"You've got a good group," Molochko was saying. "I especially approve of your choice of Lt. Commander James. She's very good at her job. I've actually had my eye on her for the last few months," he confided.

Raeder was certain he didn't react; he'd remained standing, just watching Molochko. But the operative's eyebrows went up and he straightened in his chair.

"Ah. Like that is it?" Molochko leaned forward and folded his hands on the table. "In that case is it a good idea to include her in your team?"

"Excuse me?" Peter asked, inclining his head.

"You obviously care about the young woman," Molochko said. "I find it's best not to have emotional ties with your team."

Whoa! Raeder thought, genuinely stunned. *Where did he get* that? If Molochko was trying to intimidate him by playing the omnipotent bureau-Holmes superspook, he was making a good start.

"Hmm," Peter said, moving to the table and pulling out a chair at the opposite end.

There's two heads to every table, he thought. *I admit I'd be in a better position if my seat faced the door, but when everyone is seated Molochko and I should be equal.* He hoped.

"Usually," Raeder observed, "it's considered beneficial for people in combat to have some sort of commitment to their buddies. And I do care about the people under my command." He directed a level stare at the spook. "All the people under my command. And I can't say I'm happy to hear that you're already picking them over to see if there's something you can use here."

"As I said, Commander, I've had my eye on Sarah James for some time."

"Lt. Commander James is not to be diverted from my team," Raeder insisted. "It's a little late now to be accepting substitutions."

Molochko smiled, seeming genuinely amused.

"You leap to her defense so gallantly, Commander. But don't you think she'd be safer working with me than in the line of fire in Mollie territory?"

Raeder kept his glance level as he answered. "Sir, I don't believe that anyone is safe in the service of a commanding officer who is reluctant to form an emotional bond with his people."

Molochko laughed outright at that, looking years younger as he did so.

"I like that," he said, leaning back again. "But this is a training exercise, not a recruiting mission. I assure you Commander, it isn't my intention to raid your group for personnel, not even the prime picks that you've brought us."

He checked his watch. "So let's call a truce, shall we? I think I can promise you that you'll find your time with us well spent." There was a soft chime. "Enter," Molochko called out.

It was no surprise to find the two Marine ensigns, Manning and Kushner, leading the group that entered. *I'd better give them damn firm orders about their positions in our little fighter squadron,* Raeder thought. Givens followed them closely, which amused Peter and probably the Marines. His former squadron mates, Aia Wisniewski and Alonso Barak, were next and he greeted them with a nod and a smile. Sarah entered last, behind the four pilots that Peter had mentally designated "the alternates," her eyes on Molochko. She flicked a glance at Raeder, nodded once and found a seat on the opposite side of the

table from the Marines, dead in the middle. Even Peter
could feel the power shift, with Sarah the new point on
the triangle. And while it pleased him, because he sensed
that it disconcerted Molochko, it also surprised him,
because he wasn't used to seeing her play politics.

Christa MacCauliff moved around the table, dropping
an info-chip into the slot at each place. One by one the
men and women at the table keyed them up and began
studying the information on their screens.

"It may seem like very basic stuff, ladies and gentlemen," Molochko said. "But there are more than two
hundred different types of access hatches on commer-
cial freighters, depending on where they're from, who
manufactured them, or even what eccentric bargain some
handyman owner may have encountered to replace an
unrepairable part. Remember, you're not just blowing
things up anymore; you'll be boarding ships and taking
control of them. I and my team will teach you how to
handle most of them. We'll give you a video course on
the more unusual types of which we may not have any
examples. Christa," he said as she slid into the seat beside
him.

"I would advise you not to assume that there is anything that you won't be encountering," she said, her face
serious. "It might be easier to remember a hatch that you
have actually used, but knowing the parameters of every
known type might save your life. So I urge you to study
the chips I've given you most diligently."

"We'll also be guiding you in the use of the cobbled
together looking suits you'll be provided with," Molochko
told them. "They have all the usual safety provisions that
every Commonwealth hardsuit contains, and a few useful attributes that most do not." He treated them to a
little, secret smile. "And we'll teach you how to behave
like pirates. Without, naturally, breaking any Commonwealth or Star Command laws."

"There's a section in your briefing dealing with pirate
and smuggler ships, organization and slang," Christa said.
"Learn these names and terms and begin using them
immediately in conversation so that they become natural

to you. We'll also be showing you videos of pirate hang-
outs so that you can get a feel for how they interact."

"Often it's all very juvenile," Molochko drawled. "But
just because most of them are cases of arrested devel-
opment doesn't mean that they aren't gifted with a
certain animal intelligence. And I've often found that a
shrewd man can outsmart a brilliant one." He looked
them all over carefully. "Most of you fit into the gifted
to genius category, so I'd advise all of you to be extra
careful about your preconceptions."

Several of the pilots shifted in their chairs. Raeder and
Sarah crossed glances, then looked away quickly before
their amusement over Givens, Manning and Kushner's
discomfiture became apparent. Peter was actually surprised that the Marines would give themselves away like
that.

*Then again, maybe they're those shrewd types he was talk-
ing about and they're trying to lull the rest of us into a false
sense of security.* Because they were certainly bright, and
weren't the kind to be insecure about their abilities.
Oswald, on the other hand, was the type of guy who was
always trying to prove himself.

The meeting bumped along like that, Molochko or
Christa occasionally remarking on this or that pirate
characteristic in such a way that they implied a lack in
the group around the table. Raeder was certain that even
he must have reacted at some point to a velvet-coated
barb. If only by visibly noting the reactions of others.
He began to watch Sarah, looking for some telltale twitch
or glance, but she remained calm and professional looking throughout.

I'll bet Molochko can read her like a book, though, Peter
thought. *This meeting has probably told him more about all
of us than we would ever want him to know.*

The briefing went on: "And finally, I'd like to warn you
about the interaction between pirates and holo-fiction
accounts of piracy."

"Mmm . . . I'd assume that the holos are pure fiction,
and the actual pirates are greasy thugs?" Sarah said.

"Not necessarily," Molochko said. "Human beings all

have their illusions, particularly about themselves. Life imitates art. Greasy little bandits usually like to *think* of themselves as dashing, romantic figures. In practice they may be borderline sociopaths and plain no-hopers, but they like to *think* of themselves as romantic rebels against overbearing authority, a different breed from the conformist sheep . . ."

"And someone that twisted would probably take a lot of their self-image from pop-culture depictions," Sarah said thoughtfully.

"Exactly," Molochko said.

I think I followed that, more or less, Raeder thought. He decided to simplify; as the spook had said, everyone here was very bright, but most of them were more . . . well, straightforward than Molochko or Sarah. Or him.

"What the Lieutenant Commander and our host mean is that real pirates like to imitate holo pirates because it makes them feel like holo heroes."

"Essentially correct, Commander!" Molochko said, brows raising in slight surprise. Well, that's all we have to say. Go forth to study or eat or exercise or whatever you please. Tomorrow at oh seven hundred we'll begin your instruction. Meet in the ready room adjacent to the hangar deck."

He and Christa rose.

"Oh," the spook said, seemingly in afterthought, "the information contained on your chips is not identical. So there'll need to be quite a lot of discussion to determine where the differences lie." He gifted them with another of his sardonic smiles, then left, the lovely Christa in tow.

Raeder and his team remained seated by unspoken agreement.

"Well," Peter said, "you've all been here longer than I have. Has anybody managed to get oriented yet?"

"Not me, I'm afraid," Sarah said with a grin. "I've spent all my time checking out my Speed. I've found the supply shack," she shrugged, "but it was empty."

"The supplies came over with me," the commander told her. "So if there's anything you need it's probably there now."

"Ensign Kushner and I have found the galley, the weapons locker, suit storage, the lifeboats, the main bridge, engineering," Manning said. She rubbed one dark eyebrow. "But I've no idea where Mr. Molochko is lodging."

"Right now I'd prefer to know where the galley is," Raeder said. "So if you'd like to brief us all on the layout, I'd appreciate it, Ensign."

He was pleased. *Maybe Scaragoglu was right about these two,* he thought. *There's nothing I like better than having a first-class scrounger in the outfit.* As opposed to having a first-class scrounger preying on your outfit.

"I'm going to check on how our techs are doing," Peter told them when the marines had finished their report. "I'd like you to study those chips this afternoon. We'll all meet in the galley at eighteen hundred for dinner and we'll try talking in pirate." That got him some grins. "Dismissed, people."

They all rose. Wisniewski and Barak came over to him, smiling and he held out his hand.

"Good to see you again, Commander," Aia said, giving his hand a firm shake, her gray eyes looking honestly pleased.

"Been too long," Barak agreed. He nodded. "Looking good, Commander."

"So do you," he agreed. "You heard about Esme?"

They both laughed.

"Light enough candles and drink enough herbal teas and I guess you can never tell what will happen," Wisniewski said with a wry grin.

Barak pursed his lips, "I think it more likely had to do with Esme and her husband . . ." Aia whacked him before he could finish and they all chuckled.

"We should club together and send them a baby present," she suggested.

Raeder and Barak looked at each other over her head. It was plain that they were both thinking, *Buying presents. That's such a woman thing.*

On the other hand, it was a good idea and definitely something he wanted to contribute to.

"If you'll do the shopping," he said to Aia.

She nodded, with a smile and a look in her eye that said, *I don't get this antishopping business, must be a guy thing.*

"Gotta go, see you folks at eighteen hundred," he said. They nodded and Raeder went to find his techs with a light heart.

"Arrrgh, matey!" Givens said to a very unimpressed Ensign Manning. Kushner smiled tolerantly at him from the opposite corner of the galley, blue eyes twinkling as he watched the smaller man trying to make time with his partner. It was more entertaining than trying to figure out the nonstandard autochef, which seemed to have a particularly vicious variety of neo-Sumatran as its primary culinary template. He liked riijstaffel himself, but not dosed with jalapeños.

"Matey?" she asked. If words were dirty diapers she'd have been holding this one by the cleanest corner with just the very tips of her fingernails. "I take it you didn't study your chip?" she inquired in a deadly voice.

"Aye, lass," he said, laying a confident arm across her shoulders and leaning close. "Time enough for study later, ye ken? Fer now let's eat, drink and be merry. Arrrghh!"

"Yank fire, spleeb!" Manning barked. At the tone and the look in her dark eyes, Oswald jerked his arm away. "Unless you want an oh seven six glicken up your life you'll keep your grip on your own quip." At his somewhat puzzled expression she sneered, "For a translation, Oswald, read the chip." Then, with a poisonously sweet smile, she turned and walked away.

Givens watched her go, looking both stunned and perplexed.

"Ak-shuly I think she kinda likes you, Lieutenant," Sam Kushner rumbled from behind him.

Oswald turned to look up at the smiling blond.

"Oh, yeah?"

Kushner looked at Peggy drawing herself a cup of coffee.

"Sure," he said. "She smiled, didn't she? Tell ya what

man, you better do what she says, though, the ensign's
got no time for zoinkers."

"Zoinkers?" the lieutenant said, frowning. Whatever
they were they didn't sound good.

"Yeah," Sam said, smiling benevolently. "You go out
there half prepared, like you are now, and that little
nuzzle's gonna bite your treats off."

Some remarks require no interpretation. With a slightly
sick smile, Givens assured him, "I hear ya."

Sarah James turned away, and her eyes met Raeder's
equally amused glance. It was all she could do not to
laugh out loud.

"There's a guy who's kissing the A-H," he remarked
softly.

"That wasn't on my chip," she said. "What's the A-H?
Something anatomical?"

Raeder laughed. "Maybe, but on my chip it meant
touching the antihydrogen, thus courting disaster."

She quirked her eyebrows judiciously. "I think she was
too generous; he was acting more like a squeege than a
spleeb."

Raeder spread his hands and said, "And the difference
is?"

"A spleeb is a jerk, a squeege is a creep."

He shook his head and spread his hands again. "And
the difference is?"

Sarah laughed. "Small, but significant."

"So he was being a zoink?" the commander asked. He
hadn't had time to study his own chip all that closely,
might as well pick one of the finest brains in the room.

"No, no. Zoink is a verb, it means to con someone.
A zoinker is someone who can be conned." She narrowed
her eyes. "So how was your chip?"

"It had a long section on this pirate hangout." He
shook his head. "It was like a frat party for psychotics."

Sarah shrugged. "Most frat parties are."

"No, no, no," he said, shaking his head. "*Real* psychotics. You would not want to be a waitress in one of these
places. Hell, you wouldn't want to be a patron in one
of these places. The entertainment was torture."

She looked at him, impressed. "You mean they actually . . . ?"

"Worst band I have *ever* heard," he said, shaking his head.

With a "tsk!" Sarah rolled her eyes and walked away.

"She doesn't understand," Alonso Barak said, handing him a cup of coffee. "I've got the same clip and I agree. If you needed proof that these people are total degenerates, that music would do it."

"I can't believe they let the band live," Aia agreed, coming up behind them.

"Who says they did?" Peter asked. "Maybe they were just waiting for them to stop playing so they could beat them to death with their own instruments."

"I don't think I could have waited," Alonso murmured.

"Nor I," Aia agreed.

"Watch your grammar," Barak corrected.

"Me neither," she amended obediently.

"I'll have to show this clip to everyone who didn't get it on their chip," Raeder said.

"That could qualify as oversharing," Aia commented dryly.

"Hey, it's not like it's the men's room," Raeder said with a grin.

"Unfortunately that's what I got," Sarah told them, returning with a cup of tea in her hand.

"Ugh!" Wisniewski said with a shudder.

Sarah made a little moue. "Oh, it's not so bad. At least you can't smell it. But I could hear the band in the background, and frankly that's as closely as I'd like to be acquainted with their sound." She took a sip. "I never thought I'd feel lucky to have watched a tape of a bad-bar men's room."

"I like a woman who knows how to look on the bright side," Alonso said gallantly.

"Nuzzle," Aia said.

Barak looked at her in surprise. "Is that an offer?"

She laughed. "You should probably have called her a nuzzle instead of a woman."

"Ah."

"So nuzzle means a woman?" Raeder asked.

"No. A person you're attracted to," Sarah said, smiling. "Of whatever gender you're attracted to." She looked thoughtful. "We'll actually have to be a little wary of using too much slang. It's not really natural to talk this nonsense all the time."

"Probably why Molochko wanted us to start using it right away," Raeder remarked. "Smart, that."

"I suspect he knows his business," Sarah said, worrying him.

"I suspect he intends for us to grow better acquainted with his business, too," Aia said with a grin. "I do love upgrading my resume."

Both of the men snorted and the two women caught each other's eyes; no need to wink, it was a moment of perfect understanding.

A bell softly chimed eighteen hundred and they drifted over to collect their trays and line up for their dinner. Peter was pleased at how well everyone seemed to be getting on. Even the Marines were putting themselves out to be pleasant.

This is going to work, he told himself. *We can make it work.*

CHAPTER EIGHT

"This is getting to be a bit much, Mr. Molochko," Raeder said with an edge in his voice. The suit sucked the sweat off his forehead and ran a cleanser film across the faceplate.

The operative, though a man of no known rank, was in command of Raeder and his team for the duration of this training mission. Each team had successfully cracked eighteen different types of hatches and Peter was damned proud of them. But they'd also been out of vehicle now for six hours without a break.

Space Command safety regulations called for a break every four hours because being outside was *hard*; every movement required effort and concentration. Which inevitably led to fatigue, which inevitably led to deadly errors as the human brain resisted putting effort into thinking about such ordinary actions as stepping, reaching, grasping. It didn't care that in space you shouldn't let your reach exceed your grasp or you'd find out all too soon what a heaven was for.

Young Lieutenant Joe Mainini, the alternate with whom Raeder had been paired, was starting to make little omissions from the routine. Omissions that the commander himself was feeling terribly tempted to make. But out here all shortcuts led to disaster. *And I'm supposed to be setting an example,* he thought, suppressing a sigh and the impulse to straighten up and watch the multicolored tapestry of the stars instead.

It wasn't the fault of their equipment. The suits were first-rate; though they looked like broken-down wrecks, they were warm and unusually flexible. Even after hours of hard use the recycled air still smelled fresh and the jet-packs were as energetic as when they'd stepped out of their first lock. It was human failure as the men inside them tired rapidly.

"Of course, Commander," Molochko responded after a pause. "After this last one, then." The voice implied that they just weren't trying.

"We can do it, Commander," Mainini said, suit to suit.

Raeder turned his head away and rolled his eyes. This was why the lieutenant was an alternate. He was a good pilot and brave as a lion, but all too easily manipulated into proving his worth at any cost.

"We've already been out here too long, Mr. Molochko," Peter pointed out.

"I estimate that it would take you longer to traverse the hull to your last point of entry than it would for you to open the hatch you're standing on, Commander," the spook said with exquisite reasonableness. "Suit yourself, however."

"We can *do* it, sir," the lieutenant repeated.

"The point *is*, Lieutenant, that we shouldn't *have* to. We've been out here far longer than safety regs allow and Mr. Molochko could open this hatch at his pleasure." Raeder's voice was clipped with annoyance.

"The point is, Commander," Molochko drawled, "that you are being trained for a mission wherein no one is going to just pop the hatch and let you in. No matter how tired you happen to be."

"Well, what do *real* pirates do when the victim won't cooperate?"

"They blow the pressure hull open to vacuum when

they get annoyed enough," Molochko said. "I really wouldn't recommend that. So you'll have to be *better* than pirates at getting hatches open without cooperation."

"I agree. I'd also like to think I'm a better planner than to take my people into a fight totally exhausted, Mr. Molochko. Especially if I have a choice. As I will on this mission."

Raeder refused to call the spook anything but "Mr. Molochko," and that worthy, no doubt amused by Peter's covert rudeness, referred to him only as "Commander."

"This lock is one of the simple ones," Molochko said, half encouraging, half complaining.

O-kay, Raeder thought, angry but composed, *I guess we know who's holding all the cards here, don't we?* Molochko didn't want to concede the point, regs and safety be damned, and so he'd keep them talking like this until they ran out of air. *So we'll open this stupid lock and then I will confront this smug, sleek bastard and get a few things straight.* Like the fact that from now on safety regs were going to be observed or the fur was gonna fly.

Without a word, Raeder hunkered down and began to unload lock-picking devices from his pack.

"Ve-ry *good*, sir," Mainini said enthusiastically and bent to help.

Peter rolled his eyes again out of the kid's sight. *I was never that young and bouncy, was I? Someone please tell me I wasn't.*

Molochko had been right about the lock. *I didn't know anyone actually made them like this anymore,* he thought. It had an elastomer rim on the door and matching seal on the interior, and it went airtight simply by pressing one against the other via a hydraulic cylinder, controlled either by the little system that controlled the lock, or by a backup manual dogging wheel. Archaic . . .

"Four minutes fifty-three seconds," Raeder said dryly as he preceded Mainini into the cramped chamber and tugged the younger man down beside him. The lieutenant pulled the hatch lid to behind him and swung the manual locking bar shut.

"That's an antique, isn't it, sir?" he asked with a grin.

"I'll say," Raeder mumbled. He was concentrating on getting the almost unbelievably archaic lock to cycle. *This couldn't possibly be a mockup of an actual working, functioning piece of equipment,* he thought. *It's barely computerized.* He turned another dial and, finally, the readouts on his faceplate informed him that the chamber was filling with atmosphere.

"Aw, thank heaven," Mainini said and released his helmet lock, pulling it off wearily. "In gravity this thing weighs a ton!"

"Don't . . ." Raeder began as he turned; the lock wasn't finished cycling and it was against regulations to separate your suit under those conditions.

Then the outer hatch burst and Mainini, his helmet and Raeder were blown out into space by the explosive rush of air.

Raeder's artificial hand clamped onto the frame as they went out and a flailing left hand caught the lieutenant's boot. He tugged the younger man towards the hatch and guided him through; the junior officer's face was a screwed up knot as he clenched eyes and mouth shut, the struggle not to take a breath obvious as droplets of blood from burst veins in his nose formed little balls and floated off. Raeder followed, pulling the hatch cover after him.

"Mayday! Mayday!" he shouted into his mike. "Explosive decompression, get a medic and a stretcher to this lock, stat." Raeder tried to seal the hatch but it wouldn't close. A quick search proved that his artificial hand had dented a section of the metal where he'd grabbed it and he was forced to spend precious seconds pressing that section flat and smoothing it so that the lock would seal.

"Open the inner hatch," he shouted when the readouts showed minimum pressure.

Mainini was on his knees, eyes tight shut. In the ship's gravity blood was running profusely from his nose and open mouth. There was enough air now that he could take a breath. Not much oxygen in that breath but at least it wasn't vacuum. The lieutenant's whole body heaved as he gasped for air.

"Open the hatch, *now!*" the commander roared.

"Absolutely," Molochko said quietly.

The lock pinged as it completed cycling and the door swung open; outside was an emergency medical team. That's when Raeder knew for certain. This had been no accident.

"We've got him now, sir," the medic said as they exited the lock with the lieutenant strapped to a stretcher, zipped into a portable pressure chamber.

"Where are you taking him?" Peter asked. Then realized that the medic couldn't hear him. He released his helmet. "Where are you taking him?" he repeated.

"Sick bay's on level seven, sir. There's signs that will direct you." They went off at a pounding run, avoiding ducting, tubes and color-coded conduits.

Raeder watched them go, forcing himself to take deep, supposedly calming, breaths. Explosive decompression was no joke. With luck Star Command's intensive training had countermanded instinct and the lieutenant had the presence of mind to keep his eyes shut, minimalizing damage to those delicate organs. But there was probably some respiratory damage and certainly a whole lot of discomfort facing him. Possibly a regeneration tank.

The commander was enraged because he was certain in his soul that this "accident" had been planned by Molochko. He'd seen the lieutenant pull the lever home himself; according to the plans they'd studied that hatch should have remained sealed. If it hadn't then either the spook or his minions had tampered with it, or alternatively Raeder and his crew hadn't been given full information about it. *Either way puts Molochko in the wrong.*

He marched off to the suit hangar. No sense in trying to confront the dried up little spleeb in ten kilos of space gear. *Besides, it'll give me time to calm down. I don't want to do what Paddy would and tie the bland-faced squeege's nose into a knot.* He entered an elevator and spoke the floor he wanted. *Actually I* do *want to do that, I just can't. Conduct unbecoming an officer and a gentlebeing and all that.*

When he entered the suit locker it was to find a subdued group aiding each other out of their bulky equipment—taking off each other's meant you didn't have to wait until the exterior temperature of the suit came back into the range bare skin could tolerate. Every head turned on his arrival and eyes silently asked for information, for every one of them had heard the tone of Raeder's voice as he called for emergency medical help. But the expression in his eyes silenced them.

He took another deep breath and announced, "Mainini took off his helmet before the lock had finished cycling. The lock blew and we were propelled into space. I got him back. Now the medics have him. I'll tell you more as I know it."

They glanced at each other, all except Kushner and Manning. Free of their suits already they moved towards the commander.

"Help you with that, sir?" Manning asked.

"Yeah," Raeder agreed after a moment.

Manning took away the helmet, Kushner started to work on the seals.

"Molochko?" the Marine asked quietly.

Peter shot a glare at him and Kushner's lips tightened.

"I'm no doctor," the Marine said, "but I wouldn't hesitate to call that spleeb a psychotic."

"In other words," Manning said as she returned and began working the seals on the other side of Raeder's suit, "if you think the spook is responsible, you're probably right. He has a reputation for teaching object lessons."

The commander stopped breathing for a moment, then he bit out, "If you two have *any* information about Molochko, even if it's only rumor, I want you to give it to me now. Before someone else goes out the air lock without a helmet."

The two marines pulled the upper half of the suit over Raeder's head, looking each other in the eye as they did so.

"Sir, there's not much known about him, even by rumor," Peggy said, brushing back her hair.

Kushner, returning from storing the upper half of the suit said, "He's kind of like General Scaragoglu, he's got a free hand." The big man shrugged. "Unlike the general he really likes to push that though. Someone always gets hurt on one of his training missions. I honestly thought you knew, sir."

Raeder held on to his fury by an incredible effort of will.

"Never assume that I know something," he said at last, barely managing to unclench his teeth. "One of your jobs on this mission is to keep me informed. You can't *do* that if you're going to assume that I already know everything. I would rather have too much information than, as in this case, none at all."

"Yes, sir," they mumbled together, each pulling off a magnetic boot.

"It wouldn't have helped to know, sir," Manning said after an awkward moment looking him hard in the eye. "Someone *always* gets hurt, it's like Molochko's trademark or something. Knowing would've just upped the anxiety level."

"Usually nobody gets killed," Kushner said, eyes downcast.

Raeder glanced behind them to see seven appalled faces looking back.

"*Usually?*" he asked.

Good hard training is one thing. If you trained realistically, there were always accidents—a small price to pay for the blood saved in combat. *Deliberately endangering lives is another.*

They shrugged and nodded. "I need a shower," Raeder told them and, after wriggling out of the lower half of his suit, headed for the bathroom.

Jeeze, he thought, *this guy has been getting away with actually* murdering *Space Command personnel, and no one has called him on it? I knew I was down the rabbit hole, I didn't know it led to hell.*

"Ah, Commander," Molochko said, laying aside his stylus and folding his hands before him on his desk. "Come to beard me in my lair, have you?" He grinned, and his eyes were eager.

Raeder took a chair from a grouping to the side of the office and plopped it down before the desk where there had been none.

"We need to discuss your regimen," he said after studying Molochko for a long moment.

Molochko raised his brows and leaned back in his chair. He spread his hands.

"But you know my agenda," he said reasonably. "We'll teach you how to crack locks, avoid booby traps, interact like pirates, collect intelligence." He shrugged. "There you have it."

Raeder looked at him, as though waiting for him to go on. "Hmm," he said at last. "My impression of your personal agenda in this case is that you intend to terrorize and perhaps, if it suits some obscure purpose of your own, to kill members of my team."

"That's ridiculous." Molochko waved the notion aside with one well-manicured hand.

"I saw Joe Mainini seal that lock," Raeder said grimly. "I watched the bar slide home. That lock should not have blown."

"Lieutenant Mainini removed his helmet before the lock was through cycling," the spook said dismissively. "Very dangerous thing to do, you must agree."

"That lock should not have blown, Mr. Molochko."

"We-ll," he said and pulled a wry face, "you're also here to learn about booby traps."

"But not today," Raeder insisted. "Today we were told that we would simply be opening those locks. We've barely begun to memorize the manuals on them and we've been given no instruction whatsoever in finding and disarming booby traps. Which you are well aware of."

"Don't you understand?" Molochko asked, leaning forward. "I am trying to teach you to expect the unexpected!"

"But that's not your job," Raeder informed him, also leaning forward. "Your job is to teach us to open locks, to identify and disarm booby traps and some intelligence on pirates. If anyone is going to teach my people to expect the unexpected it's going to be me, not you. You don't have time to teach that too, so you just leave it to me and I'll take care of it in my own good time. Do we understand one another, Mr. Molochko?"

The spook had leaned back while Raeder was speaking and he watched the commander with hooded eyes, his chin resting lightly on one upraised fist.

"No, I don't believe that we do understand each other, Commander. What you fail to grasp is that *I* am in command of you *and* your people for the duration of this training mission. You will all do as I say, and you will do it without question."

"I don't think so." Raeder stood and, placing his hands wide apart on Molochko's desk, he leaned forward. "I am not prepared to agree to that. So I will tell you how it's going to be. You will give me an agenda every day, detailing your plans for our activities. If there is something there that I do not like, such as Mainini's trip out the air lock, then it will be removed from the agenda and it—will—not—happen. In fact there will be no more planned accidents of any description from this point on. Now, is that clear?"

Molochko looked at him with contempt.

"Tsk," he said. "You're in no position to make demands of me, Commander." The spook gave a quick, cold grin. "I repeat, I am in command, and you will do as I tell you." He spread his hands and, smiling, cocked his head. "You simply have no choice."

"Now there's where you're wrong," Raeder said, straightening and resting his hands on his lean hips. "I do have a choice. If you will not agree to my terms and if you do not stick to those terms I'll simply drop out of this mission." Peter shrugged and folded his arms across his chest. "Easy."

"You can't do that," Molochko said, laughing. "Even if you wanted to you couldn't. You expect me to believe that you'd voluntarily take a clerical job, sitting in a cubicle day after day after day, while everybody else does the real fighting. Not you, Raeder. Doesn't fit your profile."

"I'd rather sit in a cubicle than sit by and watch you

maim or kill people that I'm responsible for." Raeder's voice had the ring of sincerity and his gaze was unwavering as he stared at the spook. "I'd like to think that's in my profile."

"You can't."

"I can. I will."

"And so will we," Sarah James' voice said from the intercom, followed by a chorus of "Yeah!" from the other fliers.

"I'm sure you know that there's a very brief window to prepare for this mission," Peter said, suppressing a smile and trying to hide his surprise. "I doubt that General Scaragoglu would be pleased if we felt compelled to drop out of this mission en masse because of your intolerable behavior."

No expression marred Molochko's face as he stared back at the commander. Then he blinked.

"Very well, if you're all so dead set on being melodramatic about it. I will accede to your conditions. I'd just like to go on record as saying that you don't know what you're missing."

And I hope I never do, Peter thought.

"Thank you, Mr. Molochko," he said aloud. "When may I expect to see that agenda?"

"It will be delivered to you at nineteen hundred," Molochko sneered. "Will that be convenient?"

"Absolutely." With that Peter turned, congratulating himself mentally on not going for the runt's throat. *Not that I think for a minute that I could get ahold of it,* and left the office.

Sarah James lifted her finger from the intercom as he came through the door and smiled at him. Christa, her hands folded on her desk, looked at him askance, but the rest of his team grinned like demented chipmunks.

"Just a sec," Raeder said. He opened the office door again and leaned in. "By the way, Mr. Molochko, these rules extend to my technical and support crew. Do you understand?"

"Don't be tedious, Commander," Molochko answered in a bored voice. "Of course it's understood."

Peter closed the door quietly and turned to his command.

"Well, what are we doing here?" he asked. "Don't we have some studying to do?"

Grins and nods all around as they left the office, heading for their computers. Raeder followed more slowly, thinking, *That was too easy. Gentlebeings be damned, an officer who doesn't stand up for his people is unfit to command . . . but it was still too easy.*

The next day's schedule, in detail, arrived every evening after dinner.

"And I haven't seen Molochko in two weeks," Peter muttered to himself, looking over the last day's lessons. They were mostly concerned with how to camouflage the Speeds—not simply physically, but by avoiding Star Command methodologies without losing combat performance.

"So far so good . . . but I haven't seen him at all in two whole weeks." *Implying, perhaps, that my persnicketiness has denied my team the full attention of the Lord of the Spooks?* Peter shook his head as he watched the image of the *Aardvark* grow smaller on the com screen. *Doesn't* feel *right,* he thought. *This can't be the last of it.* And with that grim thought he turned the com screen back to the report he'd been writing.

One thing was certain, Scaragoglu was going to be informed of Molochko's bad habits. Hopefully that would mean that the gray little lunatic would be stopped.

CHAPTER NINE

No time this trip for contemplation of the coolness on his face as Raeder debarked onto the *Invincible*'s main deck. It was swarming overloaded chaos: two Speeds in bays meant for one, a cursing group of men and women wrestling with a launch rail amid skittering waldos and trails of sparks, lifters with loads of high-impact synthetic boxes labled with arcane number-letter combinations . . . the feel of a ship getting ready for a combat cruise.

Or as if the Invincible *is pulling away from the station unexpectedly,* he thought. Odd. There'd been no indication until now that there was an emergency situation. *But then,* he shrugged, *emergencies are sudden and unpredictable.*

"All senior personnel report to the captain's briefing room," came over the intercom. Raeder handed his duffle to Paddy, saying, "Do you mind, Chief?"

Then, barely waiting for the answering nod, he jogged off to the connecting elevator. In a case like this he was willing to bet that Captain Knott wouldn't hold to his rule that senior officers travel on foot, where speed seemed to be of the essence everywhere else.

"Sir!" Lieutenant Robbins squeezed into the elevator

beside him. "As I've been in command of Main Deck for the last two weeks I should probably come along to brief you. Readiness status is as follows . . ."

Po-faced efficiency her trademark, Raeder thought, *Odd, there's actually a human being there, if you look.*

Raeder relaxed and let her talk, knowing Main Deck was in good hands with Chief Petty Officer Jomo arap Moi. With her thumbnail outline of what had been accomplished while he was gone, backed up by the full report Cynthia handed him, Peter expected to ace any questions the captain might have. *Essentially, it's "we're ready."* Back when he was simply a Speed pilot, he'd taken that for granted. Never again!

"Good work, Lieutenant," he commended her, meaning it. The doors opened, revealing the corridor from the briefing room, and a few of the department heads hurrying towards it.

"Thank you, sir," Robbins said, stepping back. The doors slid shut on the faintest of smiles and the elevator whisked her back to Main Deck, where a thousand tasks cried out for her attention.

Peter grinned, pleased that he'd made her so happy. *Boy, that girl is loosening up.* A real smile—tentative enough to make the Mona Lisa look like a grinning fool, but an actual smile. Considering what she'd been like when he joined the ship . . . of course, then she'd been under suspicion of sabotage and murder.

He turned and moved towards the briefing room with determination, entering the room on the heels of Ashly Lurhman, chief of Nav/Astrogation. The captain was at his place, talking to the XO. As Raeder and Lurhman slid into their seats Knott looked up.

"Welcome back, Commander," he said.

"Thank you, sir."

"As you can see we're preparing to depart." On the words there was a subtle lurch, the barely perceptible signal that the *Invincible* had left her mooring with Ontario Station. "Correction, we are departing for the site of our mission. It's been an intensive two weeks, people," he said, glancing around the table, "but from all the reports you've given me we're as prepared as our own and the quartermaster's efforts can make us."

Genuine smiles all round at that. The quartermaster had been uncommonly generous. Another reason to smile; they were finally going to discover the reason for that generosity as well as all the emergency refitting and personnel replacement.

The captain tapped a key and the central holo display lit up, showing an asteroid field that Raeder knew he'd seen before.

"Now," Knott said, "it's time to tell you about our mission. This is the Chaos System."

"Well named," Truon Le, the Tac Officer, muttered, "it's a holy mess."

There were grunts of agreement around the table; the place seemed to be all rock. Augie Skinner, the engineer, looked particularly lugubrious, since it was his department that would be handling meteor damage, and in a system like this there *would* be damage.

"We'll be heading there to intercept a pirate that's captured a freighter loaded with chip fabricators."

Everyone at the table leaned forward with interest and dismay. Possession of such embargoed technology would greatly increase the efficiency of Mollie sensors and their missile warheads. Dodging the ones they had was bad enough.

Not a pretty picture, Raeder thought. And he'd had time to get used to the idea.

"Why the Chaos System, sir?" Lurhman asked. "There are no facilities there at all. Well," she corrected herself, "the Mollies have a small watch station there, but that's about it."

"Apparently the pirates have been using it as a back door," Knott said. "Naturally they want to escape Commonwealth notice where possible and this system is ideal for that purpose. There's smuggling activity going through there as well. Another thing we're going to try to put a stop to. According to intel the Mollies have beefed up their presence in this system considerably over the last few months. Pirate negotiations with the Mollies appear to have gone unexpectedly well, because our rendezvous has been moved up by thirty-six hours. Not that pirates are great at punctuality," Knott drawled, "but if our informant is correct we'll have to scurry to make it on time." The captain eyed the men and women around the table. They looked back, keen as young lions on a hunt. "Part of our plan," he continued, "will be to drive a wedge between the pirates and the Mollies. We've been provided with a copy of the pirate ship-to-ship code and will be broadcasting messages meant to be picked up by the Mollies sent to meet them. It is essential," Knott insisted, catching Squadron Commander Ronnie Sutton's eye, "that at least one of the enemy's ships escape to spread that doubt."

"Understood, sir," Ronnie murmured.

"Phase two of our mission involves Commander Raeder and his volunteers," the captain went on.

Sutton's eyes flashed as he glanced briefly at Peter, then he returned his attention to the captain.

When Knott had finished speaking the squadron leader slapped the table before him.

"Brilliant!" he exclaimed. "The neutrino signals and debris from the battle will completely mislead their sensors. We could drop off a hundred Speeds and they'd never even suspect!"

Knott smiled secretly. He knew Sutton would give anything to be a part of Raeder's crew. He'd probably even take orders from the commander.

"We'll be needing every Speed we've got, Squadron Leader," the captain said. "Phase three. The *Invincible* will be popping in and out of Mollie space looking for someone to rumble with."

The whole table of young officers suddenly wore a feral grin.

"Ah, well then, sir. As long as the squadron will be keeping their skills sharp." Sutton looked very relieved.

"Oh, I assure you, ladies and gentlemen, we should all complete this mission sharp enough to need a sheath." Academy rings tapped approval of the notion on the table. "Here are the briefing data. Are there any questions?"

There were, and they were answered and explored quickly, but thoroughly.

"Thank you all," Knott said at last. "You are dismissed to your, no doubt, pressing tasks."

With that they rose, saluted and left, eyes aglow with plans and expectations.

I sure hope everything goes as expected, Raeder thought pessimistically, moving out with the rest of them. His mind imagined meteor damage that couldn't be repaired or ignored, a massive attack force of Mollies waiting for them. *Which would actually be okay,* he thought, brightening briefly. Or worse yet, a missed rendezvous. An all too likely scenario that dashed him back to gloom.

Then, *Hey! I never got to file my report with Scaragoglu about Molochko's murderous habits.* And wasn't it interesting that intel had moved up the date of their rendezvous with the pirates. *Yeah,* Peter thought cynically, *interesting. As in, of course there's no chance that there's a connection.*

Captain Drongo of the cheerfully named ship *G'day* tapped his fingers impatiently on the wobbly arm of his command chair. The other hand cupped his massive unshaven jaw.

The captain had an artificial eye, shut down just now to save on the battery. It looked amazingly like a black eyepatch with its matte-black shielding down, the apparatus filling the whole eye socket. It was an appropriate look for a pirate captain, and one he cultivated with exacting care.

On his shoulder sat a brilliantly colored little omnivore with wide yellow eyes and a wickedly curved beaklike snout. It tapped five of its six legs in imitation of Drongo's hand, muttering, "Waitin', waitin'."

"Aye," Drongo growled. "Waitin' fer those lace-pantied Mollies to get up the nerve to say boo."

There were chuckles on the bridge at that and the little creature chimed in with an astonishingly loud baritone boom of a laugh. The *G'day*'s bridge was a rectangle, with an L-shaped addition at the back; the yard that had converted her from an express-freight carrier had been purely concerned with function. In fact, they'd probably never heard of aesthetics, and wouldn't have been able to find *ergonomic* with a dictionary program, and there were far more stations than on a warship of comparable mass. That was the result of less sophisticated AI and infosystems, but the cobbled-together compromise had proved quite workable. And profitable . . .

There was a very faint tang of bad meat and ozone under the usual shipboard smells of synthetics and recycled air, legacy of an engagement that had seen the survivors of the bridge crew working in vacuum suits. Drongo had been there on that occasion, and had been one of the ones who'd remembered to keep his faceplate closed.

"Shaddap, Sod," the captain said affectionately. He'd called it *the lit'l sod* for a long time after he'd gotten it, intending to find a better name eventually. But closer acquaintance with the thieving little beast, and habit, had won out and the critter had remained Sod ever after.

Everybody on the *G'Day*'s bridge wore their space armor now. Even Sod had a small square pressure chamber bonded to the back of the command couch, and was trained to get to it fast. *G'Day* didn't emphasize spit and polish, but everyone knew that their lives depended on attention to detail. Those who felt that this was too much like honest work tended to have short life expectancies.

"They're hailing, Cap'n."

"Yeah, I got eyes, haven't I?"

The screen on his console had lit up with the image of a thirtyish male dressed in white and trying unsuccessfully to hide his disdain.

Drongo thrust a finger up his nose as high as he could get it and twisted. *Give ya a reason to gimme that look, mate.* To his delight the man on the screen swallowed visibly, his whole face quivering with loathing.

"Hallo!" Drongo bellowed cheerfully, wiping his finger on his shirt. More swallowing. "We thought you was all napping." He put a little snap into that.

"Our apologies for the delay, Captain," the Mollie said. "We were attempting to determine that you were, indeed, the . . . *G'day* and that you were alone."

Sod you, Drongo thought. *Can't even say g'day without chokin' on it.*

"Well are you happy now?" he asked sarcastically. "Or should I go have me dinner and some sex n' booze or a brace of happy-pills?" *Cor, look at him,* the captain thought, maintaining his look of barely suppressed rage with heroic effort. *He looks like he's goin' to inhale his own nose.*

Sod, picking up on Drongo's true mood, boomed out that huge laugh. Drongo tapped it in admonishment and the little creature writhed into a compact knot of misery.

The Mollie continued manfully, "We need to inspect your cargo."

"Oh. Dew yew?" Drongo asked. "Dew yew indeed?"

Not that he could actually do anything if they wanted to push things. The Mollies were a task force of three destroyers and a light cruiser. More than a match for him and his crew. He'd been unpleasantly surprised at their numbers. At first he'd thought that they meant to kill him and grab the freighter he had in tow. *It's what I would have done in their place, straight up, s'truth.*

Then he'd realized that they couldn't afford to do that, much as they obviously wanted to. Without the smugglers and the pirates these nutballs wouldn't be getting any supplies at all. They *had* to deal with him, even though it was like putting their balls in a vise. So he could afford to give them some lip, and their attitude made it irresistible. They reminded him far too much of his father.

Drongo smiled, an alarming expression. He was remembering the day he'd left home; nobody had found the body until the neighbors complained about the smell.

"I'm sure that you can understand our position," the Mollie captain said. "After all," he continued with a trace of smugness, "antihydrogen is quite valuable where you come from."

"Yeah?" Drongo agreed with raised eyebrows. "And so's chip fabricators. I could sell this cargo on any of a hundred worlds and get paid a good price for 'em."

"But not in antihydrogen," the Mollie insisted, still smug.

"Oh? Like you think I *pay* for antihydrogen. Is'at what you think? *And* speakin' of which, where the hell is my barge of A-H? I don't see it beyond your lit'l flotilla, I don't."

"Autie hygygen!" Sod exclaimed. "Where's it at? Can't see it, can't see it!"

"Shaddap, Sod." Drongo stared into the screen, challenging the Mollies, his heart pounding.

He didn't like this at all. It screamed *setup* and it wasn't what he'd expected or what had been agreed upon. Although admittedly the arrangements, made through a broker, had only consisted of, "They want the stuff, they agreed to the price, here's the coordinates, here's the time." Sure as hell he'd be more careful about the next drop.

I've half a mind to chuck it and just go, he thought, unhappy and suspicious.

"We are merely being cautious, Captain," the Mollie said. "We wish to inspect the cargo. When we are satisfied we will call for the barge to be brought up and we will then exchange freighters." He smiled beatifically at Drongo. "We Mollies are an honest people, Captain Drongo. *We* keep our bargains."

Drongo sniffed.

"'At remains to be seen, dunnit?" he asked. He hiked himself up in his chair, pretending boredom. "All right, all right. How many you sendin' over?"

"I will send a group of four technicians," the Mollie captain said.

"Then I'll have six of my crew meet 'em." Drongo narrowed his eyes. "That's all right wi' you, innit?"

"Of course, Captain. When my brothers in faith are satisfied I shall call up the barge and we can make the exchange."

"How long are we talkin'?" Drongo asked, still not happy.

"Once I'm given a favorable report the barge should be here in six hours."

"SIX HOURS!"

Drongo came out of his chair, looking for something to throw and Sod, knowing from experience that it could be him, leapt from the captain's broad shoulder with a little shriek and slid into a narrow space between a comp screen and the bulkhead.

"Are you *freakin'* crazy?" Drongo raged. "Y'don't sit in space makin' a highly illegal trade like this for six bloody freakin' *HOURS!*"

"I'd better send my people along then, hadn't I?" Captain Smug said. "Soon begun, soon done," he quoted.

Drongo was fairly frothing now.

"*I am* not sittin' here for six *freakin'* hours," he shouted. "You satisfy yourselves that I've got the goods an' then I'm buggin' outta here. I ain't sittin' around like a fool! You c'n wait fer me this time."

The Mollie captain allowed himself a little moue of distaste. Doubtless he would flog himself for permitting himself the pleasure of showing his feelings like this, but he seemed to find it irresistible.

"If you remove the cargo from this site then obviously we will simply have to wait, once again, for my people to verify the cargo, and, naturally we will not call for the barge at all if you leave."

"Wha? Like I've got another freighter stuffed up me bum convenient like, just so's I c'n fool you?" Drongo flopped back into his chair, big jaw dropped in disbelief. "This is *your* idea, mate, not mine. *I* came to make a deal, fair and square. It's you goin' all fluttery over there. It's crazy sittin' in space for six hours like this." He waved a big hand. " 'S crazy."

"Crazy," said a shrill voice from the bulkhead. With a lightning-fast dart, six legs flashing, Sod got itself back into its favored position on Drongo's shoulder. "Crazy!" it reiterated.

The Mollie just stared back at the captain.

Drongo frowned. "Look," he said reasonably, "y'could send that cruiser with me to keep an eye on me, see that I don't play any games."

The Mollie captain outright smirked at that.

"Either you stay here, or we have to inspect your cargo all over again when you come back. And then call for the barge." The Mollie looked like he was getting great pleasure from this situation. Whatever he was going to pay for that pleasure, he seemed to feel it was worth it. "Take it, or leave it," he said.

"Awright," Drongo muttered. " 'S bad luck though."

"Bad luck," Sod agreed.

"Shaddap," the captain snapped.

"Cap'n," one of the pirates shouted, "message incoming from the jump point! It's in our code!"

"Ahoy mates," a cheerful voice said. "Sorry we're late. Hope we're not too late to kick a lit'l Mollie butt, eh?"

"Who the bleedin' hell is that?" Drongo asked. Everyone on the bridge shrugged and shook their heads.

"Dunno, Cap'n," Zollie said anxiously. " 'S big though, bigger 'n anythin' out there. Holy hell!" he exclaimed.

"Whot now?" Drongo snapped.

"They've launched a whole bloody load of Speeds—all weapons are online and they're all screamin' towards us like bats outta hell!"

"Whot the bleedin' hell is *goin' on?*" the captain demanded of his equally confused crew.

The Mollie captain frowned and turned to one of his cohorts, who read out the translated message for him.

"You damned, lying scum!" the Mollie shouted. "Battle stations," he roared at his own people. "A good thing we didn't come trusting to this meeting," he shouted into the screen, flecks of spittle spraying. "You will feel the hard hand of the Spirit of Destiny, sinner! You and your friends!"

"Whot!" Drongo screamed. "*Us?* We don't know who the hell they are!"

He stared into the blanked screen for a split second.

"Aw, bloody *hell!*" he bellowed, banging his fist on his abused armrest. "I knew we was outta luck the second they said we'd have to wait."

He activated his artificial eye, which lit up in green and yellow splendor as the shield retracted.

"Cap'n," Zollie's voice went high with fear, "them

Mollies are bringin' their weapons up too, and they're aimin' at *us!*"

Drongo flipped open a covering over a pair of buttons and his fingers hovered over them for an instant while his face twisted in misery.

"We gonna fight, Cap'n?" Zollie asked into the silence that followed.

"Fer what?" Drongo asked. "Ta help the Mollies? Stupid buggers!" He meant the Mollies and the whole crew knew it and agreed with him. "We'll never get that A-H now, even if we drove this lot of strangers off with their pants on fire. Them Mollies was suspicious to begin with, now after that message they'll kill us if they can." *And be happy they done it,* he thought bitterly.

Then with a regretful sigh he pressed both buttons.

"Cut our losses, mates," he said. "Let's bugger outta here. This vector."

The precious freighter full of chip fabricators blew in a spectacular magenta fireball seconds before the Mollie ships opened fire on the *G'day.* Drongo grinned for a second, imagining Mollie fire-control officers struggling not to swear as their consoles lit with the orange-red of *tracking lost* amid the fog of plasma and energetic particles.

"Dumpin' chaff!" the *G'day*'s Tac artist said, grinning under her bandana. "Decoys! ECM pods! Flushin' the waste maintenance system!"

"Oi?" Drongo said.

"Show the zoinkers what we think of 'em," she explained.

"Oh, right, then." *G'day* boosted, her extra drive fields ever so slightly out of synch and the hull making that subliminal groaning that always gave him the willies. Fleeing the Mollies, the incoming fighters, and away from the jump point.

For now. Once the two forces engaged with each other there'd be plenty of time to sneak out of the Chaos System.

"Catch us if ye can, zoinker spleebs," Drongo muttered.

"Zoinker spleebs, zoinker spleebs," Sod chortled.

"Shaddap!" Drongo snarled. Maybe he *should* have gone into accounting.

CHAPTER TEN

"No response from the pirates, sir," Communications Officer Havash Hartkopf said grimly.

Captain Knott glanced at him. *The kid looks like a young basset hound,* he thought, amused.

"I'm sure there's been a response, son," Knott told him, "they're just not getting online with it."

Pirates not being the brightest stars in the constellation, they might still be trying to figure out the message. *Which was meant for the Mollies anyway,* he thought with an inner smile.

"Mollie weapons are coming online, sir," Truon Le, the Tactical Officer, announced.

"Excellent," Knott murmured, tracking the tactical officer's information.

Mai Ling Ju, the XO, smiled as she called up Truon Le's data at her station.

Suddenly the computer registered a massive explosion.

"The Mollies have not fired," Truon Le said.

"The pirates must have rigged the freighter to blow," Ju agreed. She hoped no one had been aboard, then winced at her own naivete. If there'd been no one

127

aboard it was because the pirates had already killed them.

"Whup, there they go," Truon Le told them. The screen registered missiles coming from the light cruiser towards the pirate's last known position. It also showed a green dot speeding away from the site of the blast.

"They're getting away unscathed," Mai Ling said, scanning the readouts. "If that's the best the Mollies can do on countermeasures, they should call their ship the *White Cane*. Should we send someone after them, sir?" she asked.

"Negative," Knott said after the briefest of pauses. "It's the Mollies we really want."

The Mollie task force was forming up now, turning towards the *Invincible*.

And it's us they *really want,* he thought.

"The Mollies are sending us music," Hartkopf said. He sent Knott a sample.

The captain listened impassively for a few moments; it was one of the atonal Mollie battle hymns. *These people,* he thought, *are so incredibly* tedious! *A battle hymn doesn't have to sound like a basket of cats being thrown into a cold lake.* There was a particularly dissonant *blat!* and he winced. *Then again, maybe the awful music is one of their most deadly weapons.*

"Thank you, that's enough, Hartkopf," he said. "Keep me posted."

"Sir," said Truon Le, "we are in range to bring up the holo-map."

"Bring it online," Knott said.

"Holo-map online, aye," the tactical officer said.

The holo-map came to life in all its three dimensional, multicolored glory. The three Mollie destroyers glowed green, arranged in a triangle around the light cruiser, which shone yellow. Each ship was preceeded by a same-colored cone that would twist to show possible vectors. Sutton's squadron of thirty-five Speeds, which were well in advance of their carrier, were blue, the *Invincible* itself was shown in white. The pirate, just leaving the map, was pink.

The Speeds lengthened their formation to a cone shape, like a butterfly net. The pattern wasn't static—pilots kept moving within the general framework to make it harder for the enemy to get a bead on them. The two groups of combatants closed, their combined velocity mounting towards 15kps. At those values anything like a physical hit became certain destruction from kinetic energy alone.

"Tap," Knott said. "Lead squadron."

That gave him a slightly lagged version of what Sutton was seeing. Stars crawled across the screen, tracked with the color-coded lines and markers of the heads-up display. A strobing red line . . .

"*Locked,*" six of Sutton's Speeds reported.

"*Follow-ons, concentrate on the cruiser,*" Sutton's voice said. "*We're going for the tin cans.*"

A bleeping sound, *zeep-zeep-blatt!*, as the seeker missiles launched and began laying their own vector tracers across the battle-board. The lead Mollie destroyer launched a cloud of decoys, and ghost images swarmed across the screens. Knott leaned back, forcing himself to a relaxation that would cut the tension on the bridge.

The holo-map on the *Invincible's* bridge marked the actual ships with blinking white dots as ghost copies of them appeared in the tank. The missiles rolled out dotted lines behind them as they sped onward, their focus shifting, lines arcing away from the original targets.

The squadron fired again, targeting the last recorded position of the actual Mollie ships. Truon Le updated the Speeds' information from the higher-powered sensors of the *Invincible* and the squadron fired again.

"Why aren't the Mollies firing, skipper?" the XO asked, her brow furrowed.

Knott shook his head; he'd been wondering the same thing.

"Maybe they're waiting for a miracle," he muttered.

Most of the first rank of missiles flowed over and around the targeted ships. Several hit decoys and their images disappeared from the holo-map as the warheads detonated, adding to the particle fog that would steadily degrade sensor data as the engagement continued. *Hope we get lucky*, Knott thought. The Commonwealth's superior electronics gave maximum advantage in an uncluttered field. Some of the seekers found their intended targets and blew away ablative material and antennae, but none were ship killers. Sutton and his people came on, waiting tensely for the Mollies to fire. And the *Invincible* charged on in their wake, her monstrous engines flailing at the structure of space.

The tac officer on the *Invincible* calmly updated the Speeds on the position of real ships that their instruments could no longer positively identify. Knott wished distantly that there was some way to clear away the electronic clutter the enemy put out.

"Cruiser is the main target," the squadron leader reminded his people.

Not that they would, or could, ignore the destroyers. But the cruiser was a real threat to the *Invincible*, anything that could take out the light carrier would be dealt with first.

On the bridge of *Righteous Wrath* the captain stared regretfully into his own holo-map. *I have a quantum opportunity to destroy a capital ship,* he thought—the signature was nothing that the databanks recognized, but it *had* to be some sort of carrier, those were unmistakably Speeds. *And I can do very little.* They'd arrived here in an overpowering show of force to intimidate a lone pirate into accepting less than favorable terms for his cargo. And if he had fought they could have handled him. But *this!* They had empty missile tubes, and broken beam weapons with under-maintained, overused guidance systems to confront a full squadron of Speeds and what looked like a fifteen-thousand ton hull that *had* to be carrying considerable armament itself. The enemy was launching missiles as if they were free, and the performance was disconcertingly good, up to Commonwealth Star Command standards. The only thing they could do was hope the Spirit of Destiny was on their side and would guide their missiles to where they would do the most damage. He would serve the Spirit by closing to ranges where his smaller number of less-capable missiles would be more likely to strike home. If the Spirit allowed them to survive that long . . .

He watched the destroyers throw out more chaff and supressed a sigh, ignoring the increasingly anxious glances his bridge crew were throwing his way.

Pray, he thought to them. *And make every shot count.*

On the bridge of *Invincible* Knott watched the Mollie destroyers move forward on the holo-map, forming a wall between the cruiser and the oncoming Speeds with their overlapping ECM and antimissile systems. At last they outstripped the cover of their own decoys and every other Speed fired seeker missiles. The weapons, deployed by fusion-powered magnetic rail, slammed out at literally astronomical velocities.

The destroyers spit out another cloud of decoys and a number of the missiles went wild, some destroyed decoys . . .

A savage cheer went through the bridge of *Invincible*. "Hit, by God!" the tac officer barked. "Number one destroyer . . . secondary explosions . . . her drive's dropping off! Not a ship killer, sir, but she's badly hurt."

As Truon Le relayed the information the squadron leader swore silently to himself.

"Tap," Knott said. Sutton was calling his pilots:

"We're going to have to do a bit better than this, ladies and gentlemen." With a flick of his finger he switched from electronic read to passive camera. Something distant sparkled; he blinked it into high magnification. *Ah,* he thought, *visual at last.* "Target acquired," he said briskly. "Bearing follows." With a flick of his finger in its control cup Sutton sent the information out to the squadron.

"Good," Knott said softly as he followed the links. "Excellent, most excellent."

Now the Speeds had the Mollie destroyers firmly locked in their own short-range sensors, no longer needing the delayed, relayed data from *Invincible*.

"Preparing to engage destroyers with spinal energy weapons," Sutton said grimly. The immensely powerful but short-range energy cannon could gut a ship, if the Speed survived to use it. "Follow-on flight, take the cruiser!"

"Brother Captain," the Mollie tac officer said over the battle hymn, just a little louder this time.

"Yes, brother?" the captain of the cruiser replied.

"The destroyer captains request permission to go to visual with energy weapons. The electronic countermeasures of the Commonwealth ships are misleading our missiles. We are certainly in visual range," he added encouragingly.

The captain frowned. *If my brother captains need to be ordered to do something so obvious then we really are out of hope.*

Aloud he said, "Our brothers have little faith in the Spirit of Destiny. With true faith they could smite the enemy blindfolded."

That is exactly what they are trying to do, Captain, the tactical officer thought. Privately he also thought that with this man as their leader the Spirit had them marked for martyrdom.

"Brother Captain?" he said encouragingly.

"Very well," the captain said wearily.

Thank the Spirit! the tactical officer thought. *I hope it's not too late.*

"They're trying to trace with the close-in systems," Knott said quietly. He forced his hand not to close on the armrest of his couch.

Sutton's in charge, he reminded himself—that was the curse of commanding a carrier; you flew the Speeds like a hawk from a falconer's glove, and then it was up to them. If things closed to ship-to-ship engagement ranges, something had gone badly wrong.

He leaned forward, monitoring . . .

Sutton's AI informed him that the Mollie gunners were trying to target him. "Looks like the Mollies have gone to the eyeball Mark 1, people. Look alive out there!"

For himself he directed his AI to follow the pulse of
the Mollie that was aiming for him. The mechanical quasi-
mind drew markers and parallax across his vision.

Now!

The Speed bucked around him as the massive particle
gun fired, atoms stripped to their shells and accelerated
to near-light velocity. Light flared in the distance, the
system translating invisible energies for his eyes. Particles
were bending and warping around the destroyer's shields,
sucking the energy from the weapon that could open
their ship like a trout under a fisherman's knife . . . but
straining their capacities to the limit, and the flare would
leave the ship blind for crucial seconds.

"I've got him, I've *got* him!" a soprano voice carolled.

For an instant a ragged patch of the viewscreen before
him went blank as the system protected his eyes from
the savage radiation flare. No need to transform *that* into
the visual spectrum. A matter-antimatter reaction on that
scale broadcast over the entire range.

"Destroyer target one eliminated," the AI said clinically,
unaffected by the mingled horror and exultation of two-
hundred-odd lives and thousands of tons of starship
snuffed out in less time than a thought.

"Squadron leader, I have a solution on Bogey Three!
Say again, I have a confirmed solution!"

"That's negative on Bogey Three!" Sutton snapped
reluctantly. "We're supposed to let one go; that's the one
who had a secondary in his magazines. He hasn't fired
a thing except his close-in defense battery since. Paste
him with energy weapons, as if you were out of munitions, harry him to the jump point."

"Yessir." The same reluctance was in the pilot's voice.
It went against nature for a Speed to give up a target. . . .

Knott watched grimly as the protective screen of
destroyers was peeled away from the enemy cruiser.
"They're short of ordnance," he said.

The tac officer looked up. "That's what the AI thinks,
too," she said.

The task group going for the cruiser opened out the

formation and, speeding over their own front lines, folded over her like the petals of a carnivorous flower.

"That wave's going to get in with parasite bombs," Knott said, his eye on the tank. "Ops. Ready with long-range launch."

A slight quiver went through the fifteen thousand tons of the *Invincible* as her own missiles—massive things half the size of a Speed, with their own high-grade AIs and countermeasure suites—moved from the magazines to the launch rails.

"I have a solution."

"Launch." A fading rumble from beneath them . . .

The screen showed a sudden tracery of light. Fusion explosions were speckling the darkness, each one pumping a bundle of X-ray laser rods in the nanosecond before it vaporized them. *Icepicks of the Gods,* Knott thought, his stomach muscles drawing in slightly in instinctive sympathy, knowing what the enemy commander must be feeling as the bolts of energy went burning through ablative panels and into the hull frame, searing through conduits and bulkheads, into the sensitive electronic heart of the cruiser, seeking the bottled antihydrogen that would tear the ship apart from the inside. One after another the Speeds dropped their loads.

"Loss of drive energy," the tac officer said. "She's shedding hull plating and atmosphere . . . still has hull integrity and basic power systems, though. Fusion generator online, and she's warming up her A-H bottle for a jump."

"Is the solution still good?"

"Yes, skipper—we're going right down their throats, and her ECM and shields are going null . . . missile approaching detonation envelope . . . three . . . two . . ."

A ball of light expanded across the screen. "Containment failure. Target destroyed."

"He's running for it!" Sutton's wingman shouted.

Now the lower velocity of the crippled Mollie destroyer actually helped it, as it shed momentum and reversed, starting its run for the jump point. That meant running the gauntlet of the Speeds again, but those had used most of their parasite bombs.

"Okay," Sutton said. "We've got to let him escape, but make it convincing—we don't want him thinking we deliberately let him go."

The rest of the squadron doubled. A particle beam from a Mollie gunner slammed into Sutton's wingman and the Speed exploded into flame and twisting fragments. Sutton cursed bitterly, under his breath.

"Apache, Onion, Penguin," the squadron leader said, "harry our mark to departure. He sent an aiming pulse at the ship he meant and left it to his men to drive it to the jump point.

From the captain's chair of the injured destroyer *Fight Temptation Strongly* Second Lieutenant Prayerful Stubbins stared with shock-filled eyes around the ruined bridge. His forearm had been broken when the ship was hit and he'd gone flying over his own console. But he was in excellent condition compared to most of his crewmates. He also appeared to be the highest ranking surviving officer.

The cruiser and one destroyer were gone, their missiles were gone, the ship was badly damaged, leaking atmosphere and for all he knew blood. There was blood everywhere on the bridge. His head whirled and he grayed out for a moment. When he came back to himself his eyes found the holo-map and he saw pirate Speeds coming for them. Not as many as surrounded the brother ship, but in their present reduced state more than enough to finish them off.

The Interpreters must be warned of the pirate's treachery, he thought. There would be no reward for such a warning, he knew. They would punish him for leaving the fight, but he knew his duty.

"All about," he shouted. "Full speed to the jump point!"

Across the bridge his brothers in Ecclesia moved as swiftly as shock and injury would allow. The destroyer, her engines miraculously uninjured, sped towards escape followed by Speeds. Their missiles exhausted, the pirates fired particle beams but they were too far from their target to strike with any force. The shields flared and glowed, surrounding the ship in a nimbus of protection and blinding attacker and defender both.

Even so Prayerful cradled his injured arm and begged for intercession from the Spirit of Destiny. Each nibble the enemy took of their damaged ship might be one bite too many and he trembled with fear as well as shock. The disaster that this mission had turned into shook his faith.

Could *we be wrong?* he wondered. *Are the Interpreters guiding us astray?*

They entered transit and he lost consciousness. The traitorous ideas would prove harder to lose.

Sutton and his people bore down on the remaining destroyer. The ship maneuvered with great skill and when she fired she hit something. They'd lost two more Speeds to the Mollie's marksmanship. He'd noted the pilots successfully ejecting and was grateful.

"Mollie destroyer," Captain Knott's voice came over the com, "you are surrounded and outgunned. We call upon you to surrender according to the rules of war. We guarantee the safety of your crew." There was a long pause. "Please respond."

"Lying, treacherous pirates! You dare to talk of rules of war? You shall never take us alive!"

"What shall we do, sir?" Sutton asked the captain.

"We'll wait a bit," Knott told him. "I'm sending out a rescue boat to bring in our survivors."

They knew there would be no Mollie survivors. The Commonwealth had learned early on that there were no emergency suits provided for any but the bridge crew and then they rarely used them. Intelligence reported that such suits were considered to show a dearth of faith and therefore likely to bring down the wrath of the Spirit upon them.

Why would anyone follow a religion like this? Knott asked himself. Of course the younger ones hadn't chosen it, they'd been born into it, and brainwashed into believing it was the only way to live. *Which is very likely the real reason their Interpreters don't want us taking prisoners.* Finding themselves for the first time among people who didn't hurt them and demand that they adhere to impossible standards was mind-boggling for the few Mollies they'd managed to take prisoner.

The destroyer hung in space, leaking atmosphere, Speeds all around with weapons locked. Suddenly they sent a high-speed transmission to the lone Mollie outpost in this system, there was a burst of music, one of their battle hymns, and then the destroyer blew wide.

Drives flared as Speeds reversed thrust away from the explosion and every heart fell at the unnecessary deaths.

There was a moment of total silence. Then Knott got on the com and said, "Commander Raeder, prepare your people."

"Acknowledged," Raeder responded.

He and his people had been watching the action, yelling advice and encouragement, speculating about the Mollies' curious reluctance to fire. But the Mollie self-immolation had silenced even the Marines. That silence lay heavy for long moments, until he straightened and spoke.

"Well," Peter said, turning to them, "I doubt there's much more we can do to prepare. You've got your ditty bags all packed?"

There were grins and nods in response.

"Then we should all go over our vehicles and manifests one more time, because if we don't bring it with us, it won't be there when we need it. Be ready for departure at fifteen hundred. Dismissed."

They stood as one and saluted, then departed crisply for their final checks.

Raeder smiled at their formality, but took it as a good sign. *We're as pumped as we're gonna be,* he thought. *We're going to cause some trouble here.*

CHAPTER ELEVEN

Raeder keyed in the lock's *open* sequence again. And again, nothing happened. The *Invincible* had dropped off their little flotilla just outside the asteroid field. A decision the commander had applauded. *I mean, why look for trouble?*

The area was an enormous field of floating rocks. Granted, they were far too far apart to see with the naked eye; this was an asteroid *field*, after all, not the rings of a gas giant—a distinction the entertainment holos always had trouble making. A ship the size of the light carrier would still make a much larger target, and thererfore be prone to more extensive damage than the sleek Speeds or even the chunky cargo carriers would take. The velocities involved were . . . well, astronomical.

"Commander?" Knott's voice came over the com.

"It's still refusing to open, sir," Raeder told him. "I think we're going to have to send a team out to look at it."

There was silence for a moment, then a sigh.

"Well," the captain said, "it's been several decades since

anyone was here. I suppose it was too much to expect that the lock would work perfectly."

He didn't say that it would be a shame to have to call off the mission because they couldn't get into the secret hideout. It wouldn't be a shame, it would be ludicrous.

Raeder glanced over at his technicians, belted down in their seats. They looked back, clearly wondering which of them he would tap for this.

"Sure, and it probably only needs to have new batteries," Paddy said.

There was relief on some of the faces beside him. Not everyone enjoyed working outside, and this clearly settled it. The crazy New Hibernian would go.

"Or it might be a wee bit of meteor damage," the big redhead went on. "It'll be the work of minutes, I'm thinkin'."

"We're going to send someone out to give it a look, Captain," Raeder said.

Knott, who had heard the lilt of Paddy's voice, though not what he was saying, smiled.

"Excellent, Commander. Try not to take too long though. The Mollies will be sending reinforcements as quick as they can."

We need to be gone by then went without saying.

"Yes, sir," the commander said crisply. "We're on it. Out." He turned to Paddy. "Okay, let's suit up, Chief. What do you think we'll need?"

In under fifteen minutes Raeder and Paddy were attached to repair scooters not unlike the one Peter had flown on the *Africa* on his way to join the *Invincible*. These were newer and a lot more high tech, which was to be expected from the military.

They sure have a lot more pep than the Africa's, Raeder thought. Stars cartwheeled around them as he applied boost. He had let Paddy lead and the New Hibernian's headlight illuminated quite a lot of the gigantic hatch. The Chief was exploring the rim of the recessed door with a handheld spotlight.

"The mechanism will be obvious," he was saying. "A

wonking great thing. If it was operational it should be lit up, too. So I'm bettin' it's a dead battery after all."

Raeder grunted. "I thought those things were supposed to last a thousand years," he said. "At least that's what the maker's ads said."

Paddy laughed. "And if they did then who'd still be makin' 'em? Are you still believin' what the recuiter said too, sir?" He flashed the light around a bit more. "Ah! Here we are!" he said cheerfully.

Paddy parked the scooter on the hatchway itself, the magnetic wheels gripping, and moved himself over to the lock mechanism using handholds extruded from the foamed metal of the door when it was installed. Raeder parked beside him and watched the Chief move carefully over the face of the hatch.

"Do you think you'll need help?" he asked. The real reason he was here was because the rules said, when working outside, you must have a buddy. But if there was one thing Raeder was certain of, it was that Paddy Casey didn't need anybody's help with any machine ever built.

Paddy was at the broken lock now and clipped his line to a ring meant for just such occasions.

"We-ll," he answered after a few experimental prods, "I was goin' to say no, but . . . This here is an old thing, I've never seen the like." He took out a tool and began to unseal it.

"Let me take a look," Raeder said. "I've just had this intensive course in opening obscure lock designs."

"Mary and the saints!" Paddy exclaimed when he'd opened the covering.

"What?" Raeder asked, hearing a note of horror in his voice. Bending his knees he pushed himself off and floated over to Paddy's position, grabbing the Chief's arm to stop himself. "What?" he said again.

"Tis a bomb, sir."

Raeder yanked aside the cover and stared at the neat bundles of explosive that filled the large box where the lock mechanism should be. *Fulgurite B!* he thought, his mind starting to gibber. Blasting explosive, in use for centuries—the ads for *this* called it the "ultimate chemical explosive," for good reason. Then his eyes noted that the fuse didn't seem to be reacting to having the door opened. It looked dead, in fact.

He laughed uneasily. "It's a dud. I think. Hell, it's been here for over forty years. But I am so *sick* of dealing with bombs—at least this isn't one of Larkin's."

Paddy laughed too. "Sure it's no wonder the door wouldn't open."

"Could there be another lock mechanism?" Raeder asked.

"I hope so," Paddy said. "Because I don't want to mess with this lot. If it did go off it'd take half the damned asteroid with it, and you and me just incidentally." He slammed the door of the lock housing and it bounced back open. There was a flash of green before he automatically tapped it closed.

They looked at one another in dawning horror. Paddy slowly opened the door again. Inside, the fuse mechanism glowed with little lights, turning slowly from red to green.

"That isn't good," Raeder said, dry-mouthed.

"No, sir. Not good at all."

Raeder's mind ran through possibilities. If they tried to remove the fuse the bomb would probably explode. Of course the gel might be inert after all these years . . . but the makers of Fulgurite B *also* claimed it would last a thousand years, and they were probably nearer to the truth. Then again, jostling it might not set this one off, but if it was wired to other bombs planted throughout the hutch then even if this one didn't explode its cousins might.

How could we have forgotten that miners are experts with explosives? Or that these particular miners were very, very angry when they left here.

On the other hand, they surely knew that someday, someone they didn't hate might return, so there probably was some simple way to defuse this thing.

"Manning, Kushner," he said over his com. The Marines were their demolitions experts, let them earn their keep.

"Sir," they responded simultaneously.

"We have a bomb," Peter told them.

"Sure," Manning said calmly.

Oh, yeah, of course, sure, Raeder thought.

"Whaddaya mean, 'sure,'" he snarled.

"Old miners' trick," she told him. "Stick a number four screwdriver in the hole between the last two red lights. That usually stops the countdown."

"Usually?"

"Well, it's old stuff, sir. But it *should* work."

"Do we *have* a number four screwdriver, Paddy?"

Blue eyes stared into his from behind his face shield.

"Well . . . not on me," Paddy said.

"On the cart?" Raeder asked, one eye on the diminishing red lights.

"Oh! Aye!" And Paddy launched himself over to his cart, opened the back panel and rummaged in its guts, tossing out neatly stacked and tied tools. "Here!" he cried and pushed himself off, while Raeder pulled in the Chief's line. There was a tense moment while Paddy tried to free the screwdriver from its tray with clumsy suited gloves.

Pad-dy, Raeder thought impatiently, but did not say, though he almost cracked his teeth holding his mouth shut.

Paddy shoved the screwdriver home just as the second-to-last light went green.

Raeder's heart almost stopped, and his breathing certainly did. Then, after a very long moment he let out his breath in a rush as he realized that they had indeed stopped the countdown.

After a moment he said, "Thank you, Manning. That number four screwdriver seems to have done the trick."

"You're welcome, sir," she said smugly.

"I'm just wondering, Manning," he said dangerously, "if you remember what I said about not assuming that I know everything?"

"Uh . . . Ah! Yes, I see, sir."

"So if I ask you what we can expect next, you'll tell me, won't you? Just assume I'm an idiot for the moment and don't know anything, all right?"

"There are undoubtedly other booby traps inside, sir. So we should send a squad through to clear the hutch. Also, this bomb is disarmed, but not defused. It wouldn't be a good idea to move it until the other traps are also disarmed."

Raeder thought about that. *Makes sense.* On the other hand, there didn't appear to be a locking mechanism, so how did they get inside to look for the other booby traps?

"What are you forgetting to tell me, Manning?" He waited patiently.

"The locking code should work now?"

Raeder doubted that he would ever again hear that note of uncertainty in Manning's voice. *So I suppose I'd better enjoy it while I can,* he thought.

"Lieutenant Commander James," he said over his com.

"Yes, sir," Sarah answered.

"Would you please try the locking code again for us?"

"Yes, sir." Sarah tapped in the code.

Raeder could feel the vibration through the handle he clasped. He reached out and grabbed the screwdriver, making certain it was secure, then flashed his spot over the lock and saw it beginning to split into four parts and retract.

"Paddy," he said.

"Yes, sir?"

"I think we'd better move those scooters."

"Lt. Commander James," Raeder said.

"Yes, sir."

"Please tell Captain Knott that we have opened the miners' hutch, but that it is probably riddled with booby traps from the time of the Consortium wars, so it's going to take us a little while to move in."

"Yes, sir."

Raeder and Paddy powered up their scooters and floated into the great maw of the hutch, casting their spotlight beams in every direction. The place was so huge that the light faded almost to nothing before it touched the surrounding walls. There were abandoned nets for gathering crushed ore floating about in huge, ragged clumps. There were even some small cargo vehicles. These adhered to old mag strips set into the asteroid's substance. Tools had drifted over time and bumped gently against the walls, ceiling and smoothed floor. A few longer objects of various shapes hung, some still gently rotating despite decades of friction.

"Commander?" Sarah James' voice said in Peter's ear.

"Yes, Lt. Commander."

"Captain Knott says the *Invincible* will wait for two hours while we check out the hutch. He'll need to know by then if this mission is go."

"Understood," Raeder said crisply. "I hope to know well before that."

"Yes, sir. James out."

"Manning, Kushner," Raeder said.

"Sir!" the two Marines responded.

It's eerie the way they do that, Peter thought. *It's so coordinated, like they're sharing a brain or something.* Perhaps those rumors about the Marines recruiting from hivemind aliens . . .

"Okay, people, you're the experts," *about bombs, among other things,* "where do we start looking? And what do we do now that our number four screwdriver is already in use?"

"Well, sir," Manning said, "according to my grandfather the inside bombs that weren't directly connected to the door trap were small and easily defused. Blue was the color of the miners' flag, so cutting the blue wire, where applicable, should prevent the bombs from exploding."

"What about the main power board?" Raeder asked.

"That will definitely be trapped, sir."

Raeder allowed himself to sigh. "What about bringing the Speeds in here? Is that likely to set anything off?"

"If they'd done something to the entrance then your scooters would have set it off, sir."

I have got to find a way to convince this woman to tell me things I really need to know, Peter thought desperately.

"We should be fine," Manning continued blithely. "Well within the acceptable risk envelope, sir."

Whaddaya mean "we," Raeder thought sourly. *"Should" doesn't sound too great, either.* Marines tended to have an eccentric definition of acceptable risk.

"Assuming the area is clear of debris," she continued.

Raeder and Paddy looked at one another. As the men on site they knew who was going to get that job.

Hmm, Peter thought. *Unfold one of these nets and drag it down the hangar, that should get most of this junk out of the way.*

First things first though. They needed to find the main power board and get some light in here. He'd studied maps of this place and had a very good idea of where it should be. But the dark, and the sheer size of the place were disorienting.

They moved forward, their rockets adding small stabs of temporary blue light to the icy darkness, reflections flickering in the distance. Finally they reached the far wall of the cavernous space. Moving along its curve to the right, Raeder at last discerned the heavy door that led to the power housing.

"We're at the hatch of the power room," Raeder said. "Talk to me, Manning."

"The door should be clear," Manning said. "The usual trick was to put a dab of gel-band and a detonator on the main power contacts, just enough to blow someone's arm off."

"Oh, nice," Raeder growled. *Though to be fair,* he reminded himself, *the miners had cause. And it was war.* "So what do we do?" he asked.

"Slip something metallic, foil would be good, between the gel and its metal contact point."

Paddy tapped Raeder's shoulder and waved a strip of metal at him.

"It's for solderin'," he said. "But it should do the trick."

"Then let's go," Raeder said and parked his scooter.

The lock on the hatch worked smoothly and their spotlights chased shadows into the corners. Across from the hatch was the switch they were looking for, and Raeder found himself licking his lips nervously. He wasn't an expert at this by any means and the explosives, if there were explosives, were old and unreliable. He took a breath and moved awkwardly across the small room, magnetic boot soles gripping the grid built into the floor, but the weightlessness still making every move an effort.

Peter sidled up to the main power board and worked off the plate that covered the switches. This was incredibly antiquated equipment, even by Consortium standards. But they'd reasoned that when a chip was burnt out, it was gone, but a mechanical part can be repaired or gimmicked into performing. And they were practically free for the taking.

With difficulty, due to the bulky helmet he wore, Raeder managed to get a side view of the switch in question. There was a large lump of gel joining it to the contact point of the main switch.

Great, he thought.

"Give me that metal strip," he said to Paddy, holding out his hand.

"Sir, maybe I should be doin' that," the big man said. "Not that I'm doubtin' yer abilities, now, it's just that I'm the more expendable, d'ye see?"

"This is an order, Chief," Raeder said firmly. "Give me that strip of metal." *Not that I wouldn't prefer that somebody else do this,* he thought. *But you're no more expert at this than I am, Chief. So I'm gonna trust me instead of you, okay?*

With a scowl Paddy handed it over and retreated a few paces.

Nice when your friends show faith in you, Peter thought sourly. He knew as he thought it that Paddy was right to withdraw and that his cynicism was just an attempt to keep his mind off the possibilities.

If this little bomb blew it would not only kill him, but probably the mission too. They could, maybe, replace the main power board with supplies from the *Invincible,* or work around it; but putting someone else in charge under such circumstances would have a . . . significant effect on morale.

He eased the strip behind the hard lump of gel with exquisite delicacy, sweat threatening to run into his eyes and blind him. So far, so good. He paused for a moment and glanced at Paddy. The big New Hibernian was squeezing his hands into fists and releasing them, his face carefully expressionless.

Raeder went back to work, pushing gently. After what seemed like eternity he was through.

Well, I guess this solder had sufficient metal in it, he thought with relief. *I'd know by now if it didn't.* He frowned, looked at the switch with its lump of gel, then cursed mentally.

"Manning," he said with terrible calm, "can I now just pry this stuff off the switch itself? Or do I need another metal strip?"

"You need another metal strip, sir."

Raeder clenched his jaw. *I should have seen it,* he chastised himself, *it's my fault. It's so obvious.* But it would have been nice if she'd cautioned him about it. It would have been a lot easier to scrape it off the switch and then the contact. *C'est la guerre,* he thought and suppressed a sigh. But when he got her in here, he was going to make her teach him how to defuse a bomb so that if this ever happened again he'd *know* what to do.

"Do we have another strip of solder?" he asked Paddy.

"Aye, sir." Paddy held one up. "Might I . . . ?" he gestured towards the open panel.

The commander paused before answering.

"Sure," he said. "Go for it." *At the moment I've only got one of those in me,* he thought.

The Chief came forward and Raeder stepped away. After a much shorter time than he had taken, Peter was sure, Paddy gave a relieved sigh.

"It's done, sir," he said with a grin.

"Make sure the contacts are clean!" Manning said suddenly.

Raeder chuckled. *By George, I think she's got it.*

"Our Marines assure me that they've gotten them all, sir," Raeder told the captain. "Manning says it looks like a hasty evacuation. We're still going to be cautious, naturally. But everything seems to be working very well; electronics, the air scrubbers, plumbing all functioning.

Which is amazing considering that this is obviously an economy operation. Just not so cheap that they were in danger of killing everybody."

"That's not the way I've heard it," Knott growled.

There had in fact been many cases where Consortium cheeseparing had killed hundreds of miners. But it was reassuring to know that this wouldn't be one of them.

"Then we'll leave you to settle in, Commander," the captain said. "Good hunting."

"Thank you, sir. The same to you."

Raeder was about to shut down when he heard someone say, "Sir! Mollie craft approaching from the vector of their outpost."

Perraglio, Raeder's communications tech, snapped into action, accessing the Commonwealth spy gear operating in the area. A screen showed an in-system shuttle sliding cautiously towards the recent battle site.

"Take him out," Knott said calmly.

As suddenly as a gasp the Mollie fired off a tight burst communication towards its base. Perraglio and the *Invincible*'s techs moved to block it.

"I think that got it, sir," the young petty officer said.

"You think?" Raeder asked with raised eyebrows.

Perraglio shook his head. "It's impossible to be absolutely sure, sir. But the odds are definitely in our favor."

The *Invincible* flowed forward with the lean economy of a leopard at full gallop. The Mollie ship was still making her turn when the single ship killer missile hit her broadside, and she was gone in a brief flare of fire and spinning debris, blinking like chips of foil as their spinning brought a reflective surface towards the light.

Raeder realized that they'd been lucky before. The small battle group they'd encountered had been so confident of their own ability to fight the *Invincible* that they hadn't bothered to send intelligence to the tiny Mollie outpost in this system.

If the shuttle's message had gotten through it would be all too easy, once the mission got underway, to figure out that the Commonwealth was behind these mysterious raiders.

"We'll leave you now, Commander," Knott said. "Once again, good luck and good hunting."

"Thank you, sir," Raeder said. *I really* hope that message didn't get through. "And the same to you."

CHAPTER TWELVE

Manning and Kushner, grim-faced, thrust another armload of musty-smelling bedding into the chamber Raeder had decided to use for storage. Which essentially meant anything that would be of no use on this mission and needed to be removed from underfoot. Lieutenant Givens clomped up behind them; the noise he was making smacking his magnetized boot soles onto the hard floor made it obvious to the two Marines that he felt that such scut work was beneath him.

They glanced at each other out of the corners of their eyes, looking for all the world like older children deciding to torment their younger brother.

"Phew! This stuff stinks!" Kushner exclaimed.

"So does the air," Manning agreed. The scrubbers were old, and substandard when new, so it wasn't any wonder that the atmosphere was fusty.

"You know what stinks," Givens grumbled. "What stinks is that pilots are doing *this!* Why aren't the techs doing this?"

Two of the tech crew, pulling huge bags of abandoned

151

tools behind them, stopped to look at him, one in disgust, one looking hurt.

"We are, boyo," Paddy said, coming up behind him so softly that even the Marines were taken by surprise, to their evident displeasure. "Why, even the commander has lent a hand."

That was true, at least before the Speeds had flown in.

"So where is he now?" Givens challenged.

"Well, I'm sure I don't know, Lieutenant," Paddy said quietly. "The commander forgot to submit a schedule to me, last time we were takin' tea together. But I can soon find out if ye need to talk to him."

"I just feel that there are better uses for my skills," the lieutenant insisted as though someone had been arguing with him.

"Well, we all have our skills, now," the New Hibernian told him.

Paddy thought to himself how young the pilot was, and didn't much trouble to keep his opinion from showing.

Givens turned to the Marines for backup and saw exactly the same expression on their faces.

"It's got to be done, sir," Terry Hunding said cheerfully. The pretty young tech hauled her bag towards the storage space. "The sooner we get it done, the sooner we can get down to business."

With a grunt and a sour look, Givens turned and walked away. To his credit he didn't jump down Terry's throat as all three of her superior officers would have bet hard credits he would.

Hunding watched him stalk off with the glow of hero worship in her brown eyes.

The two marines locked gazes with Casey and quickly lowered theirs. His had told them that he knew very well that they'd been provoking the lieutenant to indiscretion. And like all junior officers, perhaps better than most, they knew better than to fall afoul of a chief petty officer as canny as Paddy. Whatever else they might be, Manning and Kushner were survivors.

Paddy tsked! to himself as they walked away.

"Not even one day gone," he murmured, "and already there's trouble brewing in paradise."

Sarah was acting as quartermaster, choosing and organizing the preparation of the dormitories and eating areas. They'd all be eating prepared meals, but having everyone eat in the same area would help to keep the hutch clean with minimum effort.

"How's it going?" Raeder bustled up to ask.

"Fine," the Lt. Commander answered with a smile. "We've cleaned out all the old bedding and we're hanging up the new."

She indicated a crew that was arranging sleep sacks along a wall. The whole crew would end up sleeping like papooses hung in a row. Sarah hoped that nobody snored too loudly. This place was *basic* and designed for communal living. The Consortium hadn't believed in pampering the help, and the whole huge echoing tube of the asteroid base made that *very* clear.

The open plan alone would take some getting used to; Welters, the nickname for Commonwealth citizens, liked their privacy. She'd certainly come to appreciate hers as the commander of the WACCIs, and she'd missed it immediately when she was required to share quarters with one of the other pilots when she'd transferred to the Speeds. But this . . .

We'll certainly lose some of our mystique as officers, she thought wryly.

Raeder looked gloomy.

"Thank God it's only for a month," he muttered, as though responding to her thought, then grinned at her smile. "I'd better go check on our techs' progress in setting up," he said and turned away. "Oh." He turned back, suddenly serious, "be prepared to put your helmets on at a moment's notice. We're expecting a Mollie task force any time now."

"Yes, sir," Sarah said. "We'll be ready."

And they would be. It was still too cold to be comfortable working without their suits on anyway, so everyone still wore them. Though helmets had been removed they were at hand, and gloves dangled from special catches at their wrists, ready to be put on instantly.

One of the Commonwealth's spy devices would signal them when the jump point delivered the Mollie task force. At that point the generators would be shut down, the air and heat and light would cease to circulate. They could live with that . . . provided it didn't go on too long. They could live in their suits . . . for a while.

Everything's timing, she mused.

Raeder stood behind Petty Officer Mike Pellagrio and watched the information coming in from the electronic spies intelligence had planted in this sector. He paced behind the stations of the other two techs, who had been relieved of any other duty but watching for Mollies. So far, all was quiet; nothing from the Mollie outpost, nothing coming through the jump point.

"Sir!" Pellagrio said. "The jump point's hot! Something coming through—mass in the hundred-k range."

Raeder moved back to the young petty officer's station. Columns of figures scrolled down beneath a holo display of the warped space around the jump point; that looked like a vaguely obscene flower, or a very distorted trumpet.

"I've got warship-type neutrino signatures coming through," the young tech said.

"Oh, mother take me home!" Raeder said, with a whistle as the AI started assigning ship classes. *A Mollie fleet carrier . . . two battlecruisers . . . and four destroyers.* "Well, that's more than we're going to attack with our Speeds, right enough." A major task force, a quarter the striking power of a Sector fleet. *Uh-oh. Here comes their logistics train.*

Peter hit the alarm button; lights flashed and klaxons sounded in every corner of the base. After ten seconds he shut it off, got on the intercom and announced, "Suit up people, the lights go out in one minute."

There was a minor flurry of activity around him as the techs reached for their helmets; Raeder knew that this was being repeated throughout the hutch. He settled his own helmet on his head and then attached his gloves.

We should be all right, he told himself. *All those neutrino signals and all that debris from the battle should hide all but the smallest traces of our entry into this field.*

There'd been no sound from the Mollie outpost, arguing that they hadn't gotten that desperate message after all.

"Commander!" Ensign Manning called as she trotted into the command area.

Then she and everyone else froze as the lights went out and they were all lost in a pitch-black world with only the tiny puddles of light from the headlights on their helmets for company.

"Commander," she repeated and continued in the direction she'd been heading when the lights went out.

A helmet-light turned in her direction and Manning homed in on that.

"What is it, Ensign?" Raeder asked. He knew in his heart that he wasn't going to like this. *That's what it means when someone like Manning says "Commander!" in just that tone. She might as well have been shouting, "You're not going to like this!"* What really worried him was the idea that this was something that the Marine herself didn't like.

"Sir!" Manning declared and saluted smartly. As smartly as one can salute in full EVA gear in zero g.

Raeder returned the gesture, a little bit of ice growing in his stomach.

"Sir, I regret to inform you that I had completely forgotten the bomb located in the lock mechanism outside the hutch." Manning's eyes were straight forward, her slim body pulled up into attention.

Raeder's mouth formed a surprised O. *The screwdriver!*

"Nice work, Manning," he said through gritted teeth. "But thank you, for informing me."

He was justifiably angry. It *had* been a stupid mistake. First, it was a huge bomb that hadn't actually been defused and second . . .

"If the Mollies do know about this place and come here to check it out, Manning, then our cover's blown."

He'd wanted to stay with the Marines for at least the first few bomb disposals, but he'd been needed elsewhere. *How could she* or *Kushner have forgotten something this important?*

That number four screwdriver might as well be quivering in the heart of the mission; it would wave a big red warning flag under the Mollies' noses.

On the other hand, he thought, his usual sense of fairness resurfacing, *if they* do *know about the hutch, it's best we find out now.* If they did know, then the mission was effectively off. Because the Mollies weren't as boneheaded about everything as they were about theology. They'd know quick enough where the mysterious raiders were coming from. And they would handle the problem with their usual merciless dispatch, too.

"We can't turn the generator back on," he mused aloud.

"There's a workman's door built into the larger one, sir," Manning said. "It cost too much energy to open the big one too often."

"You know where it is?" Raeder asked.

"No, sir. But I can find it," Manning promised.

"Get what you need," the commander said. "I'll go with you."

He could see by the way she lowered her eyes that she didn't like the idea of him being her buddy outside. *Tough,* he thought. He'd vowed she was going to teach him what she knew about demolition and this was as good a time as any to start learning.

"Just hold it steady, sir. Please," Manning said politely.

She was using what looked like a piece of wire to pry the fuse apparatus off the gel-band, while Peter held the screwdriver steady in its hole.

"What is that instrument you're using, Ensign?" he asked.

"It's a piece of wire, sir."

"Oh."

Well, that's just what it looked like. Raeder smiled ruefully. *Maybe I'm getting the hang of this.*

The Marine pulled the mechanism towards her, revealing a complicated mess of color-coded wires. Raeder looked at it with interest. You couldn't see anything out here with the Eyeball Mark One, but the skin between his shoulder blades was uneasily conscious that close by was enough Mollie firepower to sterilize a planet—hell, enough to turn an average Earth-type planet into an asteroid belt like this. He kept his attention firmly on the booby trap.

"I've never seen anything like that outside of historical films," Peter said in astonishment. "How did they manage with such primitive equipment?"

"Badly," Manning said, her voice distracted. "But that was part of the Consortium's plan. The contract miners sure weren't going to build a jump-capable ship and escape from here with this stuff. They were able to do the work, but they were totally dependent on the Consortium for supplies."

She gently slid the board towards herself, Peter keeping pace, letting her direct the placement of the fuse. Manning held up a piece of wire from out of the tangle and he took it with his free hand. Then the ensign unclipped a cutter from her belt and, lifting the light blue wire out of his clasp, prepared to cut it low down, where the cut end could be tucked under the board and so appear whole.

"What happens," Raeder asked, "where it's already disarmed, if you cut the wrong wire?"

Manning looked at the commander in surprise.

"No one ever asks questions like that when you're actually defusing a bomb, sir. It's considered bad luck."

"Ah." *Sounds reasonable. Probably because it's a distracting question.* Not that he'd been able to keep it to himself. *I mean, what does happen if she cuts the wrong wire? Inquiring minds want to know.* That was because inquiring minds had their suspicions.

But his hands were steady as he held the board, with its attached screwdriver, in place for her. A needle burst of laser light and the question was answered. Or rather shelved, since she appeared to have cut the correct wire.

Manning slid the apparatus back into place and, taking Raeder's hand, gently slid the screwdriver out of the hole. Only then did she let out her breath in a relieved hiss.

Well, well, Raeder thought, equally relieved, but too high on the pecking order to be allowed to show it, *so the iron maiden had her doubts.* He wasn't sure if he was amused or retroactively scared spitless.

"Let's get inside," he said, gently closing the lock mechanism's small door. "We don't want to get caught here with our pants down."

Manning looked at him uncertainly.

"No, sir," she said. "I mean, yes . . . sir."

"It's an old expression," Raeder explained, catching on to the reason for her confusion. "It probably had something to do with politics."

"Ah," she said knowingly.

Funny how everyone always agrees with that, Peter thought.

Peter hurried back to his post behind Perraglio. The sensor array was presently running on accumulators and was completely passive, doing nothing but receiving emissions; those of both Mollie communications and the Welter spy sensors that watched the enemy's every move.

Unfortunately for all of them, the Mollies were currently broadcasting a battle hymn in honor of their fallen comrades.

It's loud enough that I'll bet their dead can actually hear it, too, Raeder thought, twisting his head inside his helmet as if that would help him escape the noise. It was certainly enough to speed even the most reluctant soul towards paradise. *Where I hope they've got better music.*

Perraglio and the other techs were monitoring on other bandwidths, looking for any signals sneaking below or above the official broadcast. But the Mollies took this sort of thing seriously and there had been nothing for over half an hour.

Finally, and none too soon, the captain of the carrier gave a rousing speech, praising the Mollie martyrs and their bravery in battle as though he'd been there to see it. His catalogue of events was a bit off the mark; he had the pirates firing the first shot, for example. But to Raeder and his crew that was all to the good. He ended his speech by condemning the Welters to the darkest pits of hell.

"May their bones burst from the heat of the black fires that forever roast the damned!"

"Ee-yu-ck," Aia Wisnewski said, wrinkling her nose.

Alonso Barak glanced at her out of the corner of his eye and grinned.

"They're a strange combination of Christian mythos and secular mysticism, aren't they?" he said. "But they've taken to the concept of hell like a cat takes to naps." He shook his head. "What an unhappy bunch of people."

Raeder glanced at them and they quieted down. True, they'd been talking suit-to-suit and the Mollies were still fascinated by the rantings of their leader, but it was best to stay quiet.

"Go forth, my brothers! Seek and ye shall find our enemies! Look also for any of our brethren who may have survived."

I was wondering if he was going to mention the possibility of survivors, Peter thought. *Not that I'd want to be one.* He could imagine the kind of debriefing these fanatics would consider appropriate. *It makes my intestines ache just to think of it.*

It was unlikely that the *Invincible* had missed anybody, though. Knott had made a very thorough search for any of their own people who might have survived and had probably picked up any Mollies out there.

They watched quietly as the Mollies searched, listened to the enemy's laconic comments back and forth. Then Raeder's stomach went cold as he watched one of the destroyers heading towards the asteroid field. He was clearly following their particle trail.

Oh, no, Peter thought, his heart thumping into overdrive. *I can't believe this! They're not supposed to have sensors that good!*

Pellagrio tapped a few keys and the view switched as new spy-eyes were brought into play. The Mollie ship moved slowly, carefully. Occasionally its close-in defense systems would fire; an invisible pulse of energy and a burst of light from a rock unlucky enough to be on a dangerous trajectory, stripped to atoms by the beams.

Then . . .

"That isn't a chunk of rock!" he hissed. He called up a closer view; there was enough ambient energy being put about by the Mollie ship's beams and reflected off everything and sundry that the passive receptors were nearly as good as active seekers. The AI obligingly drew a three-dimensional picture of the piece of debris.

What the hell is that? he wondered, narrowing his eyes in concentration. Suddenly it lit up and spun violently for a second or two. His jaw dropped. *It's a Speed engine!*

A punch on his arm nearly toppled him, and he spun indignantly to his left, to be greeted by Paddy's twinkling eyes, set above the biggest grin he'd ever seen on the New Hibernian's habitually smiling face. Peter grinned back at him, knowing instantly that the CPO had some-how, somewhen managed to push that engine out there to fool the Mollies.

He turned his attention back to Pellagrio's station and saw that the Mollies had indeed been fooled.

"The neutrino signals leading into this asteroid field can be attributed to a Speed engine that appears to have broken loose from one of the wrecks around the *Path-finder*, Brother Captain. We request permission to with-draw from this field. We've already taken minor hull damage, sir."

"Are you certain, Brother?" the carrier's captain asked. "Our instruments indicated a fair amount of mess lead-ing in there."

"The engine is still sputtering, sir," the Mollie destroyer answered. "That would easily account for it."

There was silence for a moment. Then a rock struck a major antenna and the signal wavered.

"Brother Captain, we are taking damage," the destroyer captain said, his voice laced with static.

"Very well, you may withdraw."

The destroyer had braked to a full stop on finding the

Speed's engine and her maneuvers to withdraw from the field were neat and quick. She seemed to quiver with impatience as she slowly, warily withdrew from the chaos of the asteroid field.

There goes one relieved bunch of men, Raeder thought. But he was uneasy in his mind about the carrier captain's reluctance to let the destroyer break off the search. *Will he remember that he suspected something wasn't right when we get down to business?* he wondered. Possibly. *But part of the plan is working perfectly,* he reassured himself. *They definitely attribute the attack on their little fleet to the pirates.*

Therefore, they should attribute any future attacks to the same cause.

If they knew *about the hutch,* Raeder soothed himself, *that captain would never have called off the search. Regardless of how messed up the destroyer was getting.* He shook his head. *At any rate this is no time to start second-guessing.*

The Mollies loitered around the site of the battle for several hours, prompting Raeder to wonder exactly what they were hoping for. Perhaps they expected the pirates to come back and gloat over the scene of their crime? Were they counting the spinning pieces of wreckage? They'd been silent for some time, perhaps they were having a prayer meeting?

Finally, with a last hymn blatting and pinging in tribute to their fallen, the Mollie task force left the system.

"Did you notice?" Raeder said. "They never even tried to contact their outpost."

"It's probably a punishment post," Sarah said. "In which case, they wouldn't."

"Yeah," Peter said with a sideways nod of his head and a half shrug. "They do take their punishment seriously in that outfit."

He waited fifteen minutes more and when nothing else happened he said, "Okay, power up."

One of the techs started the generator and the lights went back on. It would be a couple of hours yet before they could take off their helmets and breathe the funky atmosphere from the hutch's air pumps, and it would be too cold to take off their suits for a few hours after that.

But they should be able to sleep in just their ship suits before thirteen hundred.

"We've done a good job today," Peter said, looking at the assembled faces of his tiny command. Behind them the tunneled-out asteroid stretched, the Speeds clipped neatly in place. "This place is now stripped down and ready for action. And there's going to be plenty of action in the next thirty days." He paused.

"We've all fought pirates. Before the war that was what Star Command did for the most part. They're all scum and we're even doing the Mollies a favor by taking them out of action. If all goes right, when this mission is over, we will have compromised an important source of supply for our enemy and given the pirates good reason to think twice before attacking a Commonwealth ship for the benefit of the Mollies.

"We may well shorten the war from this base. It's important that each and every one of us remember that. Because we're going to be working to ten tenths of capacity every day; even when nothing comes by we must be totally prepared. We cannot let down our guard for one moment because this mission is too important.

"We'll be eating prepared rations." Groans came through his earphones and he smiled in honest agreement. "And we'll have little leisure and no privacy. We're going to get on each other's nerves. But we will hold to discipline, we will never lose sight of our goal. And when our thirty days are up, *Invincible* will return and take us out of here." There was a brief spate of cheering at that.

"Just remember, people, there isn't a man or woman on that carrier who wouldn't gladly trade places with you right now. Because what we're doing is important!" He paused for a moment and then smiled. "The stories you tell your children about this will have them boasting about you for the rest of their lives." He looked at the people around him and a lump came into his throat. *Get a grip, Raeder,* he told himself. "So let's make some history," he said. "Raeder out," and Peter shut down the com with cheers ringing in his ears.

CHAPTER THIRTEEN

Aia Wisnewski and Alonso Barak harried their target. It dodged and jinked, trying to take advantage of the high concentration of nickel-iron rocks to get out of the combined fire-cones of the two deadly little vessels . . . and failing. The Star Command Speeds were monitoring its transmission channels as well; nothing was getting out to the pirate's friends, but they could enjoy every word.

"My, my, he does have an extensive vocabulary, doesn't he?" Aia said, monitoring the pirate vessel. "I'm blushing."

"Fortunately, he doesn't have a very good ship," Alonso replied.

Neither of them was willing to call it a Speed. It was intended to fulfill the same purposes, roughly; a small one-person craft with a powerful normal-space drive and heavy armament. The pirate dodged, still cursing non-stop; he'd executed every maneuver his bastardized Speed had in it.

"Your turn," Barak drawled with cool courtesy.

"My thanks," Aia responded as her computer lined up the pirate in her sights. A strobing star surrounded the pip her AI had drawn, and she triggered a subnormal pulse from the Speed's main spinal particle beam. Light flared around shields; her instruments told her they were near overload even from that little love-tap.

"I surrender!" the pirate screamed.

He isn't a complete fool, she thought. *Probably saying to himself:* These people fought like Welters, probably Star Command. Which meant they were supposed to take prisoners. No sense in dying when the worst that could happen was a little prison time.

"Open your com," Wisnewski ordered calmly. "Transmitting . . ."

Her AI blinked for a minute and then came up: enemy locked out of controls. system slaved to your command: instructions?

"You guys are good," the pirate observed cheerfully, his voice full of the relief of a man just reprieved from certain death.

In the same calm, unemotional voice Aia upbraided him with the filthiest language that Raeder, listening in from their base, had ever heard. He raised his brows in surprise. This was most unlike his ladylike former squadron member. Courtesy forbade him to ask, but he couldn't help being taken aback by her vehemence.

"AI," she said, when she'd begun to repeat herself. "Following trajectory. Cut all compensators and dampers."

The pirate vessel began to corkscrew, and its pilot to retch heavily.

Maybe Barak knows, Raeder wondered and filed the thought away for later consideration. Having vomitus pitching around inside your helmet wasn't any fun at all, although if the suit was anything near spec it wouldn't be fatal.

The battle was going well for the Welters. Six pirate Speeds had been destroyed, one was blasted apart by a missile fired from the pirates' own converted freighter. Raeder had decided that they might all be drunk or drugged from the way they were fighting the vessel. After

all, their usual prey rarely fired back; this was supposed
to be a safe place to fence the loot; and pirates were
seldom models of discipline at the best of times.

Pellagrio and his crew of intent technicians stymied the
pirate's every attempt to call for help.

Oh, no you don't, Reader thought as the Commonwealth Speeds prevented the freighter from running for
the jump point. He knew the pirate's captain was
capable of jumping and leaving all their Speeds behind
to fend for themselves and had taken it into consideration in his planning.

*That freighter's going to be your prison. No pirates sharing
the hutch with my people.* While he could leave them in
their Speeds almost indefinitely he really didn't like the
idea. *It'd be just my luck that one of those spleebs would be
able to break the lock we've put on their controls.* Not that
they could go very far, but they might just decide to go
out in a blaze of glory. *With us providing the biggest part
of the blaze.* In any case, it was too much of a loose end
for this mission to afford.

"Surrender," Raeder demanded as more and more of
his Speeds were freed to skip agilely around the belea-
guered freighter. "Give up now and maybe we'll let you
live."

"Yah, right," the pirate sneered. "Like Welters shoot
their prisoners."

"You're not prisoners," Raeder pointed out. "Until you
surrender, even Welters could kill you."

"Whaddya mean, *even Welters?*"

"Who says we're Welters?"

There was a long pause after Raeder's laconic question.
The commander had no doubt but that their captain was
checking for any sign of Star Command on the Speeds
besieging him.

They wouldn't find anything.

How's it feel? Raeder thought maliciously. *Not much fun
wondering who's gonna board you and what they're going to
do to your precious behind, is it, squeege?* He really couldn't
tell if they'd give up without more of a fight. There was
always the possibility that they were just drunk or

drugged enough to be dangerous, even if it was only by accident.

The last of the pirate Speeds was shut down by the squadron and the pilots flung themselves into the fast-moving net of Speeds surrounding the pirate ship.

"Surrender," Raeder said coldly. "Now."

The silence lasted for only a few seconds more.

"Yeah," the pirate captain said at last. "We surrender."

"My people are going to board you and pilot your ship. One shot from one of you at any time and I pull my people out and we blow you wide open. Do you understand?"

"Yeah, we understand." The pirate's voice was sullen but resigned.

"Good." Raeder paused for effect. "Now, open your bay doors so that we can pilot your Speeds back inside."

There was no acknowledgement, but the big doors slid open. One by one Raeder's people remote-piloted the pirates back into their berths.

"Now I want all of you to go to your galley and stay there," Peter commanded.

"There's too many of us," the pirate protested. "We can't all fit."

"So get real friendly," the commander sneered. "Your lice probably are already. Just go there and stay there."

What the pirates didn't know was that Pellagrio had gained access through their open com to every computer-controlled area of the pirate ship. Including the freighter's unused security system, which now indicated the position of every crewman by his body heat.

"On our way," the pirate said.

Pellagrio indicated a bulky figure on one of the screens on his console. "That's probably the captain, sir," he said.

Raeder nodded as he watched the pirate crew huddle together for a moment and then move off the bridge. Most went to a large area near the bridge and crowded in. But a few snuck off towards the bay where the Speeds were. He watched the Speed crews enter the lock in parties of four. When they'd cycled through the welcoming party awaiting them gestured, then backs were slapped and the pilots proceeded to the galley. Finally everyone was there but the six pirates waiting by the lock.

No doubt armed to the teeth, Peter thought. It was equally certain that they intended to take hostages. Raeder sighed. *And I guess we're supposed to walk into their open arms like we're just some bunch of zoinkers.*

"Close the hatch in that corridor," he said to Pellagrio. "Then patch me through their com."

The pirates crouched in the corridor, weapons cradled in their arms, their eyes keen. Even keener, now that they'd all swallowed the "come-downer" pills he'd ordered; those left a vicious headache, and it was payback time.

Captain Crusher knew that he was dealing with Welters despite the lack of identifying marks on their Speeds. *Yeah, they're freelancers, sure. Freelancers who just happen to have uniform high-performance Speeds and operate according to the Standard Manual of Tactics, two-Speed teams, the whole nine meters.* He giggled slightly, a residue of the Exctazine.

The cold fact was that these zoinkers were good fighters, but they were soft in spite of all their tough talk. If these were real pirates there'd be a lot more Speeds floating in pieces outside the ship . . . and the ship would be atoms and gas itself, unless there was something worth stealing aboard. *So, take a few prisoners, bruise 'em a bit and they'll be eating out of my hand.* He was more than a little curious as to why there happened to be a crowd of Welter Speeds waiting here for him.

A faint vibration in the deck beneath his feet told him that the Welter Speeds were landing. His lips peeled back in a predatory smile. This was gonna be fun.

The hatch at the other end of the corridor shut, and the waiting pirates froze.

"Who did that?" Crusher demanded over his com unit. "Everybody's supposed to be in the galley. This ain't no time to get funny, anybody runnin' around out there, get back where you belong."

There was a pause, then, "We *are* all in the galley, Cap'n." Another pause. "All excep' you guys."

"Then who shut the hatch down here?" Crusher asked.

"I guess that was me," Raeder said.

"Who said that?" the pirate snapped.

"You just surrendered to me less than forty minutes ago, spleeb! Who do you think it is, the tooth fairy? More important, what are you doing down there when I told you to go to the galley?"

Crusher laughed weakly. He licked his lips and looked nervously at his henchmen.

"Hey," he said ingratiatingly, "it's my ship. You know how it is, we just had to try. Y'know?"

Raeder waited for a minute, then he asked, "I've got an even more important question for you: what are you going to do when I order my people to blow that lock right out of there? Oh, and no, the space doors aren't closed. Just in case you were wondering."

"You wouldn't," Crusher said. His voice was contemptuous and defiant, but his eyes were uncertain.

"Is that a challenge?" the commander asked politely. "Shall I order it done so that you and your crew know for certain just how hard I can be? Just say the word, big guy, and we're there."

"You wouldn't," Crusher repeated.

"Oh? And why is that? Do we need you for something? Well, to be fair, you are the guy that helped us win this battle by blowing away some of your own people. So I guess we owe you something for that."

"That was an accident," the pirate snarled.

"Oh," Raeder said, sounding mildly surprised. "Well there goes that thought. Wisnewski, take out that lock with your laser."

"Aye, sir."

Almost instantly a spot of red appeared at the top of the lock; metal rumbled as it expanded locally with the heat.

As one man the pirates raced for the hatch at the end of the corridor. They smashed together in a cursing, clawing knot of desperate men. The hatch remained locked and there was a hiss of escaping atmosphere from the direction of the airlock where the red spot had progressed to a short, molten line.

"We surrender!" Crusher bellowed. "Let us out! We surrender!"

"Ah, but you already surrendered," the commander reminded him. "But you changed your mind."

"You can't do this!" the pirate insisted. "You can't!"

"I'll bet that's just what the original owners of this vessel said when you took it from them," Raeder said grimly.

There was a pause, then Crusher said in a shaking voice, "I bought this vessel, I have papers. Stop it!" he screamed as the laser cut a corner and the metal buckled, leaving a large gap. "We'll do what you want, we'll do whatever you want!"

"Cease firing, Wisniewski."

"Aye, sir."

The only sound was atmosphere rushing from the corridor. The pirates, wild-eyed, stared at the cooling line of molten metal, while their chests grew tight from the thinning atmosphere.

The hatch opened at their backs. One man fell through and the others stepped on him in their scramble to get out.

"Go to your galley and stay there," Raeder commanded.

"All *right*," Raeder said, looking around the bridge of the ex-merchanter.

It looked like a standard high-boost mixed freight-and-passenger model; from a provincial dockyard, not Earth or the inner systems. The sort of craft that knitted the Commonwealth together, and occasionally took a flyer outside settled space. The modifications were extensive, though; a central thronelike crash-couch surrounded with repeater consoles and screens, some of them very good and all nonstandard; and the Tac and Weapons bays jammed in among the usual Nav and Life-Support. He walked over and touched a screen. Decision-trees and power cascades sprang into light, and he raised a brow.

"Well, well, well, somebody made a lot of money that an honest shipyard shouldn't," he muttered. "You getting all this?"

The tech nodded. "Full specs and a complete download, sir. Intelligence ought to be able to trace a lot of it, even without any smoking guns."

"Speaking of which."

He keyed a relay, and got a view from the helmet of a member of the working party. The outer hull of the pirate vessel stretched away, smooth foamed-metal plating covered with ablative armor and studded with the marks of sensor arrays, launch rails and beam-weapon lenses.

"How's it going?"

"We'll have the lot physically disabled in about an hour, sir," the cheerful reply came.

"Good." He turned back to the tech. "I want everything not essential to life support physically disabled." He didn't entirely trust software lockouts; there was always the chance of some evil hacker genius . . . Mostly something for the holos, but you never knew. "Then let's weld the hatchway shut."

He ducked through it, looking at the assembly of personal weapons laid out by an impressed pair of Marines. *Not surprised, just impressed.* Peggy looked as if she was tempted to pick up a few of them.

"Found their armory, I see," he said.

"Hell, sir," she said. "This is just what we found on 'em and in the crew quarters." She wrinkled her nose. "Only clean stuff there—it was like a frat house gone bad."

There were vibration knives and thread-edge metal ones, knuckle-dusters and little rings that threw a pulse of ultracompressed air to make a punch hit like a mule's hoof. Handheld lasers, plasma guns, half a dozen varieties of slug-thrower . . . and what looked like a compact makeup case.

"Careful, sir!" the Marine said as he reached for it. "Half a dozen contact poisons!"

"Poisoned *lipstick*?"

"Well, what can I say . . . don't kiss any of them."

"Wasn't planning on it."

Raeder was still shaking his head when he came to the crew lounge. He picked a carton of entertainment chips off the scarred table, read the labels, and pulled his eyebrows back down with an effort of will, keying the com to connect him to the galley. Heads came up as his own image appeared on a wallscreen.

"We're going to leave you alone now for a month," Raeder told the pirates. "And when I say 'alone' I mean it. So if you've got any bright ideas about setting the place on fire and having us rush in to save you, forget it. Likewise, poisoning yourselves with any expectation of our rescuing you is a big mistake. And in the unlikely event that you could get out of the secured area, we've also drained off all your antihydrogen and taken critical parts out of your drive, and physically disabled all communications equipment. You have ample food, water and air. How you entertain each other is your problem. Try to be alive when we come back. If you aren't, I won't cry."

There was silence after Raeder finished his announcement, then Captain Crusher squeezed his way to the hatch of the galley, which had been shut and closely guarded for the last ten hours. It opened easily under his palm.

He made his way to his quarters on the run, as his crew flowed out of the galley behind him. There were cries of anger from all sides as the pirates discovered that their secret caches of arms had been discovered.

Raeder followed the pirate captain's movements via his helmet tap, grinning like a shark when the burly man made for the "secret" cache behind his bunk. Crusher's rage was quieter, he swore softly but continuously as he searched for the ship's papers and his own identity chits. Everything was gone.

"My ass is cooked!" he swore to himself, unaware of Raeder's monitoring presence.

"*Parboiled*," Raeder added to himself.

The Star Command shuttles had just finished hauling the pirate's destroyed Speeds into the asteroid field with the aid of the ore nets from the hutch when Pellagrio summoned the commander.

"Sir, we have an incoming craft."

"On my way." Raeder dropped the torture device he'd

been looking at onto a tray with the others and wiped his hand on his coverall. "Store these for evidence," he said to Hunding.

The pretty tech blinked with alarm and Paddy said, "I'll take care of it, sir. Hunding, you can see to that Speed over there that Lieutenant Givens was flying."

He winked at Raeder, who rolled his eyes.

He's in love, Peter thought. *I guess he wants everybody else to be in love too.* Not that he imagined for one minute that Givens would give a mere petty officer like Hunding the time of day. Otherwise he'd have put a stop to it in a flash. *I don't want anybody getting distracted.* His own thoughts stopped cold as an unseeing Lt. Commander Sarah James crossed in front of him. He didn't even realize he was smiling until she passed from his line of sight.

Like that, he thought ruefully. *I want everybody's mind on their job.*

"Sir, we have another pirate," Pellagrio said as Raeder came up behind him.

Looking into the screen over the tech's shoulder Raeder saw a sleek vessel, not unlike a scout ship. She styled herself *The Goddess,* the paint overlaying an area where a longer name had been scoured off the hull.

"Speed squadron," Raeder said over the com, "report to your craft immediately, we have another customer." He clicked to a private channel. "Paddy?"

"We've rearmed all but two, sir. Nobody took any significant damage so, while they aren't as polished as I'd like, we're ready."

"How long to prep those two?" Peter asked.

"Half an hour, or less, sir. We've already begun loading missiles."

"Good, Raeder out." He tapped another few keys. "Lt. Commander James," he said, for Sarah was leading the squadron. "Two of your Speeds are still being loaded. They will follow you in approximately half an hour."

"Aye, Commander, half an hour. Understood. James, out."

And be careful out there, Raeder thought at her. He imagined her plugging in, testing systems, Commander Peter Ernst Raeder a million miles away from her thoughts.

With a brief sigh he turned his mind back to the pirate, watching her glide slowly in-system.

"She's cautious," the commander commented.

"Aye, sir," Pellagrio agreed. "She's using her sensors."

Peter winced. There was a lot of garbage out there for sensors to pick up. The lingering traces of explosions, of armor and metal-foam stripped to ions by beam hits . . . Anyone who'd ever been in combat would read those signals like print.

"You've blocked their communications?" he said.

"Aye, sir," Pellagrio said, giving him a glance. Body language that all but said, *No, sir, I'm sitting here waiting for you to tell me how to do my job.*

Raeder nodded, watching the monitor. *I hope she doesn't run,* he thought. *It could ruin everything if this one gets away.*

"What have we got on *The Goddess*?" he asked Pellagrio.

The tech brought up a sidebar with the pirate's vital statistics. No more than four Speeds, crew of fourteen, all women. Armament . . . Raeder pursed his lips; antiship lasers, defense lasers, particle beam weapons, and she'd apparently been fitted out with a clumsy-looking but effective missile array. *The Goddess* was ugly but loaded for bear. She had a reputation, too, of being light on her feet and a hard, smart fighter, willing to take risks for a good haul.

I guess this means that we can't expect them to shoot their own Speeds for us, Peter thought with a sigh.

Intelligence stated that Arianna Wesley, captain of *The Goddess*, preferred an all-female crew because "they keep discipline better." She'd also been heard to say that she had no intention of remaining a pirate any longer than necessary. Wesley thought she'd stick out the war, while Star Command was safely occupied by the Mollies, but when it was over, she was gone.

No wonder she's cautious, Raeder thought. She was also going to be a whole order of magnitude more dangerous than Crusher. He glanced at the monitor showing his squadron approaching the pirate and breathed a sigh of relief.

Cautious as she was, Wesley was too far from the jump point to avoid a rendezvous with Sarah.

Lieutenant Commander Sarah James sternly told herself to keep her mind on business. *Let's not understimate the enemy,* she thought. *Even pirate scumbuckets.*

A glance at her ready screen told her that the squadron was fanned out in an extended star formation, coasting on ballistic trajectories towards their intercept. A command, and the AI brought up the cones that represented possible courses available to both parties. They were gently coming together, their merging at the edges representing the area where *The Goddess* would have to run the gauntlet of her Speeds.

"Uh-oh."

The pirate was coming live; power plant raising its output to combat levels, ready to drive screens and launch rails. *Uh-oh again.*

"Launching. Say again, enemy is launching Speeds. Live boost, everyone. Follow me."

The screen flared as her Speeds' drives came live, kicking them ahead at multiple Gs. *Not too much,* she reminded herself—if the combined velocities were too high, a target stood a better chance of surviving the brief passing engagement.

"Woah!" someone said. Sarah blinked agreement; *The Goddess* had flipped end-for-end and was vanishing in a fog of energetic particles from her own drives. *Somebody's awake, there.* They were going to try and kill their velocity and then boost for the jump point right away, no questions asked.

"*Woah!*"

This time a targeting sensor was bathing one of her Speeds. The little craft's vector-line curved away from the squadron's, just as something broke free from the pirate craft and accelerated towards it; missile, from the profile. But the enemy Speeds weren't far behind. She calculated their boost, and her eyebrows went up. *Just like Peter's*, a moment's thought reminded her. These weren't intership shuttles making do as gunboats; they could *move*.

"Let's see how maneuverable they are," she said grimly. "All right, Section One goes for their Speeds. Two, stop that ship. I don't want it to reach the jump point."

"Cripple?"

"If you can. Kill it if you can't, and don't hesitate."

Crusher had been a police action. Now they were going to have to *fight*.

It had been an uncomfortable few hours working on the pirate ship for the tech crew. Even wounded and severely beaten *The Goddess*'s crew had radiated menace.

Raeder and Paddy were making a last-minute inspection as the crew finished off the last of their work.

Suddenly Crusher's bellowing voice came through the com: "What the hell are ya doin' to my ship ya bastards? You said ya was gonna leave us alone!"

Arianna Wesley looked up sharply. "You're putting us in here with *Crusher*? That hophead maniac?" A bitter twist to the thin lips. "I protest!"

"You're next to him, not in with him."

"I still protest. I was at a captain's conference with him once; there was something that needed a couple of ships, and *nothing* got done until he passed out. We'll have to listen to him: that's cruel and unusual punishment in itself!"

"Wesley! You ball-bustin' bitch!"

Raeder considered not answering, then considered the nuisance of having the pirate captain screaming through the com every time they brought new prisoners aboard. He cut the second pirate captain off with a wave and spoke himself:

"This isn't *your* ship anymore, squeege; actually it never *was* your ship. But right now, it's *my* ship and I can do what I want with it. Like, I might decide that you don't really need air up there. So it might be a good idea not to call attention to yourself, you know?" The commander paused for a moment to allow the pirate's mind to catch up to his ears. "You keep your nose out of my business, Crusher, I'll keep my nose out of yours."

He turned away from the com to find Paddy looking at him with concern in his eyes.

"Commander," the big New Hibernian said quietly, "I have to tell ye, I'm not easy in me mind about puttin' those wimmin in here side by side with that bunch up there."

Raeder snorted with laughter.

"Chief, considering how much better those *wimmin* can fight, I'm not sure we're doing the right thing leaving Crusher's men alone with *them*." He slapped Paddy on the back. "Don't worry. Your people are sealing them off tight as a drum, tighter I should hope. The only thing they'll be able to do is call each other names over the com."

Paddy looked up and Raeder followed his gaze to the grille on the bulkhead.

"What about the air ducts?" the Chief whispered. "There's a connection there, right enough."

"Pad-dy, this isn't a bad holo where the ducts are always big enough to crawl through and nobody remembers it. These are *real* ducts. They're twelve inches wide by six inches high. Nothing human could get through there. Ill will and ruthlessness will take you a long way, but it won't get you down to that size. The best they could do would be to sic killer rats on each other. Relax, it will be all right."

"Still," Paddy said, rusty eyebrows knotted together, "I don't like it."

CHAPTER FOURTEEN

Invincible drifted like a rock at a distance from the unnamed star that left it merely one bright point among many, her systems damped to the minimum necessary for life support, not even the tiny stabilizing rockets that adjusted her progress active. She was as silent and deadly as a crocodile in a calm pool; waiting for prey, her bridge a cavern lit only by the blue-tinged glow of her instruments.

Mai Ling Ju, the XO, suppressed a sigh of boredom. They'd been here for ten days, after all, and *nothing* had entered their trap. Twenty-four days into this operation and they hadn't seen action since day one. She glanced over at the captain and found him glaring at a screen, looking as alert as if they'd just begun their waiting. She frowned. Intel said that this was a very busy jump point. So where was the traffic, already?

Tactical Officer Truon Le was feeling much the same as the XO. But he had begun to wonder if there was some decisive action taking place in Commonwealth space while they sat on the *Invincible* with their thumbs up their butts. Of course it was impossible to find out because they were too far from Welter space and, well, they were stealthed. He allowed himself a sigh, and when he looked up he caught the XO's glance, raised eyebrow and all. *Oops,* he thought.

Knott combed through yet another report with his jaw clenched so hard that the muscles rippled. He was going to have to stop that. It couldn't be good for his teeth. But where *were* they? *Light carriers, long-range raiders, Hussars of Space, the daring cutting edge of the Commonwealth's might. Bah.*

Surely their little raid in the Chaos System couldn't have frightened the whole Mollie navy back to their homeworld. He could see them being more cautious, traveling in larger convoys and so forth. But not traveling at all hadn't been in the equation.

The other four jump points they'd inspected had also come up empty; showing no recent activity at all. This one had seemed their best bet given the enthusiastic description from intelligence. That and the fact that it was clearly a waste of precious fuel to just keep jumping around.

He typed in a question and electronically returned the report to Augie Skinner, the chief engineer. Augie loathed writing these things and often took shortcuts; such as assuming that everyone else thought like an engineer. It made his writing both opaque and sketchy. Usually Knott got the gist and was satisfied with that. But right now the captain was as bored as everyone else, though he couldn't show it, so he was forcing himself to be more thorough.

Besides, he thought, *it's a good idea to pull in the reins every now and again.* The captain glanced around, noted that his people were quietly busy. *Boy, I wish something would happen.*

"Sir," a petty officer on the sensor array watch said calmly. "There's some activity at the jump point. Sensor's indicate that something is coming in."

"On my screen," Knott said.

Ju moved to peer over his shoulder. The split screen showed the dark, quiescent jump point and beneath it a computer-enhanced view that showed a power surge such as an incoming ship would cause.

Ju frowned at the numbers.

"That's either a very large ship, sir, or multiple . . ." She blinked rapidly as her eyes and brain had a disagreement about what she was seeing. A Mollie battlecruiser, a cruiser and four destroyers slipped into real-space, the nimbus of their passage giving way to the massive neutrino signatures of active drives.

"Ships," she finished numbly.

Knott rubbed his index finger over his upper lip.

"Too big a bite for the *Invincible* to take on by herself," he said. "Yellow alert, but maintain stealth."

The Mollie convoy formed up and the battlecruiser sent out a powerful Identify Friend/Foe beacon; standard procedure when a ship entered a new system from hyperspace.

Certainly *Invincible* had given them no reason for alarm. She had gone so long without firing her engines that there were no recent signatures to pick up. And in an innovation peculiar to the *Invincible* the signal should indicate that the Commonwealth ship had the configuration and substance of a large rock.

The captain and his crew calmly observed the Mollies, pleased to know that this jump point was still active and happy to wait for a better opportunity.

The IFF beam struck them and Hartkopf, the communications officer, actually changed expression in shock.

"Sir! The *Invincible* is transmitting in response to the Mollie IFF!"

The entire small fleet of Mollies turned towards the Commonwealth ship in response to a beacon that confirmed them enemies.

"Battle stations," Knott snapped. *Be careful what you wish for.* "And find that beacon and silence it, dammit!" *You might get it,* he thought ruefully. The *Invincible* had nearly been destroyed by a deep-cover Mollie agent on her last cruise. Evidently, somehow, not *everything* the spy had planted had been found, despite a refit that tore the ship down to her hull plates.

Klaxons sounded and feet pounded the deck as all personnel raced to their stations. The bridge remained an island of calm, the blue-lit dimness brightening slightly as more crewfolk slid into their couches and fastened their restraints.

"Start the engines, Mr. Skinner," the captain said. "Get us out of here as fast as she can go. Following vector."

"Aye, sir," the chief engineer said.

Immediately there was a return of the near-subliminal hum that told them the *Invincible* was live once more. One of the many advantages of antihydrogen as a fuel was the way it could bring an engine from standby to full service in the blink of an eye. She was off like a gazelle pursued by greyhounds.

Knott listened to the treasonous beacon blaring forth all of the *Invincible*'s secrets; her defensive capabilities, her weapons, the number of Speeds she carried. He stared at the screen showing the Mollies trailing behind them, his eyes blazing with cold fury. The captain knew sincere regret that John Larkin was well and truly dead and far beyond the things that Knott wanted to do to him.

"Hartkopf," he snapped, "haven't you located that beacon yet?"

"Sir, there's one on every level, set so that the signals overlap in such a way that I can't pinpoint any of them. The only thing I'm certain of is that there isn't one on the bridge."

"Do you have any idea what one would look like?" Knott asked.

"I have an idea, sir. A couple of ideas, actually," the young communications officer answered.

"Inset rotating three-dimensional pictures of 'em into every screen in every department, on every deck, now. Then give me a general broadcast channel."

Almost instantly the captain's own screen showed the pictures he'd asked for; taking up about an eighth of the screen, overlaying the Mollie cruiser and one destroyer in the upper left corner. The dimensions of the two transmitters showed beneath them, each was roughly palm-sized.

"You have an open channel, sir," Hartkopf told him.

"This is the Captain speaking," Knott began. "On your screens you see two beacon devices, one or both of which are currently broadcasting classified information about the *Invincible* to the enemy. I'm informed that there's one on every deck, spaced so that the signals overlap. Therefore we can't tell you where you'll find one. Dedicate as many people as can be spared to the search. Those beacons must be found and destroyed. Knott, out."

Chief Petty Officer Jomo arap Moi and Second Lieutenant Cynthia Robbins stared at the images on the screen and then, with similar frowns, at one another.

"There *can't* be another traitor on board, can there?" arap Moi asked.

Robbins grimly shook her head, dark eyes troubled.

"No," she said, with certainty. "It was Larkin. No question."

She felt discouraged. Bad enough that they were being chased by an enemy battle group big enough to grind them to hamburger. But this felt like her nemesis was reaching out from the grave to complete what he'd started. Mentally she shook her head and sniffed in contempt at the sheer conceit of her feelings—as if the danger the ship faced mattered only to *her*. Typical of her home world, though, none of this showed in her face or manner.

"It's going to be hard finding something that size hidden . . ." The CPO gestured helplessly, indicating the enormous area around them. "Especially since the guy who hid it had a license to go anywhere on the ship."

Cynthia shook her head.

"Not so difficult. Maybe Hartkopf can't trace them from the bridge, but a hand-held unit, tuned to the frequency the beacon is broadcasting should locate them. It's what Peter, uh, the commander would do," she said. "If you can't locate the problem, find a way to make it sit up and bark."

The Chief wrinkled his brow.

"Yeah that sounds like Raeder's philosophy all right.

But, what hand-held unit?" arap Moi asked. "We don't have anything like that."

"We will in a few minutes," she said, heading for a workbench. "I've got an idea."

"They're trying to get a bead on us, sir," Truon Le told the captain.

"As we are on them, I should hope," Knott snarled.

"We're mutually out of range, sir," the tactical officer said.

The captain snorted in reply. Then said, "For the time being, let's keep it that way."

He rested his chin on his fist and stared hard at the ships hurtling towards them. Too many to fight; even with the Speeds the odds were not in the *Invincible's* favor. There was no way to fire on them without bringing themselves into firing range. There was nowhere to shake them, and even if there had been the beacon would have made hiding impossible.

He got online with engineering.

"Skinner, what's the status of our fuel?"

"We're burning it up fast, Captain. No help for it at this speed."

"Knott out," he said.

The Captain compressed his lips. He wanted to ask if anyone had made any progress finding those damn beacons but restrained himself. If they'd found any the crew would have told him. No sense in interrupting the search to be told what he already knew. And he hated every erg of fuel wasted in what was surely a futile flight through clear space away from the escape offered by the jump point.

"Sir!" the sensor technician almost shouted. "I don't know *how* they're doing it, sir, but that cruiser is moving forward. She's pulling ahead of the pack and into range!"

"Tactical Officer?" Knott said calmly.

"I have her targeted, sir."

"Fire at will," the captain told him. "We have a small advantage here in that you can't easily escape what you're running towards."

What's more the Mollie would be outrunning his own countermeasures. Knott couldn't resist a smile at that. It would take some fantastic maneuvering to avoid a missile locked onto you at the speeds they were traveling. At this range he might well be wasting ordnance, but it should at least make them jump, and might slow them down.

The XO shook her head.

"They *must* be red-lining their engines," Ju said. Foolish, and terribly dangerous went without saying. "These people never cease to amaze me," she murmured.

"This doesn't make sense!" Robbins said.

She turned in a circle, holding the cobbled-together instrument at arm's length, reading the tiny screen. Cynthia drew it back, frowning, and tapped a few keys, then held it out again.

"There's nothing down here actively broadcasting," she said. "According to this, all we're getting down here is some kind of echo effect."

"Are you sure that thing's working?" arap Moi asked, looking over her shoulder at the readings.

"Yes, I'm sure!" She glared at him for a second, then looked abashed. "Sorry."

He waved it away.

"So you're sure there's nothing active on this level?" he asked her.

The lieutenant drew in the instrument once again, tapped, held it out and swept the area around them.

She shook her head.

"No, definitely not." She tapped again, held it out. "Passive reflectors only."

They looked at each other.

"Let's try another level," arap Moi suggested.

"Sir, the cruiser has fired."

Knott watched as his screen showed a cloud of sensor-deceiving chaff exploding in *Invincible*'s wake. The missile would choose among the phony targets presented and expend itself uselessly. There was an expanding globe of energy and plasma, and he nodded in satisfaction. Then sat up stiffly; almost through the fire came the cruiser, much closer than he'd have believed possible, and she fired a volley of ship killer missiles at, in astronomical terms, point-blank range.

"Evasive maneuvers!" Knott commanded.

"Evasive maneuvers, aye," the helmsman responded.

Truon Le released another cloud of chaff, and two missiles peeled off after phantom targets. One came on like inexorable death.

Truon Le tapped the console that controlled the weapons locked on the oncoming cruiser; four missiles should have streaked outward carrying fire and death to the enemy. Instead they armed themselves but stayed in their berths. Cold flashed through his belly, and he supressed a grunt like that a man punched under the breastbone would make.

"Sir," the young tactical officer said in a voice amazingly calm. "Our missiles are armed, but they have not fired."

Knott turned to look at him.

"They are armed and in their tubes?" the captain asked. Knott carefully kept the horrified disbelief from his voice. If they were hit even a glancing blow those missiles would tear *Invincible* apart.

"Aye, sir. I've dispatched technicians to the site."

"Very good, Mr. Le. Keep me posted." His eyes went to the Mollie speeding towards them and his hand closed into a white-knuckled fist.

Regina Bach, Junior Petty Officer third class, aimed her diagnostic instrument at the malfunctioning missile tube. She blinked as the words, "*To play solitaire . . .*" scrolled across the small screen. With a shake of her head she disconnected from the tube and moved on to the next, then the next. Regina tried all four, then moved down the line until she'd tested all twelve missile tubes in this section.

"Sir," she said from the call station.

Truon Le answered her, just a light film of sweat on the wide brow indicating his tension.

"Yes, Bach," he said tersely.

"Sir, the missile tube computers have somehow become cross-indexed with the games files. There appears to be no remaining trace of the original programming. All twelve of the tubes in section three C are offering me the instructions for playing solitaire."

"Stand by," Truon Le instructed.

His hands flashed over the board as he ordered the missiles to disarm themselves. He paused. The missiles still showed red on his screen. Still armed and without even an acknowledgement of having received his instructions.

"Sir," Le said aloud.

The captain turned to look at him.

"Sir, I'm going to need an executive override on these." He tapped a few keys and connected his station to the captain's.

Knott spoke the override code quietly and the computer acknowledged that he was indeed the captain and did indeed have the authority to override the missile's programming. The missiles ignored him.

Truon Le turned back to his com.

"Bach, can you open the tubes and manually disarm the missiles?"

"Negative, Sir. The missile tubes can't be opened when they contain a live missile. It's a fail safe. Conversely, if the tube is opened it should prevent . . ." She watched the lights change on the missile tube beside her, showing an armed missile within. "Open the tubes!" she shouted and crewmen leaped to obey, only managing to open three. "Sir," Bach said, her voice shrill, "opening the tubes will prevent the warheads from arming!"

Le opened the com. "Attention all missile bays. Open all missile tubes and retract warheads. Repeat, open all missile tubes and retract warheads." Even as he spoke he watched light after light come on as the missiles armed themselves.

Almost absently he noted the cruiser attempting to lock on to them again, and he flung another cloud of ECM in their faces. His brain was frozen, replaying Givens'

Speed shooting Drongo over and over. *Think!* he mentally roared at himself. *What are you, simple? Think!*

Simple? That was it, the key. The missiles brains were simple. Clearly they'd been programmed to ignore a direct command to disarm, but—if the command was broken down into steps. . . .

Truon Le tapped in a command to one missile to power down its drive and a request to confirm that action had been completed.

"Yes!" he hissed as the acknowledgement came. In all he gave four commands, at the completion of the final order the light switched from red to yellow.

"Bach, open missile tube four," he said over the com. Then he sent the list of commands to all the remaining armed missiles. One by one the lights went to amber, then dark as the tubes were opened by their anxious crews.

An awful thought occurred to him as he watched the Mollie cruiser closing.

"Attention laser crews," he said. "Check your weapons for tampering. They may not fire properly."

His heart sank as the laser crews called back to confirm his suspicions. All the laser cannon were offering to play solitaire.

He checked his screen. The Mollie fired again. He flung out more chaff, checked a gauge. *We can't keep that up forever,* he thought. The Mollie was too close, anyway. One of their missiles was sure to get through with the close-in defense system down.

Truon Le turned toward the captain. "Sir," he started to say.

Within five hundred kilometers of its prey the Mollie burst apart from her engines forward; her overstrained containment fields had burned away their shielding, the antihydrogen met its opposite and a sunbright fireball blossomed in their wake.

"That's why you're not supposed to red-line the A-H power system," Knott murmured.

But an enemy missile came on.

"Brace for impact," Knott said, and the call went out to every deck.

The *Invincible* dared not fire antimissile missiles and lay helpless before the assault.

"Impact will be in the aft sector," Truon Le announced.

"Could you be more specific, Mr. Le?" the captain asked.

"No, sir. Not quite yet."

"Keep me posted," Knott growled.

The bridge crew strapped themselves in.

"Impact in twenty seconds," the tactical officer announced.

Cynthia and the Chief jumped back into the elevator. Level four was clear.

The lieutenant tapped her nose uncertainly and said, "Bridge."

As the elevator rose, bypassing floors, arap Moi looked at her askance. "They're not going to let us just waltz onto the bridge, Lieutenant. Not while they're fighting a battle."

Robbins shook her head.

"It was Larkin who planted these devices, Chief." She glanced at him, then looked back to the numbers indicating their level. "If you were Larkin, where would you plant something like this?"

One corner of his mouth came up and he shrugged.

"On the bridge. I guess you're right. Knowing the contempt he had for us."

"We don't even need to leave the elevator," Cynthia said. "If it's there it will register from in here."

Then a klaxon sounded and a light began flashing while a voice intoned, "Brace for impact. Brace for impact."

"Level seven!" Robbins called out and the elevator ground to a halt at the next stop. "Doors open, emergency override," she snapped.

They slid apart with agonizing slowness and Robbins and the Chief pushed through before they were quite open. Cynthia turned to the emergency shaft beside the elevator and began to open the door.

"No!" arap Moi insisted. "Brace for impact means just

that, Lieutenant. If the ship is hit while we're climbing to another level we'll break our necks."

She looked him in the eye, seeing that he meant what he said.

"You're absolutely right, Chief."

He nodded, "I know it."

Cynthia yanked open the door and started to climb. Arap Moi swore softly and followed her.

"Where do you estimate impact?" the captain asked again.

"The aft port drive base," Truon Le answered.

"Get those people out of there," Knott ordered.

It was the least that could be done if impact was inevitable. There was no good place to be hit, but at the engines was one of the worst. If containment was lost . . .

The image of the Mollie cruiser going up was like a raw wound in every mind.

It was just so hard to maneuver in space, and even a *light* carrier had an unwieldy mass. The missile itself definitely held the advantage here.

Nothing had stopped the ship killer missile, nothing had deflected it. The Mollies on the other ships must be beside themselves with joy.

Truon Le let out an audible, "Ohhh," of relief as he saw the last light go amber and then dark. At least their own armament wouldn't be helping the enemy to destroy them.

The helmsman suddenly fired all the topside maneuvering thrusters at once and the *Invincible* bobbled for a moment; the missile struck at an oblique angle and shattered. The impact pushed the ship into an uncontrolled spin. Everything not nailed down suddenly became a missile in its own right, and personnel who weren't belted down found themselves airborne. In seconds there were enough severe injuries to keep sick bay busy for a week.

"A dud!" Truon Le shouted. "I love Mollie technology," he said more quietly, his voice shaking.

"Helmsman," the captain roared. "Get us out of this, now!"

Knott was all too conscious of how much ground they were losing with every uncontrolled revolution. And *Invincible* could only take so much of this kind of punishment. His traitorous imagination supplied him with an image of the ship breaking in half, men and women tumbling helplessly out among the stars.

Augie Skinner was on the com. "The aft port engine has gone into automatic shutdown," he said. "She doesn't look to have taken damage though. We'll have her online again in about four minutes and then we should get more forward momentum, sir."

"Carry on," the captain said. "Get me that engine, Skinner. Make it in two."

"Yes, sir. Skinner, out."

"Hang on, Lieutenant!" the Chief shouted.

God knew it was all he could do to keep his grip. At the first impact his feet had flown out from under him and he'd dangled high above the deck while centrifugal force threatened to pry his hands off the rungs.

"Take your own advice, Chief," Cynthia shouted back.

She'd slid one slender leg over a rung and hooked her foot to the one below. Still she found it hard to hold on one-handed. She had a deathgrip on her cobbled-together unit with the other. How long could this go on?

"We've got to get out of here," she said.

"I can barely hold on!" arap Moi shouted. "I can't climb! And don't you try it either! Sir," he finished lamely. Sometimes it was damned hard to remember that someone half your age and a head shorter was your commanding officer.

"The point is," Robbins said, hooking her encumbered arm around the ladder and reaching for the next, "I'm getting too tired to hold on much longer. We're only about fifteen rungs from the top." She paused, panting, to get her breath. "We can make it."

"Sure we can," arap Moi said. *Just like I can fly.*

He tried to look past the lieutenant. It sure looked like a lot more than fifteen rungs to him. Then he reached for the next rung; his head was beginning to spin like the ship.

✧   ✧   ✧

Skinner's voice announced, "We have the engines back online, sir."

"Very good, Mr. Skinner," Knott replied calmly. Despite the crash harness, his knuckles were white from holding on to the armrests of his chair.

"Dinna fire the main engines until I have her spinnin' under control, sir," the helmsman cried. "She canna take the strain!"

The captain glanced over at the lieutenant as his hands raced over the helm controls in a virtuoso dance. The computer which should handle the delicate firing sequence of the attitude adjustment rockets was unresponsive for some reason.

More of Larkin's work? Knott wondered. Were they going to have to strip this ship to her bulkheads to get rid of that man's interference? The captain heartily wished that all of his people had Lt. Robbins' sixth sense about defective parts. He watched the helmsman's performance with genuine admiration.

"Where are the Mollies, Mr. Le?" he asked. A glance at his screen made him close his eyes, since it doubled the spinning sensation.

"Ten megaklicks and closing, sir."

Knott gripped his chair's arms more tightly still. They were almost within range. His glance found the helmsman again, and he forced himself to remain silent. No order or suggestion of his could make the man work harder or faster. Mentally he cursed Larkin to the deepest of the Mollie hells.

Then, feeling almost sudden, the wild spinning slowed, stopped.

"What's our heading, Ms. Lurhman?"

Ashly Lurhman, the astrogator, gave him the numbers. Facing away from the Mollies.

Thank God for small favors, the captain thought.

"Mr. Skinner, fire the engines, give us all the speed she's got in her."

"Firing engines, aye, sir."

Knott saw with approval that the tactical officer had

jettisoned another cloud of chaff and decoys. Their pursuers hadn't fired as yet, but they would. This might help for a few moments anyway.

The emergency door opened beside the elevator and Second Lieutenant Cynthia Robbins literally fell onto the bridge. Chief Petty Officer Jomo arap Moi followed and helped her to her feet.

Knott had spun his command chair around to face her and his gray eyes were fierce as he demanded, "What the hell are you doing on my bridge, Lieutenant?"

Arap Moi swallowed hard, and he looked at Cynthia desperately, obviously willing her to have the right answer.

Robbins herself briefly ignored the captain as she tapped instructions into her unit and waved it around.

"It's here!" she exclaimed. "Sir," Cynthia said eagerly, looking up at last, "the beacon is broadcasting from the bridge."

"No way!" Hartkopf objected. "My instruments show . . ."

"It must be very well shielded," Robbins said distractedly, waving the instrument around. "But every other deck has only a passive reflector. Therefore, by the process of elimination, it has to be on the bridge."

Cynthia tapped in a few more commands, and the instrument began to triangulate on the location. She followed the signal and when she looked up, she was standing directly in front of the captain. She blinked. Then, somewhat diffidently, she tried to pinpoint the location of the device, hoping to find it in the captain's computer, or com link. To her intense regret both were cleared. Reluctantly she directed it towards the captain again.

Cynthia bit her lower lip, then looked at Knott decisively.

"I'm sorry, sir. But I believe it's in your chair."

Knott stood slowly and, without taking his eyes from her, stepped away. Robbins approached and ran the unit over the chair. She looked up.

"It's under the seat," she said. She reached into her pocket and failed to find the tool she needed.

Arap Moi stepped forward and handed her a screwdriver. Cynthia went to work and in moments pulled the seat off its stand, revealing a small, and decidedly incongruous, metal box. The captain reached in and picked it up, flung it to the floor and stamped on it, hard.

"The beacon has stopped sending," Hartkopf said.

"Well, that's one thing taken care of," Knott said. He picked up the seat of his chair. "Lieutenant," he said, holding it out to her, "if you wouldn't mind?"

Cynthia tore her gaze from the captain's screen, where the Mollies were shown to be much closer now, and looked down at the cushion.

"Oh!" she said. "Yes, sir, of course, sir." And taking it she proceeded to reattach it to its base.

"Two things accomplished," the captain said, taking his chair again. "Now if we had something we could throw at the Mollies to slow them down we'd be in business."

The Chief blinked.

"Ah," he said, uncertainly.

Knott looked at him.

"You have a thought, Chief," he encouraged.

"Sir, we have these mines," arap Moi said.

"Oh!" Robbins exclaimed, looking as stricken as though he'd suggested flinging a passel of orphans at the enemy.

"Mines?" the captain said, his voice rising in disbelief.

The Chief shrugged.

"It's the last thing they'd expect," he said a bit defensively.

Knott looked at him consideringly, then he began to grin.

"You're absolutely right," he said.

"I like it, sir," the XO said, laughter in her voice. "It's not unlike that movie."

"I know the one," Knott agreed, and chuckled. "All right, Chief. Get yourselves down there and prep and launch those mines."

"Yes, sir," Robbins and the Chief said.

"Now!" Knott snapped.

And the two of them scrambled for the elevator.

CHAPTER FIFTEEN

Captain Will-to-Be-Chaste Oppenheimer sat bolt upright in his captain's chair. His gaze was fixed on the Commonwealth ship with an unblinking malice; if the evil eye had actually worked, the screens would have shown only an expanding cloud of plasma.

In no way had he indicated his extreme displeasure when their missile had failed to detonate. To Oppenheimer it merely indicated that the Spirit of Destiny had rejected the sacrifice of the cruiser. Doubtless some of those on the doomed ship had offended the Spirit through some unconfessed and unrepented sin.

His own ship was pure. The captain's hand curled slowly into a fist. He had taken exquisite pains to assure himself of that. How did the Word of Wisdom go?

Punishment produces fear, fear produces obedience, obedience produces discipline, discipline produces virtue. Therefore, punishment produces virtue. He permitted himself a small smile to encourage his crew.

When the time came, and the filthy Welter turned like a rabid dog to fight the men of the *Destiny's Arrow*, his people would be found worthy.

Chaste bowed his head and prayed briefly that the Spirit would forgive his pride. As ever before battle he laid their lives on Destiny's altar. Then he watched in contempt as the fleeing ship spat out another cloud of chaff. Oppenheimer had no intention of firing until he *knew* he could make a kill. But he would pursue them to hell itself to make that shot.

Meanwhile, he recorded the information that some brave Mollie had provided them. Doubtless the Interpreters of the Perfect Way would find use for the information.

"This *doesn't* make sense," Lt. Robbins said, her voice rising. She blinked, hard, and began reading again.

"That's because you're reading the manual," arap Moi told her. He slapped a small door shut in the side of the mine he'd been working on and walked over to her.

"Well how am I supposed to know how to arm this thing if I don't?" Cynthia asked.

"Flip to the illustrations," he suggested.

She tapped in the instruction.

"Now what?" she asked, looking up.

He reached over and tapped a single key.

Instantly a disembodied pair of hands ran through the process of arming the mine.

"Oh!" Robbins said. "I've never noticed that before."

"Kinda neat, isn't it? You verbal types usually ignore this function. I like it because it saves time. Which we're wasting," the Chief said with heavy emphasis.

"Right," she agreed, licking sweat from her upper lip.

They and six volunteers loaded the bulky mines onto pallets and maneuvered them over to the great outer door. Six of the smooth heavy spheres sat in a row, waiting to be deployed—an unorthodox procedure, but nobody was going to let their only remaining functional weapon fall into the grasp of the malignantly reprogrammed launch systems. The mines themselves were by nature entirely passive and would have to be manually thrust from the ship, but the pallets they'd been attached to had a small amount of fuel and would be used to direct them into position. Cynthia checked to make sure that their suits all had safety lines attached to rings in the deck.

"Ready, Captain," the lieutenant announced.

"Deploy mines," Knott replied.

Cynthia raised the crash doors a quarter of the way and one after another they shoved the mines out, guiding the automated pallets that held them into position behind the ship, and then shut them down.

"Think this will work?" arap Moi asked her.

"I *really* hope so," she replied. "It would be almost like the holo."

The Chief rolled his eyes at the stars in hers.

"Well, for that and several thousand other reasons," he said, meaning the captain and crew of the good ship *Invincible*, "I hope it works too."

"It was your idea, Chief," she said.

The other volunteers grinned and nodded, giving him a hearty thumbs-up.

"Don't remind me," he said. He wondered what Raeder would say when he found that all of his rare and precious mines had been expended. *I think he might actually pout. But only because he missed the show.*

"Brother Captain," a technician said respectfully.

After a brief pause Chaste acknowledged him.

"Report," he said laconically.

"Brother Captain, the Commonwealth ship has expelled a far heavier than usual cloud of chaff. I'm concerned. They might be firing on us and we could not predict the path of their missiles, nor their number or targets."

"How much time would we lose by going around this obstruction?" Oppenheimer asked his astrogator.

"As much as an hour, Brother Captain, possibly more; the cloud is spreading out as we speak."

Oppenheimer frowned. The Welter might be preparing to make evasive maneuvers, waiting to see how *Destiny's Arrow* and the destroyers moved in order to put greater distance between them.

"We must not lose the ground that Destiny has gifted

to us," he said portentously. "They are desperate and this is a ruse meant to confuse us. We will proceed."

"Yes, Brother Captain," his crewmen said in unison.

Chaste was pleased by their deference, and then sternly reminded himself that it was not due to him, but to the Spirit *through* him.

"They haven't budged an inch, sir," Truon Le said excitedly. "They're barreling right up the middle."

"And the mines?" Knott asked.

"Right *in* the middle," the tactical officer said with a smile.

Don't count your battles before they're won, kid, the captain thought. But there was a certain amount of gleeful anticipation in his own heart.

"When will we know?" Robbins asked.

She and the Chief had crowded in behind the desk in Raeder's small office. He'd created a program to tie into the bridge's pickup and they were shamelessly making use of it.

"Any minute now," arap Moi said quietly.

It was hard to see through the chaff Truon Le had put out, but the flare of an explosion would stand out even from that fog.

"There!" Cynthia exclaimed, pointing.

"Brother Captain!" a tech shouted.

Oppenheimer turned to glare at him. Shouting was not permitted on his bridge, regardless of the circumstances.

"Report," he said through clenched teeth.

"The *Martyr* has just been destroyed." The crewman looked at his captain, his face pale.

The captain stared back at him, allowing just a trace of his anger to show. Somehow the news didn't completely surprise him; the *Martyr* was a notoriously unlucky ship.

"Why was I not informed that the Welter was firing on us?"

"Brother Captain, there is no sign that they *have* fired

on us. It could be the chaff confusing the sensors, but I honestly don't think so."

"Could they have been attempting the same sacrifice that our brethren made?" his XO suggested.

Chaste looked at the XO with dislike. This ambitious underling frequently neglected to refer to him as Brother Captain. He turned away.

"Is there any way to determine that?" Oppenheimer asked the technician.

"Not with any certainty in this electronic fog, Brother Captain. Under these circumstances it's only possible to determine that the enemy has fired when the ordnance itself locks onto us as a target."

"Return to your station," the captain told him with a thoughtful look.

The crewman, more pale than before, sat down at his screen.

Almost immediately he announced, "Brother Captain, the *Light of Ecclesia* has been destroyed."

"They're throwing something out with that chaff!" the captain said. "Astrogator, plot us out of this, now! Contact our remaining escorts, they are ordered to remove themselves from this course immediately. They are to proceed with dispatch, but extreme caution."

"What do you suppose they're using?" the XO mused. "Brother Captain," he said at Oppenheimer's glare.

"Just get me a straight shot at them and it won't matter," Chaste snapped.

"The Mollies are moving away from the minefield," a technician announced.

The captain nodded in satisfaction. That should buy the *Invincible* some room to maneuver. Two destroyers and a battlecruiser were much better odds as well. *Or will be when we get our weaponry online.*

"Another mine has been struck, sir," a technician said. "There's too much interference to determine which one of them it is."

Then, one after another, the two destroyers leapt into clear space.

"Sir!" Truon Le said, disbelief in his voice. "They're firing. I show fifteen seeker missiles coming from one of the destroyers."

Why? Knott wondered. At this distance it seemed a waste of ordnance. Then again, only one had to actually hit to kill the *Invincible*, or slow them down fatally. Even the unexploded missile that had struck them had closed the gap between them.

Perhaps it was impulse; anger over the loss of his fellows? Mollies were inclined to such gestures. It was one of the things that made them so dangerous; you literally could not predict what they would do next.

"Have we got anything we can throw at them, Mr. Le?"

"Checking, sir." The tactical officer connected with Bach. "What have you got for me, Petty Officer?"

"Sir, the missiles themselves appear to be fine. It's all new ordnance, delivered after Mr. Larkin's time. It's the missile launch tubes that are compromised."

He looked up at Ju, the XO, who stood at his shoulder. She chewed on her lower lip thoughtfully, then leaned forward. "Stand by," she told Bach. Ju tapped into the general com on Main Deck. "Lt. Robbins, please contact the tactical officer's station immediately."

"Yes, Mr. Le," said a surprised Robbins, who blinked at seeing both of their faces on her screen.

"How did you deploy those mines?" Ju asked.

"We put them on pallets and guided them out behind the ship."

"Have you got any of those pallets left?" the XO asked sharply.

"Dozens," the lieutenant said with a shrug.

Ju grinned for the first time in what seemed like an eternity. Le, with an answering smile, patched Robbins and Bach into one link.

"We can't use the launch tubes," Ju told the lieutenant. "But if we load them onto your pallets and get the missiles outside the ship they can be fired at the enemy."

"They'll have low velocity."

"That's better than *no* velocity! I leave it to you two

to work out the details, but it needs to have been done five minutes ago."

"Yes, sir," they said in unison.

The two women started talking, agreeing to access ordnance from the missile storage areas adjacent to Main Deck.

While they worked it out Ju turned to the captain and reported.

Truon Le sent out another cloud of chaff. They were now critically low on ECM.

Knott watched most of the missiles destruct in the diminishing field of chaff. One alone continued towards the *Invincible*.

Not again, the captain thought.

"Brother Captain!" the technician shouted in surprise.

Captain Oppenheimer glared at the man, his eyes becoming somewhat maniacal. *I do not permit shouting on my bridge!* he thought furiously.

Bad enough that they had blundered into a *mine* of all things, taking out a whole battery of maneuvering rockets, not to mention six laser emplacements. He would not, absolutely *would not,* countenance a breakdown in discipline.

Chaste turned slowly towards his XO.

"Put that man on report," he said with deliberate calm.

Oppenheimer snapped his gaze to the technician, who sat frozen at his station, then back to the XO, surprising a look of pity on the Executive Officer's face.

"Do you have something you'd like to say?" the captain asked with a curl to his lip.

"Only that I wonder what caused the technician to exclaim like that." The XO's face was once again impassive. "Brother Captain."

How Oppenheimer *hated* that infinitesimal hesitation.

"Well!" he snapped, breaking his own rule against shouting. "What is it?"

"The enemy has been hit, Brother Captain. One of the missiles from *Sin's Enemy* has crippled them; it appears that at least one engine has been disabled."

The captain schooled himself to stillness. This was pleasing news, but no less than he'd expected. Destiny was, after all, on their side.

The trouble was that they themselves were crippled. He frowned. That shouldn't matter. But it worried him; he disliked going into combat with any disadvantage.

As soon as he thought it, Chaste mentally flagellated himself for his lack of faith, and he resolved to throw himself into Destiny's arms and combat with the infidels immediately.

"What do you advise?" he asked his XO.

"Pursue them and destroy them," the man answered. "Brother Captain."

Oppenheimer nodded. "Yes," he agreed.

"The best I can say, sir, is that we've maintained containment," Augie Skinner reported, his face grim behind his face shield. "Two main engines are out. We might be able to get one of them online in an hour, the other will need station facilities. The entire aft engineering crew is dead, over sixty seriously injured in adjacent compartments."

Knott took it in without a change of expression, but inside he was shocked. He'd known it was a significant hit, but ... *The entire aft engineering crew. That's a hundred and seventy people!* Sixty seriously injured and probably a hundred with wounds that wouldn't completely incapacitate them. *Two of the main engines down isn't exactly good news either,* he reminded himself. He had to think of the ship first and last, or *everyone* was going to die.

It seriously compromised their ability to maneuver, to say the least. Putting it well within the capacity of those two destroyers to catch up to them. And though one of them had spent all of its missiles he wouldn't put it past them to ram the bigger ship. It was the sort of thing Mollies did.

"Sir," a technician said calmly, "the Mollie battlecruiser is coming into view. She shows damage."

"How bad?" the captain asked.

"Portside, forward," Truon Le said. "I'd say she's lost

several laser emplacements, and probably a great deal of her maneuvering ability. The destroyers are coming into range," he added.

"Fire when ready, Mr. Le."

"Aye, sir."

And let that be soon, Knott prayed.

"The destroyer has fired," the tactical officer said.

"Captain!" Knott glanced at his screen and saw Ronnie Sutton, the squadron leader, gazing back at him from a corner of it.

"Squadron Leader," the captain said in acknowledgement.

"Sir, my people and I are ready to fly at your command."

Suppressing a smile, Knott nodded.

"I'll keep you posted," he said.

Sutton nodded and his image flicked out. He'd obviously been in his Speed, ready and waiting. Knott understood that, but he was reluctant to commit his Speeds in a running battle like this. He genuinely dreaded the thought of losing someone out there in the dark. If the relative velocities were wrong, you *couldn't* make pickup.

Still, if the XO's idea fails, they may be our only hope.

"Captain?" The image of Ashly Lurhman, the astrogator, appeared on his screen.

"Ms. Lurhman," Knott said.

"Sir, I'd like to propose a plan."

"Go ahead."

Lurhman was a fidgeter, but when she was presented with a meaty problem all that nervous energy was channeled into solving it. Just now she was as still as a hunter on point. The captain knew that she had something worthwhile to offer him.

"Sir, I've been turning us towards the jump point for awhile now. The Mollies don't seem to have noticed. And in about a minute there won't be a thing they can do about it even if they do."

"Good," the captain said. "But they can follow us for one jump Ms. Lurhman, and with one engine down and one severely damaged and offline we won't be making another right away."

"Ordinarily not, sir," the young astrogator said. "But in this case we want them to follow us." Her usually gentle gray eyes held a surprisingly evil gleam. "The system I have in mind was only just listed by one of the last exploration vehicles a few months after the war started. It's extremely dangerous because there's a neutron star just adjacent the jump point. It was only by some very fine piloting that the exploration team escaped to tell about it."

Knott narrowed his eyes in thought.

"Considering the damage we've sustained, Ms. Lurhman, could even the best piloting you've got in you get us out in time?"

"Sir, we'll be expecting it. According to my calculations we should be able to slingshot around the star and use that momentum to jump us out of there. With the damage that battlecruiser has sustained, and not knowing what's waiting for them, there's no way the Mollies could escape to pursue us."

"And the risks?" Knott asked.

"As I see it there are two, sir. The gravitational pull of the neutron star could be stronger than reported, which is highly unlikely, or our engines might deteriorate further."

In either case, we'd be reduced to a film on the neutron star's surface—one so thin even our atoms would be crushed.

"Sir," Truon Le interrupted, his voice a bit shaky. "The antimissile missiles that Lt. Robbins deployed have succeeded in intercepting the Mollies' fire."

"What about the ship killers?" Knott asked.

"They were too big for the platforms," Truon Le said. "Lt. Robbins has suggested just pushing them out into space."

Knott suppressed a sigh. He felt like they were throwing rocks.

"Carry on," he said.

"Sir," Lurhman said, reclaiming his attention. "The only other thing we can do now is send out the Speeds."

Knott shook his head. The enemy were close enough, and they were all going fast enough, that the much slower Speeds would be left irretrievably behind in minutes. They wouldn't have a chance to do their job.

"Plot it," he said aloud. "Alert the helmsman." *And God help us all.*

The XO leaned forward and murmured in Chaste Oppenheimer's ear, "The enemy are headed for the jump point." He straightened. "Brother Captain."

Chaste was sure that he'd seen lightning flash at the corner of his vision.

"No matter," he said at last, controlling his voice with difficulty. "There's nowhere they can jump from here that won't put them in the Ecclesia's space." He smirked. "And they've only got one jump in that tub."

The XO placed his hand on the arm of the captain's chair. Oppenheimer stared at it as though it were a loathsome insect.

"They might leap to some, as yet, uncharted destination. Brother Captain."

Oppenheimer slowly looked up and measured the XO through narrowed eyes.

"Are you suggesting that we *not* follow them?" he asked, his voice silky.

"Not at all, merely that we pursue them with extreme caution. Brother Captain."

"You coward!" the captain spat. "You have no faith in the Spirit of Destiny at all, have you? You're just like the rest of your puling generation; pretending to have faith to get ahead, waiting for better men to die so that you can take over and spread your rot!" He ground his teeth with fury. "If I thought there was anyone amongst these *idiots* that could replace you I'd have you thrown in the brig even now, in the midst of battle!" He flung the XO's hand away. "Be grateful that I allow you one last chance to serve Destiny. Stand away from me," Chaste said with a sneer. "And watch how one of the truly faithful goes to battle."

✧   ✧   ✧

Knott swallowed the slight nausea that transition to jump still gave him and asked, "How long will our transit be, Ms. Lurhman?"

"Eight hours, sir. Very short."

"Attention, attention," Knott said over the general com. "This is the captain speaking. Stand down from combat readiness. Only essential personnel are to remain on duty. The rest are to eat and rest. You will report back to duty at oh seven hundred. All untreated wounded personnel are to report to the auxiliary infirmary on deck six. Knott, out."

He looked up at Ju, who had come to stand at his shoulder.

"Sir, you should also eat and rest," she said.

Knott grinned at her.

"Sorry, Ms. Ju, but I consider myself essential personnel." Her lips quirked. "You're right, though. We should rotate our people, give everyone at least two hours off. If someone were to bring coffee and a sandwich to my ready room in two hours, I might just take a break and consume them."

Ju nodded. "Yes, sir, I'll see to it."

He turned back to his screen and lost himself in the ongoing reports about repairs and casualties. A couple of hours later, Augie Skinner contacted him.

"Captain, we've got the jump engine back online. And considering the damage we've done a pretty good job." He shook his head grimly. "But she won't take much stress, sir."

"I take it the damage was worse than you first thought," Knott said dryly.

"Aye, sir. Considerably worse."

"Well, Skinner, I'm sorry to tell you this, but I suspect we're going to need that engine. Do whatever you must to bring it up to capacity. Failure is not an option. Knott out."

The chief engineer turned to his crew.

"Break out your tools, people. We've got a miracle to perform."

The tired faces slowly curved into weary smiles. They had two choices; they could groan and then do it, or they could just do it. If the Chief wanted miracles, then they were going to perform them.

"You didn't tell me this was a pulsar, Ms. Lurhman."

Knott's hands gripped his chair arms, the knuckles whitening, then he forced himself to relax his grip.

His split screen showed two very different scenes outside the *Invincible*; one was what the naked eye would see, serene and empty space; the other revealed the pulsar that the sensors were reading, something like a lighthouse gone mad, whirling like a top and flashing darkness instead of light.

It was also flashing death, in the form of powerful radiation; although *powerful* was a rather weak term. It made any energy weapon a ship could mount about as significant as a flashlight.

The light carrier's shielding was second to none and there were "storm cellars," heavily shielded shelters, throughout the ship in the event of something catastrophic. But even they could only do so much if the *Invincible* were unlucky enough to be caught directly by one of those beams of radiation.

"I'm sorry, sir," Lurhman said. "I should have mentioned it. But it's figured into my data, and we should be in no danger."

We should be able to fire on our enemies, too, the captain thought. *But we're here, two engines down, instead of blowing them off the grid.*

"In future, Ms. Lurhman, we'll let that be my decision." Knott called up the com. "Attention, attention, this is the captain speaking. All nonessential personnel are to report to the storm shelters. Infirmaries are to lower shielding immediately. Knott, out." He glanced around the bridge and called out a half dozen names. "Report to the storm cellar."

He returned their salutes as they left with a crisp one of his own. If they were unlucky this would be the last time they'd see each other alive.

That's an optimistic thought, Knott remarked to himself. *Must be old age creeping up on me.* He watched the screens as they slid rapidly towards the neutron star and almost smiled when he realized that his feet were pressing into the deck, as though that would slow their descent. They were aiding the grip of the pulsar's gravity, which allowed them control of their descent, but they were still moving incredibly fast.

"Skinner," Knott said over the com. "I haven't heard from you in a while, Chief. I can't help but wonder if that's a bad sign."

"We're doing very well, sir. Frankly I'm surprised at how well." Skinner looked tired, but almost cheerful.

"Well, according to the astrogator, we're going to really need that engine in nine minutes," the captain remarked dryly. "So I want it online in five."

"Understood, Captain." The chief engineer nodded. "Skinner, out."

Knott went back to staring at their progress towards the neutron star and its radiation and crushing gravity. *Oh, for some distraction,* he wished.

"Sir! The Mollie battlecruiser and one destroyer have just exited the jump point, destroyer is firing."

Knott frowned. *It's getting eerie the way action keeps following thought around here.*

His eyes automatically noted the data on the missile's path and he saw that he had nothing to worry him. The pulsar's gravity had it; there was no way the missile could strike them unless the *Invincible* deliberately leapt into its path.

Like the missile, they were well and truly committed; the only way they could survive now was if Ashly Lurhman's self-confidence was justified.

"Brother Captain," the XO said, not shouting, but with a sternness that showed that he wanted to. "We *must* withdraw! If we are caught by the pulsar's gravity we will be sucked in. This ship is too damaged to . . ."

Oppenheimer stood and, whirling, slapped the XO square in the mouth.

"Destiny," Chaste hissed, "will intervene. Destiny will save us, and allow us to smite the infidel. Because," he bellowed, "Destiny is on our side!" The captain glared at his executive officer, allowing all of the loathing he'd hidden to show. "If you have nothing worthwhile to contribute, be silent." With a haughty glare Oppenheimer took his seat again. "Report!" he called out to his techs.

"They're coming on," Ju said, shaking her head. "Poor fools."

Knott was forced to agree with her. Approaching this close to a neutron star in a ship that damaged was suicide.

The moment of truth was on them with heart stopping suddenness. They swung round the star, just as Lurhman had plotted. Every crewman held their breath as the helmsman fired the engines.

The captain felt the change in the ship that indicated another engine had engaged. He smiled, not needing Skinner to tell him that the engineer had succeeded. He could feel the smoothness in the *Invincible*'s new vigor and knew they'd win this fight.

"Full marks, Mr. Skinner," he said when the chief engineer's face appeared on his screen. "Well done."

"Thank you, sir. Skinner out."

The *Invincible* shot out from behind the tiny pulsar and roared for the jump point.

"Brother Captain," the tech said, his cheeks pale, ears still ringing with the screams of his comrades. "Our destroyer companion has been . . . absorbed by the pulsar."

Every man on the bridge turned to look at Oppenheimer, and because every one of them knew that *Destiny's Arrow* would soon share the destroyer's fate, their eyes were accusing.

The captain sprang to his feet, his fists clenched before him, his face pale with rage.

"It is because none of you have *faith*!" he cried. "Had

you truly *believed* then the Spirit of Destiny would never have deserted us!"

"No," the XO said with the chilling calm of a man who knows he will soon die. "It is because *you* are an idiot."

Chaste swung around to confront him, his teeth bared.

"*You!*" he said in a tearing whisper. "I refuse to die with scum like you on my deck!" Oppenheimer began to advance on the XO. "You I shall kill with my own hands!"

The younger man struck him to the floor with contemptuous ease, and when the captain looked up in astonishment it was into the tiny barrel of a needler.

"I think not, *Brother Captain.*" The XO's eyes narrowed slightly. "I believe we'll send you ahead to ask a question of the Spirit for us. Ask it for us; why, if Destiny was on our side, did it make a fool like you our leader?"

The Executive Officer looked up at the men around him and saw agreement in every face. One of the techs caught his eye, looked at the needler in the XO's hand, then up into his face and mouthed the word, "Please."

The XO raised the weapon and fired, then one by one he killed the others. As he raised the needler to his own head, he felt a flash of pity for the rest of the crew, and their horrible fate as they rushed towards the neutron star.

If it isn't merciful, at least it will be swift, he comforted himself, and pulled the trigger.

The *Invincible* lay quietly in a deserted section of Mollie space, and every crewman prayed that there *was* such a thing as a deserted section of Mollie space.

I know there is, Knott thought. *Space is very large indeed, even the slivers we humans presumptuously think of as ours are larger than we can really grasp.*

He gazed around the conference table at his officers; all of the younger faces looking back at him bore the stamp of exhaustion. There was none of the giddy relief that victory brings anywhere around him. The cost had been far too high.

To bring their weaponry back online would take a degree of expertise that the personnel of *Invincible* just couldn't supply. Even the redoubtable Robbins declared it beyond her capacity; at least, within a reasonable time frame.

But the worst news came from the chief engineer.

"Captain," he said, eyes downcast, his face pink with shame. "The second real-space engine pod has burned out." His lips thinned to a line. "It will have to be completely replaced." Then he took a very deep breath and looked Knott right in the eye. "The worst news, sir, is that we only have enough fuel to get us back to Ontario Base."

A horrified stillness settled over the table and everyone froze in place.

"Thank you, people," Knott said, carefully laying down the stylus with which he'd been taking notes. "Ms. Lurhman, you will lay in a course to Ontario Base for us. Is there any other business?" he asked. Cold gray eyes swept the table; there were no takers. "Then you are dismissed."

They filed out quietly, all except Mai Ling Ju who kept her seat beside the captain, her dark eyes watching him.

When the door closed at last Knott put a hand to his face and rubbed his burning eyes. He, too, was exhausted. *I know I'm too young for retirement,* he thought, *but I feel so damn old.*

"We're leaving a lot of good people to starve out there in the dark," he said gloomily.

Ju snorted and when he raised a brow inquiringly she shook her head at him admonishingly.

"You *must* be tired, sir," she said, a smile playing lightly on her lips.

He straightened in his chair, his eyes demanding an explanation.

This time the XO outright grinned at him.

"Are you forgetting who you left in charge on that asteroid, Captain?" Ju shook her head again. "I wouldn't be so quick to count Commander Raeder out, if I were you, sir. Nor would I expect him to wait until his people try to eat their boots. I fully expect that somehow the good commander will come riding home in triumph. He's got more than just skill or intelligence on his side."

"Oh?" Knott said after a beat. "And what would that be?"

Ju grinned till her nose wrinkled.

"He's got luck, sir!"

CHAPTER SIXTEEN

"Gak!" Raeder said as he came aboard the prison ship and cracked his helmet seal. "What *is* that?"

"Ah, well," Paddy said wearily, "the boyos up atop have decided to object to hostin' so much company and they're makin' their feelin's known."

"With what?" the commander gasped, rubbing his nose.

"I haven't wanted to know, Commander," Paddy answered.

"But they're breathing this stuff themselves!"

"Ah, weel, they're that upset," the Chief said with a shake of his head. "Though I don't imagine it's as bad for them as it is for the rest of the ship. The air exchanger up there is designed to carry away fumes, where the rest of the ship is supposed to be just storage, so it's a much more primitive system." He shrugged. "The sweetness of the air didn't matter, y'see."

"Suggestions?" Raeder asked.

"Short of breakin' down their door and cleanin' the ducts ourselves?" Paddy shrugged again.

"Is there any way to reverse the flow of air without depriving them of oxygen?"

"Y'mean so's the smell gets in to them and no one else?" The Chief thought about it for a moment, blue eyes half shut. "Aye, it can be done." His eyes slid towards Raeder. "The others'll probably figure it out and give those spalpeens a taste of their own medicine, y'know."

"Poetic justice if they do," Peter said. "Don't let it go on for more than a week, though.

He grinned. "This'll be the last bunch we can fit in here."

Paddy nodded. "It's been a good haul," he agreed. "But I'll be glad when it's over. I distrust a run of good luck that goes on too long, with the dice or with life," he said. "It makes me feel the fall will be hard indeed."

He was only echoing Peter's own thoughts, but the words made a chill run down the commander's spine. *It's the Irish in you responding to the prospect of gloom and doom,* he admonished himself. Still, the *Invincible was* overdue by four days.

The prisoners were running low on supplies despite Raeder being overgenerous because they were being sealed in. A couple of bored gluttons in the bunch, he'd figured, and suddenly there would have been only twenty days' food instead of a month. But he may have underestimated his gluttons by quite a few.

Some of the pirates had just taken on supplies when captured, or stolen them; others were almost out. All in all though it had worked out, until now, with a thirty-day supply for everybody. But there had been nothing to spare, and there certainly wasn't now. This bunch had come in with an almost empty larder, which would eat up the little surplus they'd held back.

As for the Welters, their supplies had been carefully calculated for thirty-five days to allow for unforeseen circumstances. *After that I guess we'll just have to eat the prisoners,* Raeder joked to himself.

The Mollie transports continued to show up, only to find empty space awaiting them. Those were allowed to return to their bases, carrying news of disappointment or betrayal, but nothing else. On significantly fewer occasions the pirates showed up with a Mollie escort and in those cases Peter made a point of taking them out. It was absolutely vital that a wedge be driven between the two parties.

Why should the Commonwealth be the only government troubled by pirates? he thought with a grin.

Their few Mollie prisoners were kept together in a separate cell on the freighter. But the way things were going the next freighter they took was going to have to be pressed into service as an overflow jailhouse.

"It's done," Paddy said from Peter's elbow. "I expect we'll be hearin' protests from that lot in a little while. Though if they were smart they'd keep it to themselves."

"If they were smart," Raeder said, "they wouldn't be pirates in the first place. They'd be lawyers."

Another anxious forty-eight hours of waiting passed with no sign of the *Invincible*. Though water and ammunition were in plentiful supply, they were out of food. They had vitamin supplements, but that was it. The prisoners, having been warned, still had several days of provisions.

But when that's gone they really might eat each other, Peter thought.

He'd privately given the *Invincible* forty-eight hours leeway to get to them before assuming that they weren't coming. Now he was certain of it. The next ship with jump capability that they encountered was their ticket home. They'd have to rig up a tow to bring their prisoners with them. That and put some unlucky volunteer on the bridge to bring them through the jump with the rest of the Welters.

I hope the Mollies don't choose now to declare this system off limits. Their goose was really cooked if they did.

He supposed they could raid the enemy base for supplies and drop off the Mollie prisoners there. Then Raeder's crew could take the Mollie's quarters and fly the pirates home to justice on the freighter/prison. *But that will blow our pirates-cheating-the-Mollies scheme,* Peter thought. Returning prisoners for nothing but food wasn't typical pirate behavior. Actually, taking prisoners in the first place wasn't typical pirate behavior.

His favorite scheme involved giving the pirates a heap of supplies and leaving a beacon to guide the Mollies to them. He was pretty sure that they wouldn't be treated kindly or like innocent victims. But only *pretty sure*. There remained the risk that the pirates could point to the Commonwealth.

They'd been careful, they'd acted as much like pirates as they reasonably could. But therein lay the problem. They were forced to be *reasonable* and that alone would set off alarm bells in the thickest pirate's skull. Besides, there was no heap of supplies that could be left behind.

He sighed. *Just one more ship,* he thought. *That's all we need is one more.*

"Sir, we have incoming traffic."

Raeder dropped his feet to the floor and sat forward, peering into his screen intently. A Mollie destroyer came out of the jump point's distorted trumpet, flickering into the "reality" of sidereal space.

No question but that he's *looking for trouble,* Peter thought.

"Weapons are hot," Pellagrio said. Unnecessarily in this case; the Mollies' whole trim was aggressive. "More incoming," the tech added.

Behind the destroyer lumbered a Commonwealth freighter.

"Hey!" Raeder said when he read the name that scrolled up as the AI interpreted the engine signature. "That's the *Province of Quebec!*"

Her name was clear as a bell in the screen, the ship he'd saved en route to the *Invincible*. Had she been taken by pirates after all? The commander felt her presence here personally. If she'd been captured he'd make the bastards pay. If she was betraying the Commonwealth, he'd know the reason why.

Raeder hit the alarm button, which set off innumerable flashing lights throughout the hutch, silently alerting the pilots to scramble for their Speeds.

❖   ❖   ❖

"The freighter will be armed," Sarah James said over the com as she settled into her Speed.

"Yeah," Raeder agreed. "But they sure won't have a Star Command crew to man them. How good the merchanters who will handle 'em are is anybody's guess. Historically they weren't too accurate."

"I'm not going to rely on that, Commander," Sarah said. "Historically they haven't been armed with state of the art weapons either."

Raeder watched his people go with trepidation. This was the first time they'd faced anything like a destroyer. Up until now the Mollies had been content to send nothing more formidable than a corvette.

And there are only the six of them. It would have been better if the Mollie had come alone.

"Two, Six, you've got the freighter. Do *not* annihilate our ticket home, please. The rest of you, follow me. Let's scratch that tin can!"

She boosted hard, enduring the stress stoically and watching the distances scroll downward in the display. Their best hope was to severely damage the destroyer in the first minutes of the fight. The longer the enemy was left unscathed the more difficult the Welters' situation became. And the worst thing they could do was to drive them off. So, more important than her own safety was finding and hitting the best possible target.

"Targeting laser detected," the AI said.

"Gotcha." The destroyer was boosting away from the freighter it guarded, to intercept the Speeds and engage at a safe distance from its charge.

Her hands moved in the gloves, a dance more delicate than a pianist's. Thrusters fired, and the Speed's vector took on a chaotic unpredictability. Not enough to fool a missile, with its own sensors and maneuvering ability, but a beam had to hit precisely, and a Speed made a small and tricky target.

Distance closed with eerie speed, as it always did in a meeting engagement. She snapped off a missile as she made her pass, waited for the close-in batteries to engage it, then rolled and slammed a bolt from her plasma cannon. That spattered off the destroyer's shields, but she used the recoil to add a twisting tumble to her path. The Mollie laser cannon missed her craft by the space of a few particles. The AI flung out chaff to confuse the missile that followed on its heels, cheerfully reeling off distance until it detonated—outside the destruction envelope, but she'd be needing a course of antiradiation repair drugs after that.

And . . . *Yes!* The warhead had driven its bomb-pumped spike right into the flank of the Mollie craft. Destroyers were lightly built; the readouts showed ablative plating, foamed metal—and oxygen, nitrogen, the spectra of water crystals. "*Hit, by God!*"

The destroyer slowed as the Speeds went past, a quarter of the heavens vanishing in the flare of its drive as it prepared to come about and keep them from nearing the defenseless freighter.

Sarah was coming around for another run when she saw the freighter kill one of her Speeds. She gasped in astonishment.

That answers the question of how accurate they might be, doesn't it? the lieutenant commander thought bitterly.

Aia! Raeder thought in shock. He could feel the blood drain from his face as he watched pieces of her demolished craft spinning outward from the center of the blast.

He and Wisnewski had flown together since his first assignment out of the academy. He tapped a few keys, seeking an escape capsule.

There was nothing.

Wisnewski was dead.

"Givens, get over there," Sarah said with forced calmness. The freighter was turning already. Fleeing for the safety of the jump point. Under no circumstances could they allow that to happen.

"On my way," Givens responded.

"I want that freighter stopped, pilot," she said crisply. "Kill them if you have to."

This was not really what the lieutenant commander wanted at all. She'd noticed that the *Province of Quebec* was the freighter's original name. That might mean that the craft had only been in the hands of the pirates for a very short time. Which might also mean that there could be survivors from the original crew aboard.

She also knew that their communications were monitored and that the pirates, inveterate cowards that they were, might surrender more easily if they thought the Speeds were under orders to destroy them rather than letting them escape.

Three Speeds against a destroyer was impossible odds, but they were what she had to work with. She flung another missile after her first, hoping to deepen the hole in the Mollie's side, bringing them that much closer to the fragile heart of the ship.

"*Province of Quebec*," Barak growled. "You will shut down your engines and your weapons or I will kill you."

"Whoo!" Givens said cheerfully. "You fools are kissin' the A-H now. Do what he says, or he'll do you." The lieutenant trained his weapons on the *Province*'s bridge. "And I'll back him up." His voice was suddenly hard.

"Alonso," Raeder said, "you will not kill that freighter. That is a direct order, you will *not* kill that freighter."

All that could be heard in response was Barak's ragged breathing.

"Givens! You will stop Barak from killing that ship. Do you understand?" Raeder waited. At last a response came.

"Interfer... You... aking up... ase. Please repe... You are... aking up."

"The hell I am," Peter roared. "Givens you will obey my orders or it's your ass! Do you hear me?"

But there came only one more "... ase," in response. Then nothing.

"Damn!" Raeder snarled, then flung himself from his chair and raced for the makeshift flight deck.

✧   ✧   ✧

Sarah swore silently as she watched Kushner and Manning pull another hare-brained, hair-breadth stunt. *I wouldn't mind if they were accomplishing anything,* she thought, gritting her teeth. *But all they're doing is risking their fool necks.* Not that they had any necks to spare.

"C'mon! Sharpen up out there," she snapped. "This ain't no game!"

Manning and Kushner, who had been one behind the other, peeled off in different directions and a Mollie missile sailed harmlessly through the space where they had been a split second before.

"Stop teasing them and start shooting at them," Sarah snarled.

The two Marines looped around again; this time they did fire. Light damage, no more; the destroyer was still bleeding air and water, but the flow was slowing and there was no sign of impaired capcity.

"Tabernac!"

That must have been a missile. And *far* too close and fast. She snapped the Speed onto a vector that would open distance for a moment, wincing as the warhead went up behind her. The humming moan of the screens went to an ear-piercing whine for a second. *Not* good. A Speed's shields were notional at best.

"Think we ought to tell her?" Manning asked.

"Naw. She's doing what she'd be doing if she knew we were distracting them," Kushner replied. "We're a team, she's the logical one to plant the egg."

"True enou— Jesus!"

The expanding globe of Kushner's Speed was smeared out of shape by the velocity of the plasma and particles that composed it, but it was unmistakable.

Manning's hands writhed in her control gloves, and the Speed went into the matador dance its designers had intended. Her eyes were glaring, fixed. Kushner was *gone,* two years of combat, and suddenly *gone.*

"Gotcha," Sarah whispered to herself.

The AI had painted a pip at the most probable spot,

the place where the destroyer was weakened from her previous attack. The Speed juddered under her as the plasma cannon fired . . .

Impact. She tasted blood in her mouth, harsh salt-and-iron taste. The board was screaming at her, in its impersonal mechanical way; the fusion bottle was going red-line. Her fingers danced, but the answers came back: critical: no response: critical:system integrity breech: critical: ten seconds to failure: critical:nine:eight . . .

"I can't even *ram*," she snarled, as she hit the final control, the one no pilot liked to think about, the one that turned you from a deadly fleet piranha into a piece of flotsam.

EJECT POD.

Slamming force crushed her back. Blackness.

"I'm qualified on Speeds, Paddy," Raeder said quietly. "Says so right here, in emergency situations." He turned to face the big noncom. "Paddy, if we don't get that freighter intact, we're probably all going to die here. I'd call that an emergency. Now soldier, shut up and soldier!"

"Yessir."

The launch had none of the savage impact of going out on a carrier's rail-catapults. Raeder did his best to make up for that with the Speed's own drive.

On the Mollie bridge there was an air of quiet jubilation. There was no emotional outburst at the sight of two pirate Speeds bursting like firecrackers. Eyes did not leave the screens they were tracking, though there were smiles. All was silent efficiency and quiet pride.

Captain Honor-the-Spirit Holmes permitted himself to nod, once, in satisfaction.

"Captain," a crewman said quietly.

"Speak," Holmes said.

"The pilot ejected from one of the destroyed craft."

One of Holmes' eyebrows went up. It would be good to capture one of these marauders, to find out who they were and where based.

"Send out a team to retrieve that pilot," he said.

Then he turned his attention to the two pirates threatening the freighter. After all the losses the Ecclesia had suffered in this sector it was pleasing that the Spirit had chosen his ship, *Spirit's Praises*, to finally find success.

"Kavi, what are we going to do?" Syril asked, his prominent Adam's apple bobbing up and down in distress.

The captain looked over at her fifteen-year-old nephew and said, "We're going to sit tight. It looks like our escort will have a hand free any minute now."

"*Province of Quebec*," the com spat in a hard male voice. "This is your final warning, shut down your engines or we will fire."

Syril and Fia, her younger niece, turned to look at her, their eyes enormous. Kavi bit her full lower lip. Her uncle, Stes, had destroyed one of the pirates, so she knew they weren't bluffing. Not that she could expect any of them to live long after they'd been boarded. But the *Spirit* was already turning towards them. If she could keep these two distracted it might give the Mollies a better shot at them. Kavi took a deep breath, then she hit the com button.

"Complying," she said.

Kavi turned and nodded to the kids to begin the shutdown procedure. Then she contacted Stes and Theesa, her eldest niece, on the internal com.

"We're shutting down rather than be fired on," she explained. "The *Spirit* has already gotten rid of two of them, so if we can keep these two from boarding we might be all right. Theesa, go disable the main lock."

"Yes, ma-am," the girl said.

"Uncle, power down your weapons, but stay there. We may be able to be of some help to the Mollies when they come."

"Aye, Cap'n."

Stes shut down his weapon, then slipped over to Theesa's station to make sure hers was also cold. He shook his head at the literal mindedness of teenagers when he found it still hot. He himself would never dream of leaving something like this enabled but unattended.

If they ever had another company meeting he'd take her to task for it, and Kavi would probably give her KP for the duration of the mission.

Stes returned to his station and sat waiting for orders. In the quiet, he watched the two Speeds facing them. He pulled out the pellet gun his father had given him and checked its load, resolved to kill his children rather than let the pirates at them.

Manning fought off her shock at Kushner's death and her guilt over the lieutenant commander's by concentrating on her mission. And when she concentrated, Peggy Manning focused like a laser.

Her orders were not to destroy the Mollie ship, but to disable its jump capacity. She proceeded to obey orders.

Raeder was about to join the fray when he saw Sarah's Speed explode. Time froze. For a full minute as he flew onward he couldn't react. He saw Manning finally get on her game, he monitored the freighter as it shut down its engines.

Then he saw the signal of a homing beacon and knew that Sarah had ejected. *Whether she's safe or not is a whole other story.*

The only way to insure her safety was to help Manning injure and drive off the Mollie destroyer. It looked like Givens and Barak had the freighter sewed up.

"Manning, coordinate," he barked. "I'm coming in."

Sarah woke, so dizzy she was sorry she had. Nausea threatened, but she slowed and deepened her breathing. Slowly the feeling left her and her head stopped spinning. The lieutenant commander closed her eyes in relief. When she opened them a flickering light in the corner of her helmet display caught her attention.

Oh, great. The Mollies are coming to rescue me. She fumbled with the homing beacon on her shoulder, finally shutting it down. Then she pulled herself into a ball and put herself into a slow spin, hoping to blend in with the debris from the exploded Speeds. Even being left out here to die slowly would be better than being taken prisoner by the Mollies. The rumors she'd heard . . .

Sarah wondered briefly how the others were doing. There was a flare from the direction of the destroyer, but it seemed too small to be a Speed exploding. *Maybe they'll go back if their ship is in trouble,* she hoped. *Don't see me,* she wished. *Don't see me.*

On the three-person life raft the tech watched the homing beacon stop transmitting before he could pinpoint its location.

"Sir."

"I see it, crewman," the ensign answered. "We'll find his signature when we get closer."

They quartered the section of space where they'd last received a signal. As they worked yet another pirate Speed flashed by.

"Sir!" the ensign said over the com.

"We see him," the *Spirit's Praises* answered. "Find that pirate and get him aboard. This one seems to be leading another group of them."

Aboard the *Spirit's Praises* Captain Holmes viewed the newcomers with a cold clench of alarm. The Spirit was with them, yes, but the Spirit worked through human action . . . though Its purposes were beyond human comprehension. The first fighter group had done significant damage. One of them had bored a hole halfway to the heart of his ship, the other had taken out their jump capability. Now, this one appeared to be accompanied by three other ships.

It could be ECM, the enemy were good at such deceits. But it could also be reinforcements. Holmes debated with himself what he should do.

"Get that pirate picked up in five minutes," he said, "or get back here without him. We're heading for the Ecclesian post we have in this system. We must survive to inform the Interpreters of this betrayal by our supposed allies."

No one troubled themselves to ask about the freighter they were escorting. They were not of the Ecclesia and must take their chances. The captain regretted the loss of their much-needed cargo, however.

Sarah prayed that they wouldn't find her, right up to the moment when they pinned her in their searchlight's beam. They wasted no time asking for her cooperation. They merely stunned her with an electrical charge and one of them went out on a tether to retrieve her. Then they sped back to the destroyer.

Their little life raft couldn't hope to overtake the enemy Speed and the ensign was fearful that the captain might decide to remove the *Spirit* from danger. So they pressed their craft to its full capacity, grateful that they hadn't been noticed by the enemy as yet.

As they grew closer readings indicated that the pirates were giving the destroyer a hellacious pounding. But still they remained undetected. The ensign hung back, silent, not wishing to draw attention to himself.

Suddenly the destroyer opened up with a cloud of covering fire and the small craft hurried to find its berth in the safety of the destroyer's belly.

Raeder watched the Mollie destroyer disappear from view at speeds his own craft couldn't hope to match. *At least he's headed where I want him,* Peter thought.

"Manning, escort the freighter to base. I'm going to search for the lieutenant commander."

"Shall we return to help you search, sir?"

"Yes. When the freighter is secured."

They'd need every set of instruments, every pair of eyes that could be spared for the search. *She had her homing beacon on,* Raeder told himself. *I saw it as I came in. When did it go off? And why?* He hoped she had done it herself to escape detection by the Mollies. Peter refused to allow himself to consider that her beacon had malfunctioned, that her suit had been damaged and that Sarah was dead. *She's alive,* he insisted to himself. *I can* feel *her.*

✧   ✧   ✧

They searched for hours with no success. Raeder refused to give up. *I saw her beacon. I know she ejected, she* has *to be her somewhere.*

"Commander," Manning said.

"You've got something?" Raeder asked eagerly.

"Small craft signature, sir. Very small, maybe a life raft. They were heading towards the site of battle, and they were really forkin' out the neutrinos."

They took her, Raeder thought. His mind froze on the thought and refused to go any farther. He checked his fuel gauge automatically. Then let out his breath in a huff.

What are you thinking, Raeder? he asked himself. *You're going to go rescue her from a Mollie base, defended by a wounded but still able destroyer, with four Speeds and a couple of workboats.*

"I think they've got her, sir," Manning said into his long silence.

"I think you're right, Ensign. We'll head back to base. Raeder, out." *I'll think of something,* Raeder promised himself. *I am not leaving Sarah James in Mollie hands.*

CHAPTER SEVENTEEN

"Shell me this lobster," Captain Holmes said to his security people.

The figure in the suit put up an uncoordinated resistance, still groggy from the stun volt his rescuers had used to subdue him.

"Is there a point to this?" Holmes asked the weakly struggling figure. "We're in no particular hurry. So if you'd prefer we can always leave you in there until you run out of oxygen and let you come out on your own."

The helmeted figure slumped in the hands of the two security guards and the third removed his helmet to an accompanying swish of escaping air.

"It's a woman!" exclaimed the auditor beside Holmes in high-pitched shock.

Holmes gave him a sidelong glance. It was the auditor's job to insure that the minds of the crew remained pure and that no outside doctrine stained their faith. He could even chastise the captain himself, albeit only in private. That the pirate was a woman was an unwelcome complication. No doubt it would send Auditor Faithful-to-the-Spirit Williams into a frenzy of investigations. From this point on any man who mentioned that he missed his wife was in for a bad time.

Williams turned to his captain indignantly. He took a breath to speak, but said nothing, his hand went out in a gesture of repudiation towards the pirate woman and Holmes could almost read his little mind.

"Obviously," the captain said, "this prisoner's identity must be kept secret." He made a point of appearing to address the security force, but the way he spoke was in answer to Williams' unspoken distress. "Petty Officer," he continued, speaking to the highest ranking of the security people, "choose three other people whose discretion you trust and assign them to guard this prisoner. You will all take up lodgings in the brig and you will not speak to any of the crew unless directly ordered to do so until further notice."

"Yes, sir!" the young petty officer snapped. The man's dark face echoed the shock and dismay on the auditor's.

"If she's significantly wounded, let me know and I'll see about getting a corpsman down here to look her over."

"Yes, sir!"

"Prisoner, you might as well divest yourself of your suit and make yourself as comfortable as you can. Auditor," Holmes turned to him, "my office, I think."

"Absolutely, Captain!" Williams' eyes shone with outrage.

"This is very serious," Williams said as he paced back and forth across the captain's small office. He stopped to give the captain, sitting calmly behind his desk, an aggrieved stare. "I don't think you realize just how serious."

"Sir," Holmes reminded him gently. "It is important for the sake of discipline that you remember to call me 'sir,' auditor." He steepled his hands before him. "And I am very well aware that there is a possibility of this prisoner causing . . . ripples, if you will, in the smooth running of my ship. But of more concern to me right now is how we shall handle her interrogation."

"Methods for dealing with Commonwealth whores are well established," Williams snarled.

Holmes folded his hands as he stared off into the middle distance and resisted the urge to sigh.

"We have time," he said. "It will be some time before the jump coil is repaired. Let's take it slow."

"What do you mean, you don't know?" Raeder stared at Paddy in perplexity.

"Weel, Sir. We had no orders other than to watch 'em. And their main lock was disabled, and they've been quiet and all. So we thought we'd wait on you, sir, so to speak."

"So we don't know who they are, or how many, or how they're armed, is that it?"

"We know how many, sir. There's five, sensors told us that. Though they've got some kind of shielding in the cargo area that we can't get through. They could have an army in there, but I doubt it, since the energy signature indicates they're only heating the living quarters. One of 'em we can see seems to be a child."

"A child?" Raeder asked, startled. *One of the original crew?* It was possible, though there was nothing to say that some pirate might not have a kid. *What the hell,* he thought, *we might as well admit we're Space Command. If worst comes to worst that ship is how we're going home anyway.* And telling them might get the Welters inside the freighter with no one else getting hurt.

Kavi and her family/crew waited anxiously for something to happen. When the Speeds had left them here they'd tried to escape. After allowing them to accumulate a reasonable lead. But they'd been swarmed by workboats and messages that threatened dire consequences if they persisted.

Workboats weren't notoriously battleworthy craft, but then, neither were freighters, so Kavi took them at their word. They might well be lying, but then again, these were pirates and such would arm their bathtubs for the sheer joy of it. It wasn't the first time she'd wished for better sensors. In terms of telling just what was actually out there they were as good as blind.

"Ahoy *Province of Quebec.*"

Kavi jumped, it had been hours since they'd tried to communicate. She glanced at her uncle, his mouth tightened. She squeezed her eyes tight shut, then tapped her console.

"This is the *Province of Quebec* responding." She licked dry lips with an equally dry tongue. "Please identify yourself."

"This is Commander Peter Ernst Raeder of Commonwealth Space Command. We demand that you open your ship for a legal inspection of your papers and cargo."

If he had announced that he was William Shakespeare and he wanted her to star in his new play Kavi couldn't have been more stunned.

"Space Command," Stes said, his voice hinting at a surprising degree of relief under the circumstances.

"Space Command?" she demanded, glaring at her uncle.

"Yes, ma'am," the com answered.

"There's a big difference between busted and dead, Kavi," Stes said. "I've been happier, but I can't remember ever being this relieved."

"How do we know they're telling the truth?" she asked him, despite the open com.

"Why lie?" Raeder asked her. "We've got you right where we want you. Do you really think that genuine pirates would waste their time with psychological torture when they could indulge in the real thing? Oh, and you might remember something. You might remember a certain convoy, and an attack on the convoy, and the reason your ship wasn't captured then—and every one of you bunged out the airlock, or worse. Remember the new method of disabling enemy sensors I found? The hammer method?"

The family looked at one another, wariness on every face. Kavi "tsked!" Commander what's-his-name was right. Real pirates were into action, not talk. Which meant Stes was right too, they were busted.

"What are the odds of it being the same Commonwealth officer?" Kavi hissed, breaking the connection for an instant.

"What are the odds of a pirate knowing someone disabled a spacecraft by driving around and bashing it with a hammer?" Stes said. "Even pirates don't think that crazy."

"We're coming aboard," Raeder told them firmly. "Whether you open up for us or not, we're going to be on your bridge within the hour. But I warn you, if you fire on us we will return your fire. We don't want anyone killed here, so I'm asking you to use restraint. Will you cooperate?"

Kavi looked at her nieces and nephew, then at her uncle, who was, by expression and posture, already resigned to their fate. She sighed.

"Oh, all right. I'll meet you at our main lock," she snapped. She tapped off the com, then got up and stormed off the bridge. "Satisfied?" she snapped as she passed Stes.

"Hell, no!" he said, with a put upon, what-did-I-do-to-deserve-that expression on his face. "But we do owe him one."

She just snarled and walked on, Stes and the kids in tow.

When Sarah woke she found herself naked in an empty cell. It was small, cool and brightly lit, though there was no discernable source for the light. The ceiling, walls and floor were the same hard, gleaming white material. She felt alert and well rested, her bruises seemed of little consequence, as did her headache. She sat up and looked around.

"Ah, you're awake."

The man's voice boomed from the walls and Sarah clapped her hands over her ears.

"That won't help, you know," the voice boomed pleasantly.

Sarah cried out and curled into a fetal position; it seemed the room must explode from the sheer volume of the voice.

"It's coming from inside your head," he informed her. "While you were out, we put in an implant."

She was screaming now, but couldn't even hear her own voice over his.

"I control the volume," he continued, "and there's nothing you can do about it."

He stopped speaking and her own screaming startled her. Sarah lay on her side, eyes wide, waiting for the next blow as she tried to control her panting sobs.

"We need information," he said.

She gasped, and then relaxed as the voice came to her in a normal volume.

"What do you want to know?" she asked.

"THE TRUTH!"

The lieutenant commander blacked out from shock. When she came to, the room was in complete darkness. James lay still, not even daring to fully open her eyes as she waited for the next onslaught. But nothing came. She lay there unmoving for what seemed like hours, but no light, no sound penetrated the blackness. After a very long while, she slowly and carefully changed her position. Only minutely, knowing that they could record her movements even in this pitch blackness. She kept her breathing even, and wondered if he'd told her the truth. Had they had time to place implants in her brain?

No, she told herself, *they have not.* Then she remembered something. When she'd clapped her hands over her ears, there had been no hair. *How long have I been here?* Was it her first day, her first few hours, or had it been longer? Much longer.

There were drugs that could make you forget anything. Had they questioned her already, perhaps multiple times, while making her forget each session? From such a technique they could build up a file of discrepancies that she would know nothing about. And from those discrepancies they might be able to find their way to the truth.

I should have shot myself, Sarah thought regretfully.

"You probably think it's dark in there," the voice said.

James sighed. *I knew they'd know when I woke up.*

"But it's not. It's just as bright as it ever was." There was a long pause while she digested that. "When we return to the Ecclesia there are more sophisticated techniques that we can use. But we find that we can get good results with selective blindness."

Suddenly there was the sensation of insect legs running across her body and Sarah sat up with a startled cry. There were tiny pinpricks all across her bare body and the lieutenant commander slapped at herself frantically.

"Stop it!" she shouted. "Get them off me!"

She could see.

There was nothing there, though the sensation of tiny, running feet and biting remained. She was shaking.

"Stop it," she said through her teeth. And the feeling was gone. "What do you want from me?"

"THE TRUTH!"

And Sarah fell unconscious to the floor.

"Will she break?" Captain Holmes asked.

"Oh, yes. It's only a matter of time," Williams said complacently. "We'll be able to determine how long once we actually begin questioning her."

Holmes grimaced. She'd only been with them for twelve hours and he was already sick of the process. She was just a pirate. This hardly seemed worth the damage it was doing his soul to watch Williams enjoy himself like this. The captain was positively looking forward to executing her.

The first thing Raeder did was to separate the *Quebec*'s crew and to send people to interview them. He'd chosen to speak to the captain himself.

The fact that she was extremely attractive had nothing to do with his choice.

"What I don't understand," Raeder said, after about the tenth go-round, "is *why*. Why would you do this? And with a boat full of kids at that. How could you put them and yourself, and your ship in such danger when you could make a perfectly good living working for just the Commonwealth?"

"What do you know?" Kavi asked with a sneer. She sat at graceful ease, one long leg thrown over the arm of her chair, arms crossed below her breasts. "You're from Earth, right?"

Raeder's mouth quirked down at the corners in response to the challenge in her voice, which seemed to imply that coming from Earth was a really sleazy thing to do. He shrugged.

"Yeah," he said. "So?"

"So, just like the politicians who decided that we didn't *need* more than half the antihydrogen we'd been getting, you've never lived on a world with no breathable air."

"No," he agreed. *I think I see where she's going with this,* he thought uncomfortably.

"We cut back on everything; heating, cooling, lighting, even washing." She couldn't help a brief grin at his expression. Then instantly became serious again. "We also did everything that we could by hand, cooked food communally, used every passive energy source we could, cut back and cut back." She shook her head impatiently. "It wasn't enough. It will never *be* enough. Do—you—understand? We will die if we don't get more antihydrogen."

"Didn't the colonization board offer to relocate you?" Raeder asked. He knew full well that they had. Free transport back to Earth or any other of the self-sustaining colonies.

"Yeah, sure. And all you get to take is a couple of changes of clothes. *And* no guarantee that you'll ever see your home and everything you and generations of your family had worked for ever again. Nice deal, huh? Oh, and try to imagine how very welcome a huge bunch of penniless refugees would be on any of those worlds."

"I thought the deal was a round-trip ticket and support until the war was over." Peter knew very well that was what the deal was supposed to be. *Of course, sometimes government planning doesn't work out quite as advertised.*

"Yeah?" She raised her brows and cocked her head inquiringly. "I thought the deal was that colonies got the needed support until they were able to support themselves." In one lithe movement she swung her leg down and sat forward. "Only that's not the way it worked out, is it? As soon as it became inconvenient they left us alone to smother in the dark!"

Raeder raised his hands helplessly and allowed them to slap down on his thighs.

"You do know about the war?" he asked.

"They could have avoided it," Kavi insisted. "It's all lousy politics. Every time there's a war there's some bunch of rich jerks setting it up to make money off of other people's misery."

Raeder quirked up one corner of his mouth.

"Kavi, you're the captain of your own freighter, you're an intelligent woman. Why are you spouting this nonsense? The *Mollies*, all by themselves, suddenly decided that they weren't going to sell antihydrogen to *any* of the Commonwealth planets. They cut off the *whole* Commonwealth. Not just Earth and the older colonies, *everybody*. And they did it because they didn't like our religious views or our lifestyles. Helping them is only going to prolong this situation."

"Helping them is keeping us breathing, Commander."

Raeder couldn't argue with that. Unfortunately, neither he nor the Commonwealth could support the Wildcatter's position. *There's gotta be a way of fixing this,* he thought. Then, with an inner sigh, he thought, *But not today.*

"Obviously we won't be treating you or your crew . . ."

"My family," she said sullenly.

"Your family." He spread his hands, raised his brows. "We won't be treating you quite the same way we do the pirates. We're off-loading your cargo to make room for our people and essential supplies. We'll arrange a room for you and your family so that you can be together."

"Our cargo!" Kavi shot to her feet. "You might as well be pirates, the results are the same!"

"Hey! You're a smuggler, Captain Gallup," Raeder shouted, stung. "Smugglers always forfeit their cargo and their ships when caught. You knew that going in. You have much more important things to worry about, lady. Such as the fact that you were giving aid and comfort

to the enemy, which makes you *and* your family traitors.
And the penalties for treason are a lot harsher than the
ones for smuggling."

Kavi sat down hard.

"My family are innocent," she said numbly.

"Well, the kids probably don't have much to worry
about," Peter said, regretting his outburst. "But your uncle
is probably in the soup with you."

"What will happen to the children?" she asked.

"They'll be put in some kind of care, I guess. Don't
they have any family on Wildcat?"

Kavi shook her head.

"Everybody's dispersed." She shrugged. "I wouldn't
know where anyone is now. It's hard to keep in touch
at the best of times; now, it's impossible." Kavi gave him
a fierce look. "I will do anything, *anything*, to keep my
family safe."

Raeder opened his mouth to say that, whatever she was
offering, he had no say in what the government decided.
He just shook his head instead and left.

The trouble is, he thought as he walked towards the
bridge, *she has an argument.* Wildcat was perhaps twenty
years away from a breathable atmosphere. When that
happened the planet was, in effect, tamed and ready for
major colonization. Which meant that all those pioneers
who had sacrificed so much for generations would reap
the benefits bigtime. Stake owners would become fabu-
lously rich. *And the fact that they've had to abandon those
stakes to become refugees elsewhere leaves them in a very
vulnerable position.* Kavi was right, there would be "rich
jerks" out there waiting to reap the benefits.

So why do I feel guilty? he wondered. *I'm not a rich jerk
and I didn't start the war.* But he did hold the fate of this
one family in his hands. *They're traitors! They didn't have
to do this,* he told himself. *They killed Aia!*

Though to be fair, and he didn't want to be fair but
it was his nature, they really thought they were defend-
ing themselves against pirates.

She'll do anything to keep her family safe, Raeder thought.
And I do have certain discretionary powers . . . And Sarah

was in enemy hands. He stopped cold as the germ of an idea began to take hold.

"When do you plan to start asking her questions?" Holmes asked. He watched the quivering figure on the screen with distaste.

"Oh, not for quite a while yet," the auditor said dismissively. "Anything she'd say now would probably be a lie." He tapped at his console and the woman jumped with a little cry, then pulled in on herself, rubbing her arms for warmth.

"I've been told that even lies can be informative," the captain said, frowning. "Besides, she's a pirate. They're weak people with no sense of loyalty." He shook his head. "Why then would she lie to us?"

"Why do such pathetic creatures do anything?" Williams asked. He shrugged, his face pinched into a dismissive sneer. "Resentment, perhaps?"

Sarah lay down on her side, one arm laid across her eyes, as though to block the glaring light. Williams checked his console.

"She's trying to sleep," he said, pleased.

Holmes sighed. He loathed this. Loathed it.

"I, too, rather pity her," Williams said. "What chance did the poor creature have? If only her parents had turned to the Way. She could have been saved, made a decent woman with the proper humility and respect for her superiors." He tsked. "It's a shame. She's rather pretty in her way." His finger traced Sarah's leg on the screen.

The captain shot him a look of disgust.

"I want her questioned, Auditor. Today."

Williams nodded. "She's sleeping," he said softly, as though she might hear him. Then he struck a key and there was a loud blatt in her cell. Even the captain jumped in surprise.

The auditor turned to Holmes with a smug smile. "She'll soon be ready, Captain. Never fear, I know my job."

Holmes turned away, suddenly uncomfortable with the

knowledge that his auditor was indeed very well trained in torture and interrogation.

"All right," he said. "Call me when you're ready." He started to leave, then thought that the woman had been here for a full day now. "But be ready soon," he said and continued on his way.

Sarah sat up. She suspected that they might indeed have managed to put some sort of implant in her. They knew when she was sleeping, for example, instead of merely lying down. Or at least it seemed that they did. She had long since become confused about such things. She was hungry and thirsty, but she wasn't starving and she didn't have the symptoms of dangerous dehydration that she suspected she would experience by tomorrow. Whenever that might be.

So, she thought, tiredly, *I've been here a day at most.* And a rotten day it had been. Sarah concentrated on believing her own cover story. She embellished it, imagining a horrible childhood. Nothing too Grand Guignol, just unpleasant enough to warp a child into a pirate. She focused with all of her might, knowing that if she hit it right even drugs wouldn't pull another story from her. But it was hard. She was so tired, and it was hard.

Raeder tried to concentrate on the meeting. He hoped that by doing so it would encourage the idea that was tickling the back of his mind to come out of hiding. But frankly, this was a singularly unproductive meeting so far.

"So far as I can ascertain," Pellagrio was saying, "there's nothing incriminating in their records. No hidden files, no sign of double bookkeeping, no incriminating documents at all."

"So," Raeder said, "unless they admit to smuggling, we really have no proof that they were, in fact, selling goods to the Mollies."

People around the table looked at one another.

"Yes, sir," Pellagrio confessed, obviously embarrassed.

Raeder leaned back in his chair and stroked his upper lip thoughtfully.

Ensign Manning sat forward angrily. "Sir!" she began.

Raeder held up his hand, his eyes staring into the middle distance. Then he looked over at Paddy.

The New Hibernian stared back, puzzled. Then his eyes lit and he sat up abruptly.

"Their entire cargo area is shielded from scan," he said excitedly.

Raeder sat forward. "And they'll know the right codes."

Pellagrio caught on. "But why would they help us, when by helping us they prove their own guilt?"

"Well," Manning said, "maybe we can help them help us."

Pellagrio frowned in confusion.

Manning tapped the table. "We change our records to make it look like we've taken a different freighter. Then we say that we let them go, in exchange for their cooperation, knowing that they could be captured again virtually at will." She gave a see-what-I-mean shrug and Pellagrio slowly nodded.

"Whoa, wait a minute here," Givens said. "What are we talking about? Why should we let the dirty traitors go? And just what are they supposed to do for us that we need to make a deal with 'em, anyway?"

"Oh, Givens," Peggy Manning said, "you are so *slow* sometimes."

Alonso Barak had been sitting silent during all of this; suddenly he roared, "Let them go? Are you out of your minds? Have you forgotten that they killed Aia? Did she mean so little to you," he said to Peter, "that you'd let her killers escape justice?"

Raeder glared at his friend.

"Aia Wisnewski was my friend," he said coldly. "And I knew her longer than you did, Barak. I haven't forgotten her, and I never will. But I haven't forgotten Sarah James either. And if getting her back alive means letting this family go, then I say that's what happens." He and Barak stared at one another for a long moment. "And I think Aia would agree with me."

Barak's face changed—because it was exactly what Aia would want. He could almost hear her saying, *I can't be helped, but she can. Go get her, don't leave one of ours in Mollie hands.* He nodded slowly.

"All right," he said hoarsely. "What do we do?"

"Paddy?"

"Sor?"

Raeder stopped, conscious of the press of time. But some things had to be said . . .

"Paddy, I want your . . . I want a second opinion."

The big New Hibernian put down the microadjustor and set the small arm aside.

"Ah . . ." *I don't have time for equivocation.* "Paddy, you know I have considerable . . . regard . . . for Sarah James."

"Sir, yessir. And space is dark, sir—if you take my meanin'."

"The question is . . . am I endangering my command and the mission for personal reasons?"

The other man looked him in the eyes. "No, Peter Raeder, you are not that. Oh, yes, you're more *enthusiastic* about it, mayhap. But if 'twere my hairy Hiberian male behind that were in the hands of yon murdering madmen, you'd be doing the same. Or one of those damned Marines, who you like no better than I. As you faced down that spook for one of yours, who you barely knew. You're the Skipper; you may order us to our deaths for the mission, but you don't leave one of your own behind. Nor would any officer worth his salt."

A subtle change came over him, and he picked up his microtool and weapon again. "Now, sir, would there be anything else?"

Once again they were officer and NCO. Raeder felt iron enter his spine. "Carry on," he said crisply. "We've got a lot to do."

CHAPTER EIGHTEEN

Kavi found herself actually panting with anxiety. She took a deep breath, then a sip of water from the bulb at her elbow and told herself to calm down. The familiar surroundings of the ship had turned alien, compounding fear.

"There shouldn't really be a problem," Raeder assured her from Stes' console. "You'd already proven yourselves to be good shots."

"Against four Speeds?" she asked. Kavi shook her head. "I don't know why I let you talk me into this. They'll never buy it. They are *not* stupid people, no matter what you'd like to believe. You've only got to bargain with them to know that."

"Three Speeds," Raeder corrected her. "I was never really there, remember. Electronic trickery!" he said, waving a finger in the air. "They'll believe that, especially when you download that rigged recording on them. All you had to do was kill one more pirate and the other two ran. Just remember to come in on the offensive. You're mad at them for running and leaving you holding the bag." He raised his brows in inquiry.

"Yeah," she said shortly. It could work. The story *was* plausible, barely, and the recording convincing. But by its pounding, her heart wasn't buying into it. Kavi was damned scared. Not having her family around her wasn't helping either. Oh, she was glad they'd been left out of danger on the Space Command's asteroid base. But she missed them. *If I get out of this,* she vowed, *I will never smuggle anything ever again.*

Terry Hunding, a very petite technician who was at present playing Kavi's niece, said, "We are being hailed."

Kavi closed her eyes and tried to forget that her holds were stuffed with four Speeds, six hastily armed work-boats and a bunch of heavily armed and very determined Space Command personnel.

"Put it on my com," she said with deceptive calm.

"Freighter, you are approaching Pure Faith Base. We demand that you identify yourself or you will be fired upon."

"Everybody's so hot to shoot us," she muttered, "it's enough to give a person a complex." Kavi tapped her com. "This," she said through gritted teeth, "is the freighter the *Province of Quebec.* We were under escort by the *Spirit's Praises* when we were attacked and our escort . . . left us. I believe that's them, nuzzled up against your station," she continued with cloying sweetness.

There was a brief, offended silence, then, "Identify yourself, *woman!*"

Every time Kavi thought she'd come to terms with Mollie misogyny she found herself brought up short by their implacable attitude. *Do they have mothers?* she thought. Actually they did; they hated human biotech. But then, they hated a great deal; sometimes she thought that in their secret hearts they started with themselves. *Maybe they just crawl out from under rocks.*

"This is *Captain* Kavi Gallup," she said. "Could you put me in touch with Captain Holmes, please?"

Holmes strode into the command center of the station. There was an unpleasantly gamey scent to the air. He'd made the station's crew maintain standard cleanliness since he'd come aboard, but it would take more time for the station's air scrubbers to clear out their united scent than he intended to be here. He tried to put up with it, but every time he entered the station he was offended by how substandard these people were.

He took a stance behind the chair of Commander Gold. The commander did not acknowledge his arrival, but continued to pick his teeth as he stared blankly into his screen.

Holmes waited a moment, then shouted: "Stand to attention when I enter your presence or by the living Spirit I'll see you stripped of what authority you have remaining to you!"

Gold leapt from the chair as though he'd been stabbed. "Sir! I didn't see you there. My apologies, sir."

Holmes was not a cruel man, but he felt considerable satisfaction that he had restored to Gold an appropriate fear of the Spirit of Destiny. *Punishment produces fear...*

"Report," he suggested coldly.

"Sir! We've been approached by a freighter of Commonwealth designation. But they say they were being escorted by you. So ... I thought I should tell you, sir."

"Have they transmitted their bona fides?" Holmes lifted one eyebrow thoughtfully. Could they have escaped, or were they, perhaps, a Trojan horse full of pirates?

Gold's face turned puce and sweat broke out on his brow.

"They ... demanded to speak to you, sir, before they would do anything."

"Have you at least scanned their ship, Commander?" Holmes folded his arms and gifted the pathetic Gold with a grim stare.

"Not yet, sir. I was awaiting your arrival, sir. I'll have it done right away. Ensign!"

"Sir?" Ensign Funk's head peeked shyly around his chair, eyes like saucers.

"Scan that freighter!"

"Yes, Commander."

Holmes rolled his eyes. But in seconds the information was relayed to Gold's screen. The bridge and living

quarters of the freighter held only five people, one of
whom was small enough to be a child. These signatures
certainly seemed to fit the profile of the family that
owned the *Quebec*.

"Get them on the com," Holmes ordered.

"Yes, sir, immediately." Gold tapped at his console and
the holy symbol that graced the screen was replaced by
Captain Gallup's angry face.

"Couldn't they find you?" Kavi asked. "I know the feeling, Captain. I looked around and *I* couldn't find you
either." She folded her hands under her chin and bat-
ted her eyes at him. "Can you explain that?"

"That situation was self-explanatory, Captain. This one
is not. Can you explain how you come to be here,
unscathed and over twenty hours behind me?"

"Well, if you'd stuck around, Captain, you'd have discovered that there were only three Speeds left. All the
others were illusions. When we took out another pirate
the others turned tail. Why are we late? Would you
believe we expected you to come back? I could not believe
that our big, brave, destroyer escort had actually run
away."

"You expect me to believe that you stayed where you
were, knowing there were armed pirates in the area?"

"Of course we didn't stay there!" Kavi snapped. "We
jumped out and waited for about twelve hours. Then
we took a chance and jumped back in. My second said
that he thought you'd lost jump capability, so we figured you still had to be here someplace. So we followed
your trail. And here we are. Are you still interested in
our cargo?"

Holmes studied the woman's face looking for some sign
of duplicity. Why he even bothered he couldn't imagine.
Welters in general were accomplished liars; the people
of Wildcat were particularly adept. But the situation
troubled him. It irritated his instincts like a rash.

"You will transmit your identity codes to us," he said.

With a great sigh, Kavi complied.

The Mollie captain reviewed the information in minute
detail, allowing his expression to reveal his doubt.

"Everything seems to be in order," he murmured. "And yet . . ."

"We had a deal!" Kavi said through her teeth.

Yes they did. Holmes allowed himself a sardonic little smile. Wildcat was willing to provide all manner of proscribed materials in exchange for a surprisingly small amount of antihydrogen. But then one could do without anything except food, water and air. None of which would be available to the citizens of that benighted planet without the machines that kept their enclosed cities running. None of those machines would run without antihydrogen.

Holmes strolled out of sight of the screen's pickup and Kavi's expression changed from belligerent to bewildered. After a moment she looked distinctly troubled.

"Captain?" she said, in a much softer voice.

Holmes shook his head. They could well be that desperate. He made a decision and walked back to Gold's screen.

"I'm going to send a squad over to inspect your cargo," he told her.

Kavi looked puzzled. "Sure," she said. "Whatever makes you happy. But I think it's time that *I* inspected *your* cargo, as well."

"Certainly," Holmes said after a thoughtful pause. "When my people return, they will escort you."

"I'm familiar with your escorts, Captain. I hope we don't end up down a black hole."

"What an interesting thought," Holmes said suggestively.

Gold gave him an inquiring look. The captain tried not to show his irritation with the man.

"You'll be hearing from us," Holmes said and reached out to cut the connection.

"What are we going to do, sir?" Gold asked in obvious trepidation.

"We're going to send a team over," Holmes said with a smile. "To inspect their ship and make sure that they are who they say they are and that they're alone."

"You don't know them?" the commander said in

something like shock. "You seemed to," he said quickly in reaction to Holmes's expression.

"*She* is familiar. But I've never seen or spoken with any of the rest of her crew. Who also happen to be her family. So if the pirates did capture them, and they decided to keep her family with them while sending her on to play a little game with us . . ." Holmes could see that Gold couldn't bring that thought to a conclusion on his own. "She would do anything to protect her family. They tend to stick together that way."

"Oh!" Gold said after a long moment. "You think there are pirates on her ship."

"I think it's a good chance, yes." *Spirit,* Holmes thought, *how did this lump ever make commander?* Even in wartime and with the vast expansion of the Spirit's Arm of War, and for a punishment outpost as remote as this, were they scraping *this* far down in the barrel?

"So, what do we do now?" Kavi asked.

Raeder looked over at Manning, who said, "We have our little ways." And she stepped over to speak to Hunding.

When the Mollie craft docked it was met by the smiling and petite Hunding. Six men got off, their faces half hidden behind dark visors.

"Hello," Hunding said shyly to the debarking Mollies. "Where would you gentlemen like to start?"

The lead Mollie looked down on her from his six feet of height, then turned to bark at his men to fall in. He turned back, what was visible of his face a mask of disapproval.

Hunding endeavored to look both intimidated and in love, her small hands folded modestly before her.

"We will inspect the hold!" he all but shouted.

"Yes, sir," Hunding said, looking hurt. She turned and led them off.

As soon as they turned a corner Manning, clad in space gear, crept after them. She waited for the precise moment when Hunding opened the lock to the hold and tossed something into their midst. The sound of escaping gas was covered by the hiss of air as the pressure equalized between the hold and the outer compartment.

The six Mollies and Hunding sank to the deck, momentarily stunned. Manning and several suited figures from the hold examined the Mollies and removed any communications devices they found.

Manning took the devices and presented them to a squad that was waiting well inside the hold. Six men and one woman then progressed on a tour that encompassed cargo that wasn't there and ignored armed people who were.

By the time Manning returned all six of the Mollies and Hunding were jabbering away uncontrollably.

"Why don't you all come with me," Manning suggested.

Everyone seemed to find that a fine idea and they all rose and staggered cheerfully after her, a stream of free association flowing from their slack lips.

When you chemically suspended the will, people grew talkative as well as suggestible. It wasn't getting things out of them that was the problem, it was shutting them up.

"There's a pilot aboard the boat waiting to take them back. They're supposed to report in to him every five minutes with a code word. We found that out first thing so we've been keeping up with that, no problem. They like their captain, they hate their auditor, they miss their families, they hate the Commonwealth. They're aware that they have a prisoner on board their ship, but the captain has kept it all under wraps. The scuttlebutt is that it's a woman. Very scandalous," Manning said with a grin. "And Hunding is in love with Givens."

The pilot's head jerked up at that.

"That was uncalled for, Manning," Raeder said quietly.

"Yes, sir." Manning had the grace to look embarrassed.

"What's the status of their repairs?" Peter asked.

"They should be ready to fly in about four hours. Seems nobody wants to linger here."

"True," Raeder observed. *I sure don't. I don't even want*

to think about what they're doing to Sarah. But with every passing minute I think about it more. He tapped his fingers anxiously on the table. "How's our tour doing?"

"They should be finished in about twenty minutes, sir," Manning said.

"Let's get into position then."

In response to a prearranged code word the pilot opened the hatch door. One of the team entered, then threw up his hand and went back out. In the background a woman's voice spoke an urgent question. The pilot watched this byplay suspiciously, worried that the freighter crew might try to rush them or pull some other Welter shenanigans. He sat poised to send a warning signal to the *Spirit's Praises.*

Of course, the destroyer would then fire on the freighter. Doubtless killing the pilot and the entire inspection crew. But those who died in the service of the Spirit of Destiny went directly to paradise. So he was unafraid. In fact, he was happy. Very, very happy. He was happy it was his birthday and Mother was there with the cake, and . . .

The pilot slid bonelessly to the floor and smiled up at the big red-haired man who suddenly loomed over him.

"Happy to die," he said, cheerfully.

"Happy to oblige, gossoon," the man in the face mask said. "But some other time. Right now I need to know if there's some special code you're supposed to transmit to signal a successful completion of your mission. Or anything else you can tell me that I might need to know."

"Never," Paddy advised his commander as he flew the Mollie boat back to its berth on the destroyer, "never invite a religious fanatic to tell you anythin' he thinks you need to know."

Taut grins answered him. The boat was stuffed with Space Command personnel who'd been assigned to take the bridges of both destroyer and station and the tension level was high.

"Remember," Raeder told them. "The destroyer is our

real target. From what our prisoners have told us the crew of the station is a bunch of goldbricking misfits. If we give 'em a sufficiently terrifying threat they'll probably beg us to let them surrender. But the destroyer has a good crew, a relatively happy crew for a Mollie ship, and an able captain and officers. So we must take that bridge. Any questions?"

Fourteen men in mocked-up Mollie uniforms shook their heads. Face shields hid the upper half of their faces from him, but Raeder didn't need to see their eyes to know what those eyes held. Determination. They would get Lieutenant Commander Sarah James back or die trying.

"Permission to board?"

"Permissio—you're not Ensign Wietz!"

"No, boyo, that I'm not," Paddy Casey said genially.

One huge hand gripped the Mollie watchkeeper by the throat of his coverall and slammed him effortlessly into the side of the airlock. The other started to move and froze as the muzzles of a plasma gun and half a dozen pulse rifles centered on him; if they fired, he'd be barely a greasy smear on the foamed metal of the lock. His eyes rolled as one of the intruders slapped a patch on the side of his neck, and then he buckled and slid to the floor in a flopping heap.

"Got the visual feeds," the tech beside him said. "They're showing the scenario we had ready."

The tech opened a book-sized box and took out a thin cord. The head of it was a mass of prongs, fading down to hair-sized filaments and then into invisibility. She plugged it into the data-feed beside the lock controls and the fingers of her other hand danced over the surface of the little box.

"Got it . . . *shit!*"

"What is it?"

"They've got physical separations on subsystems and I can't route through the coordinating node on the bridge from here. I've got . . . Okay, they use the same system for internal locks and for the elevators. I'm putting in the emergency lockdown for internal pressure doors and closing the elevators off . . . *now.* That's going to get their attention! Here's the new code I entered. Sorry, Chief, that's all I can do from here. Get me to the bridge, and we're copacetic.

"All right," Paddy said, from his position on the inner airlock door. "This corridor's clear. Keep to the sides of the corridors, be keepin' alert, now."

Using everybody, there just weren't enough warm bodies to take the station and the destroyer simultaneously . . . but that was what they'd have to do.

Raeder nodded grimly. "There's probably a hundred and twenty people on this ship and *none* of them like us." An alarm klaxon began to wail. "Let's do it, people, let's *go.*"

Auditor Williams peeked around a corner and quickly ducked back into hiding. A row of the invaders was climbing the ladder to the second level. It gave him hope that they had not yet succeeded in taking the command center, or surely they would be using the elevators.

At last, the final one, a woman, he guessed, climbed out of sight and the dingy corridor was clear. If there was one thing Williams was certain of, it was that these hard-faced, efficient young men and women were not pirates.

They smelled like Welters to him—Space Command, at that.

And why? he asked himself. Why would the Welter Space Command suddenly take such an interest in this out-of-the-way station? *Because of my prisoner,* he told himself. She must be very important to them.

He sincerely regretted that he'd ever left the *Spirit's Praises.* But there were men on the station who needed correction and so he'd let his duty persuade him. Moreover, he'd reached a point in his interrogation of the prisoner where he'd needed to leave her in solitude for awhile. Solitude but not peace. He'd left an endless loop of loud blasts and flashing lights to keep her occupied.

Williams was genuinely upset by this turn of events.

He considered himself an artist and he *knew* that he had been within mere hours of a total breakdown. Without the use of drugs, without once touching her in any way, she soon would have told him anything he wanted to know. The truth, the whole truth and nothing but the truth. All in less than forty-eight hours. His best work to date. Wasted. All of it.

A shame.

As he approached the docking area he slowed. There was liable to be a considerable battle going on at the doors to the *Spirit's Praise*. Indeed, around the next corner he came upon the body of one of the station personnel. Williams picked up the man's weapon. A nice little needler. Not standard issue, but that was the Spirit's problem now, or perhaps the man's.

He listened and heard no sounds of conflict, which worried him. He considered going outside the station and finding his way onto the *Spirit* via some repair hatch. But he'd no idea what was happening out there and no way to find out.

Pure Faith Base was cheaply made, more of a military prison than a station really, and so the only place with the equipment to tell him what was happening outside was under siege.

He decided to chance it. Once aboard he'd head right for the brig. If this *was* all about their prisoner then it was imperative that she be secured.

"God *damn*," Raeder hissed.

It was *just* like the Mollies to have gunports in the approach corridor to the bridge—probably with mutinies in mind, although he'd never met people more sheeplike than the average Mollie . . .

Needles whined off the foamed metal of the wall before him. *Carnivorous sheep,* he amended mentally, and slid a probe around the corner. The needler was firing from a letterbox slit beside the door; Paddy crowded close to see, and so did Ensign Manning. She'd been very quiet since Kushner died.

"I'll take a satchel charge, sir," she said.

"That you will not, Marine," Paddy said. "No foolishness now. This is a job for two." He glanced over at the tech. "The code will work?"

"It should," she said. "But they'll be working on getting their system back under control."

"Time to go, then," Paddy said. "With yer permission, sir."

Raeder nodded bleakly. He could feel the impulse to take the job himself, but it was distant. Right now he was a machine that thought, and this was the best way to finish the job quickly. The lockdown wouldn't keep the destroyer's crew confined for long; they would find tools and cut their way through to the access shafts, if nothing else. They had to finish this on speed and momentum, before the enemy could react properly.

"Go for it," he said. "Covering fire . . . *now!*"

Weapons sprayed and hammered. Pulses of energy and slugs driven to speeds that turned air incandescent in their wake whined and growled in the strait space of the corridor. Paddy and Manning dashed around the corner; Raeder's heart stumbled as Manning did, nearly dropping the bag in her right hand, but then they were plastered against the wall on either side of the hatch to the bridge. Manning's arm went limp, blood cascading down her side in a sheet that glistened red-black under the Mollie glowtubes. Paddy grabbed the barrel of the needler in one gloved hand, and wrenched forward with strength like a pneumatic ram; his other hand stuck the muzzle of his pistol through the slot and fired as fast as he could pull the trigger.

Manning was on her knees by the lockpad. The fingers of her good hand stabbed at the pad . . .

. . . and the door swung open. With her last strength she tossed the bag through the opening and collapsed, even before its hissing contents could spread.

"Follow me!" Raeder roared.

Sarah was curled up in a fetal position, her eyes tight shut, her fingers jammed into her ears. She'd gone from uncontrollable sobbing to what seemed to be equally uncontrollable cursing.

She was tired, she was hungry and thirsty and she was *mad*.

The painfully loud noises cut out suddenly and she allowed herself to relax slightly. They'd be back in somewhere between thirty seconds and two minutes, but for now she should be safe.

But if anybody were to walk in here they wouldn't be safe! she thought. *I'd take them apart with my fingernails.*

The door slid open.

Sarah commenced a pitiful whine, she didn't fight the trembling that overtook her. Let the newcomer think she was trembling with fear or madness. Let them think they had the upper hand. Deep within her something wept and gibbered for real, but Sarah's anger kept it in check. For now. She listened intently.

Do something, she thought fiercely. Do *something!*

At last, her straining ears heard a footfall, and perhaps, in the distance, something else. Shouts?

Must be my ears playing tricks on me. For a single moment she wondered if she was hallucinating. *If I turned around would the door be open? Is there anyone there?* She fought the urge to turn over and look. She continued to tremble and to whine. That took most of her concentration. Hunger, thirst and exhaustion left her feeling numb and slow. *Hold on to your anger!* she demanded of herself, knowing the heat of it would help her survive.

There was the scrape of another footstep and the whisper of the door sliding closed. Sarah caught herself before she could slump with relief.

"Turn around," a man's voice commanded.

She gasped as if in surprise and cast a gaze of wide-eyed horror over her shoulder. Sarah made a sound that might have been "don't!" and slowly turned towards him, keeping herself hunched in.

I'm going to kill you, she thought at the man with the needler in his hand.

"I'm going to kill you," he said pleasantly.

Sarah blinked. *So that's what you look like, you cowardly*

son of a bitch! Without question this was the body behind the voice that wouldn't let her sleep.

Slowly she changed position, appearing to gather herself closer, as if in shame at her nudity; she got her feet under her, changed the balance of her weight.

The damn lights are still flashing, she thought. Which probably was helping to conceal the meaning of her movements. *So any second now the sounds should start.*

"Will you stand up, whore? Or shall I shoot you while you crouch there like a dog?"

Ooh, you're a nice one, Sarah thought. She brought a trembling hand to her mouth, bit her fingers, her wide eyes locked on the needler.

"Please . . ." she said ambiguously.

The noise went off. Williams actually jumped, as though he been poked with a cattle prod, and Sarah was on him like a scalded cat. The heel of her hand broke his nose, her other hand squeezed his treats like a suet pudding. The auditor screamed and his hands spasmed in shock. Sarah pushed herself off him and spun after the needler. She picked it up and aimed in one fluid motion, stopping herself from shooting only with considerable effort of will.

"Strip!" she snarled.

He stared uncomprehendingly and Sarah shouted it, taking a step towards him. With shaking hands the Mollie took off his shoes, his trousers and his shirt. He paused, his eyes round. Sarah pointed at his feet. The Mollie stripped off his socks, then put his thumbs under the waistband of his shorts. Sarah shot a dart at his feet and he jumped and screamed. Then he sort of hunched in on himself, doubtless in pain.

Good, James thought viciously, *I hope it's killing you.*

She stabbed a finger at him and then at the floor. He lay down on his back. Sarah raised a brow and rotated her finger to show he should turn over. With visible reluctance he did so. The lieutenant commander picked up his socks and sat on his head. She grabbed one hand and tied one end of the sock to his wrist as tightly as she could. Then she did the same with one of his ankles.

Sarah cross tied the other wrist and ankle and stood up. She watched him for a moment, wincing as the sounds grew louder. They'd stop soon, she knew.

Then she picked up his uniform and got dressed. She waited until the sounds ceased.

Then she said, "Enjoy the entertainment; it's a little loud, but it's never the same thing twice."

Then she slipped out into the corridor. She fired once to disable the lock. *Not that I expect him to get loose anytime soon, but there's nothing wrong with a little insurance.* And the longer he got to enjoy the receiving end of his own treatment the better she liked it.

Sarah tiptoed down the corridor, silent as a ghost. She hugged the wall, feeling all too exposed ... wondering if she'd ever stop feeling that way. Then, off in the distance, she *did* hear a shout. She froze, listening. But the cry wasn't repeated. James frowned. Are *my ears playing tricks on me?* She licked dry lips and waited for another tense minute. Then, with a grimace, moved on. Her luck couldn't hold out forever. She was surprised that no one had come this way yet. Edging her way to the end of the corridor she took a deep slow breath through her nose, then exhaled through her mouth. Biting her lip, she eased her head around the corner.

And came face-to-face with Peter Raeder.

Sarah screamed and jumped backward. Tangling in her own feet, she fell, but brought the needler up when Peter came around the corner.

"It's me!" he said, hands out to either side.

Her breath came out in a startled "Huh!" and then she was laughing. She couldn't stop herself, though she tried. She knew she was hysterical and there wasn't a thing she could do about it. Tears ran down her cheeks and she tried to form the words, *If you hit me I'll get you,* but she couldn't stop laughing.

Raeder looked down at her with a positively comical expression of concern, mixed with relief and growing amusement on his face. Instead of smacking her to shock her out of her fit, he went to one knee and, lifting her up, he cradled her in his arms until she began to cry.

He stroked her back soothingly, repeating, "It's all right," over and over.

As Sarah grew quieter Raeder began to talk.

"Well," he told her, "we've got a little more repair work to do on this old bus. Then we'll head back to the hutch to pick up our gear and our pirate friends and we'll blow this clambake."

"I wanna push the button," Sarah said with a sniff.

"You've got it, Lieutenant Commander," he promised.

CHAPTER NINETEEN

Kavi and her family entered the station's command center under guard and looked nervously around the somewhat shredded complex. There was a faint smell of acrid scorching, the scent a functioning console made when someone put a burst from a needler into it . . . and under that, an even fainter scent of blood; they carefully refrained from looking at some of the stains. The covers were off most of the consoles and techs were, very gently, placing small packages within their guts.

"So," Raeder said, walking up to them. "We're about finished here, and I understand that your hold is full."

Kavi held out her hand, her dark eyes shining.

"If we're careful, and we are careful, Wildcat should be able to stretch this supply for a full year." She was fairly bubbling with delight.

The *Province of Quebec*'s hold was stuffed with bottles of antihydrogen. All that had been waiting for them in the hold of the destroyer and all that had just been delivered to the station.

Raeder shook his head.

"Don't make me regret this," he said. "We're trusting you."

"Win this war in a year," Kavi said gravely, "and I can guarantee that Wildcat won't disappoint you."

Raeder opened his mouth to speak and she cut him off.

"Here," she said, handing him a disc. "This is the name of our contact, the one who arranged this whole exchange thing. We always figured him for a Mollie plant, but we were desperate enough not to care." The captain tightened her lips and then shook her head. "I can't speak for Wildcat, Commander." She met his eyes. "But speaking for myself and my family, the *Quebec* is out of the smuggling business. And anything that we can do to help the Commonwealth, we will. You have my word on that."

"Thank you, Captain. We can't ask for more than that." He gave her a salute and she returned it, obviously feeling silly for doing so. "You folks had better get going," Raeder told them.

"Commander," she leaned in close, "what will you tell them about us?"

"That you were some pirate ship that we used and that you escaped in the confusion. We fully expect to capture the *Killbird* momentarily." He smiled. "I sure hope you never run into them, they're a nasty bunch."

"Thanks," she said. Their eyes met in a moment of contact, full of might-have-beens, then she smiled. "Bye," she said and turned away.

Stes gave him a solemn nod and followed his bright-eyed youngsters, who were obviously eager to start the journey home—those who didn't want to enlist on the spot—out of the command center.

Raeder sighed. After a moment he became aware of someone at his elbow.

Manning stood there, her tongue in her cheek and her arm still immobilized under a coating of heal-seal. She was subdued since her partner's death, but since the storming of the destroyer's bridge even a subdued Ensign Manning was full of mischief.

"I've adjusted the station's records to show that they

were due for a shipment but that it had been delayed. According to the new entry we only had enough anti-hydrogen to blow the station."

"Excellent," Raeder said, beaming.

She shook her head.

"It's going to leak, sir. There are too many people in on this; we'll never keep it quiet."

"But the records," Peter said, shaking the disc at her, "will bear us out."

She stepped closer and lowered her voice.

"Sir, with due respect, Scaragoglu is not going to buy that." She smiled, but her eyes were serious and maybe a little scared.

He nodded. Her concerns were reasonable. *Reasonable, hell, they're sane, where maybe everything else about this is crazy.*

"I'll tell him the truth," he said.

She blinked. "Well, *that's* original."

"Hey, what we've done is to keep a whole planet from going over to the enemy in desperation. For at least a year. And, yeah, Space Command sure could have used that A-H. But I'd hate to think of us having to use it to subdue one of our own."

"He won't like it," Manning told him.

"Hell, *I* don't like it," Raeder said. "But at least we won't have to worry about Wildcat for awhile. They know there's no future in siding with the Mollies. Can you think of a planet more likely to be marked for purging by that bunch? But Kavi was right, when you're running out of air, you'll do anything to get some. Maybe this will motivate the Commonwealth to *do* something for the colony worlds. Or we *will* lose this war."

She stepped back and snapped him a salute, he returned it.

"Good luck, sir," she said dubiously.

Poor Manning, he thought as he watched her walk away. *I hope she finds another Kushner soon.* She seemed diminished, somehow, without her tall, burly sidekick.

Raeder looked over at Sarah James where she sat before the station he'd assigned her. Her hazel eyes never left

the image of the station on her screen. She moved slightly
and he winced as light glanced off her shaven head.

"Why," he'd asked Captain Holmes, "did you do that?"
It seemed so petty.

"My auditor wanted to attach some electrodes to her
scalp so that he could monitor her brain waves." The
Mollie shrugged. "And he said that it would confuse her
about how long she'd been with us. He seemed to feel
that was important. Interrogation is not my specialty,
Commander. I saw no reason to object, so I allowed him
to proceed."

"And did you allow your people to rape the lieutenant commander?" Raeder demanded.

"*What?*" The Mollie was clearly horrified.

"I believe it's a well known *interrogation technique.*"

Homes stiffened in outrage and would have risen from
his chair but for the weapons leveled at him.

"If you imagine that I would allow *my* people to *pol-
lute* themselves with contact with that . . ." He waved his
hand around helplessly, his face curled up into a mask
of distaste.

Raeder couldn't help but believe him, and for once he
was profoundly grateful for Mollie sexual repression.

But they had hurt her. She was handling it well, but
she was shaky and nervous. He would never forgive
himself for being too late to save her from this.

"We have achieved optimum distance, sir," one of the
techs sang out.

"All stop," Raeder said.

"All stop, aye," the helmsman intoned.

Sarah looked up and met Raeder's eyes.

"Fire when ready," he said, almost gently.

"Fire when ready, aye," she replied. She gazed at the
blameless mass of metal and plastic in her screen. She'd
been tortured on this ship, had never actually set foot
on Pure Faith Base. Yet, somehow, all of her anger, hatred
and resentment had been transferred to the grotty little
station.

She took a breath and jabbed her finger onto the firing
key.

The first charge blew out a part of the station and the tech beside her made a muffled explosion sound. Sarah laughed. The next charge brought a louder sound. Charge after charge went off until by the time the station blew wide everyone on the bridge was loudly contributing their own version of an explosion, while Sarah laughed and applauded their efforts, tears streaming down her cheeks.

There was a sudden silence and Sarah gathered herself to say in a choked voice, "The station has been destroyed, sir."

"Thank you, Lieutenant Commander," Raeder said. He swallowed. "Well, then. Let's close down the hutch, gather up our prisoners and head for home."

Sean Wu clapped the cover closed on the buoy and sighed. He and the tiny picket boat on which he served had been out here for six weeks. Repairing buoys, servicing buoys, replacing buoys. Somebody had made a crack about "buoys night out" and he'd nearly strangled her.

He was bored. So bored he was beginning to wonder if boredom could constitute a medical emergency. *I think I'd like a medical emergency about now.*

It was a plain fact that even this almost unused jump point *had* to be watched. *But why* me? He asked the gods of the service. *Why couldn't I have been stationed someplace where there was something to watch?*

"Wu? You'd better get back here. The jump point has been activated and something's coming through."

"Copy. On my way," Wu said calmly. Inside he was saying, *Omigod! Omigod! Why me? Why when I'm outside?* And he scrambled aboard his cart and headed for the picket boat.

There was no proof that being near a jump point when something came through had any effect on someone who happened to be outside clad in nothing more than a space suit. But then the sample of people who had been caught in just such a situation was vanishingly small.

Sean had no desire to become an interesting footnote in somebody's future study. *Everyone this has ever happened to has been fine,* Sean thought frantically, *with the exception of Sean Wu, whose face is in the middle of his chest and whose ass is now made of superinsulating material.*

Wu had tapped in the entry code and was anxiously waiting for the lock to cycle when the ship came through.

He turned to look over his shoulder.

"Shit!" he said aloud. "It's a Mollie destroyer!"

Raeder stared at the *Invincible* in horror. Her sleek skin was terribly mangled and there was an enormous hole gaping in her side. *It's almost enough to make a grown man cry,* he thought. She was still beautiful, though tragically marred. Raeder swallowed hard, trying not to think of Sarah James.

He'd been angry when he'd flown back with the destroyer he'd renamed the *CWS Recycled.* He'd wanted to kick ass and take names later for having been left out there with no support. But now, looking at her, he was too shocked to feel anything but sorrow over the loss of shipmates and the awful damage the *Invincible* had taken.

"Welcome home, Commander."

Raeder spun round, hand snapping up in salute to the captain.

Knott returned it, and walked over to stand by the monitor with him.

"How did you ever bring her home, sir?" Raeder asked in awe.

"We limped," Knott answered shortly. He turned to look at Raeder. "I tried, when we finally got back, to get someone out there to get you." He shook his head. "You know what it's like. Though I must admit there really wasn't anybody here who could have brought you all back." He laughed. "Of course, by the time we got back, you were busily rescuing yourselves."

Raeder smiled. He'd discovered that *Invincible* had only been back at Ontario Station for a little over sixteen hours when he'd brought in the *Recycled.*

"Which is good," Knott went on, his eyes suddenly hard, "because I don't think your mentor would have sent you any help at all." He held up his hand as Raeder opened his mouth to speak. "I wanted to warn you about him, but it was too late."

"I appreciate that, Captain. But what could I do?" Raeder raised his brows and shrugged.

"Yeah. I know you didn't have any wiggle room." He shook his head. "But maybe that nice, quiet desk on Earth wouldn't have been such a bad thing. And it probably wouldn't have been forever." He shook his head, gave a rueful smile. "Probably would have seemed that way, though."

Raeder grinned and nodded in agreement. " 'Fraid so, sir."

"Just watch your back, Commander."

"Yes, sir."

They stood in companionable silence for a moment, looking at the *Invincible*, attended by a multitude of workers.

"Well," Knott said, "at least our people will get a decent R & R this time. There's no way they can rush us off somewhere with the old girl in that condition." As he said it Knott's eyes narrowed and Raeder knew that the Old Man was aware he'd have a fight on his hands to keep his prime crew together. "All of us except you, perhaps," the captain said, giving him a sideways look. "The Marine general is probably busy planning all sorts of excursions for you."

"Yes, sir," Raeder agreed.

"You know the reward for good work, don't you, son?"

"More work, sir?"

"You're learning, son."

Scaragoglu tapped his desk and another page appeared on his screen. He read with great concentration and admirable speed. He tapped again, and again, and again.

Why do I have to be here while he's actually reading the damn thing? Raeder wondered, growing more nervous as the silence stretched on. *Probably so I'll be taut as a bowstring by the time he's finished and then he can play a tune on me,* he answered himself.

Finally Scaragoglu finished. He looked up at Raeder. His face gave nothing away.

Raeder stared back, his face equally impassive.

Captain Sjarhir, in his usual station behind the visitor's chair, slowly stroked one finger over his upper lip, wondering how long this was going to go on. The Marine general had, of course, read Raeder's report before the commander had arrived. And he had questions. But first, this . . . ritual.

Raeder sat quietly in his chair. He did not shift, he did not attempt to break the silence. Given what they knew of the commander's personality and his record, this indicated that he must be incredibly guilty of *something*.

"Your report is very complete," Scaragoglu said at last.

"Thank you, sir," Raeder replied briskly.

The Marine general leaned forward, folding his hands before him. He gifted Raeder with a warm smile.

"So complete that it's full of answers to questions I'd never think of asking," he said silkily. "Do you have an explanation for that, Commander?"

Peter took a deep breath, and Sjarhir straightened in his chair. Scaragoglu raised an eyebrow.

"Yes, sir. In exchange for their help, we arranged to deliver a year's worth of confiscated Mollie antihydrogen to the planet Wildcat."

The Marine general stared at him for a moment.

"That's the pared down version, I take it?"

"Yes, sir."

Scaragoglu raised his hand, leaned back in his chair, looked at the commander, at Sjarhir, into the distance, back at the commander.

"Let me get this straight," he said at last, leaning forward. "You gave a planet-sized supply of A-H, a *year's* supply, away on your own authority?"

"Y-es, sir."

"You took a lot on yourself, Commander."

"I realize that, sir. But I saw a real danger that we might lose Wildcat to the Mollies. And Wildcat manufactures at least one item that's vital to the war effort. So when I also saw an opportunity to prevent their defection with no real cost to the Commonwealth I acted as I was sure you'd want me to, sir."

"No, Commander, don't go attributing your actions to me," Scaragoglu insisted. "As for your move affording no real cost to the Commonwealth, you gave away a year's supply of antihydrogen. I'd call that *very* costly."

"Not if it keeps a knife from our back, sir."

Scaragoglu sat back. "Is this a test, Commander?" he asked cordially.

"Only in the same sense that you've tested me, sir," Raeder answered coolly.

"Ha!" The Marine general slapped a big hand down on his desk. "So you did know about Molochko!" He looked over at Sjarhir. "I told you he'd figure it out."

Raeder had turned to look at Sjarhir in puzzlement.

The captain watched the commander's face clear as understanding dawned and he almost pitied Raeder. He remembered many such realizations in his own past.

Peter turned slowly back towards the general.

"I suppose you've been saving up that look, waiting for an opportunity to give it to me. Well you can just save it, boy. I had to know if you'd stand up for your people. You pilots are a cliquish bunch and you were going to be in charge of all types and grades of people. I had to know if you had what it takes to stand up for someone who wasn't on your level. And I'll tell you plain, you'd be behind a desk on planet Earth right now, if you hadn't come through for that kid."

"He could have been killed, sir." Raeder struggled to keep his voice level, and his face composed. "It seems an unnecessary risk."

"I assure you it was not, Commander. Nor would he have been killed. The conditions were very carefully controlled. Mr. Molochko is a genius in his work and I trust him implicitly, which is something I can very rarely say. It's why I chose him to teach you. That boy was never in any real danger at all." He folded his hands across his stomach. "But consider the danger your people might have been in if you weren't willing to stand up for them. Consider the danger that Lieutenant Commander James would have been in, had you been unwilling to take risks for her."

Peter merely looked back at him.

"As it happens, Commander, perhaps by sheer luck, which I warn you not to press, you have met with my approval on this. The plight of the colony worlds is a growing problem. One which you have satisfactorily addressed in this case." He smiled benignly at the commander. "You've done a good job on this and Star Command sees you as its blue-eyed boy. Enjoy it while it lasts." The Marine general gave him an evil grin. "You know the usual reward for good work, don't you?"

"More work, sir."

"You're learning, boy."